Lucky Seven

"True Love Is Only Found In the Heart"

D0873433

Michael Steven Keller

Copyright © 2010, 2011 Michael Steven Keller

ISBN:978-1-60383-366-0

Published by:
Holy Fire Publishing
717 Old Trolley Road
Attn: Suite 6, Publishing Unit #116
Summerville, SC 29485

www.ChristianPublish.com

Printed in the United States of America and the United Kingdom

This Book Is Dedicated With Everlasting Love And Gratitude To...

My Family: Thank You For Believing In Me.

My Grandfather John W. Lewis: Thank You For Turning This Dream Into A Reality.

My Beloved Wife Lucille: I Love You Always And Forever Panda.

Angel & Starr: Daddy Loves You Always And Forever.

Gary Puckett: It Was A Genuine Pleasure To Meet You. Your One Of A Kind Musical Gift Will Be An Enlightening Inspiration To Me Always And Forever.

Chevy Chase: Thank You For Enlightening Me With The Humorous Essence Of *"The City Of Lights."*

Michael Douglas & Kathleen Turner: Thank You For Enlightening Me With The Essence Of Romantic Adventure.

Richard Dawson: Thank You For Many Years Of Your One Of A Kind Sense Of Humor And Genuine Nature.

Kevin J. O'Connor: Thank You For The Enlightening Truism That Has Inspired My Literary Pursuits Over The Years.

To All Of My Brothers And Sisters In Christ Who Are Living With Hydrocephalus. May The Everlasting Love Of Almighty God And His Son Jesus Christ Continue To Comfort, Strengthen, And Keep You Always And Forever.

To The Reader:
Words Could Never Hope To Express How Grateful I Am To You For Taking The Time To Share In My Vision Of One True Everlasting And Unconditional Love. I Truly Do Hope That It Brings A Blessing To Your Heart. With Love And Best Wishes From My Heart To Yours. May Almighty God Bless You Always And Forever. Please Feel Free To Contact Me Anytime To Share Your Thoughts At:
<u>romanticwriter95@yahoo.com</u>

A Portion Of Proceeds From *"Lucky Seven: True Love Is Only Found In The Heart"* **Will Go To:**

Opportunities That Arise In The Name Of Promoting Awareness, Continued Research, And Treatment Of Hydrocephalus.

The Alaska Sea Life Center: In The Name Of Promoting A Stable And Healthy Existence For The Unique And Enlightening World Of Marine Wildlife Within *"The Last Frontier."*

Wolf Mountain Sanctuary And Saint Francis Wolf Sanctuary: In The Name Of Ensuring The Healthy And Peaceful Existence Of One Of The Most Noble And Majestic Creatures To Ever Exist – The Wolf.

Opportunities That Arise In The Name Of Protecting The Right To Life For Wolves Around The World.

Devils@Cradle Tasmanian Devil Sanctuary: In The Name Of Protecting The Existence Of One Of The Most Unique Creatures To Ever Exist – The Tasmanian Devil.

Dedicated To My Beloved Wife Lucille:

Thank You For Showing Me The Cherished Reality Of One True Everlasting And Unconditional Love That I Had Only Known Through My Literary Vision – Until The Day That You Blessed My Life With Your Warm And Sensitive Kindness And Ethereal Beauty. Every Day That We Are Together Is Just Like The First In Reflection Of The Love And Tenderness That I Felt In The First Sweet Moment With You And Have Every Day Since. When I Look Into Your Beautiful Eyes, I See My Dream Come True. When I Am In Your Arms, I Feel The Cherished Love Between Us That Makes All Parts Of Our Beautiful Life Together Truly Special. I Realize At Long Last That The Love Of Almighty God Truly Did Bring Us Together. From The Luckiest Man In The World, I Am Thankful For You All Of The Days Of My Life. I Love You Always And Forever Panda!

To Almighty God Be The Glory.

For Everything That Occurs On Earth, Does So In His Time...

Thank You Almighty Father God For All Days That I Am Blessed With To Love And Serve You – And The Continuous Good Health To Sustain The Blessing - With All Of My Mind, Body, Heart, And Soul. With Your Guidance, I Look Forward To The Challenges Ahead. To Your Name Be The Glory For The One True Everlasting And Unconditional Love Of My Beautiful Wife Lucille, Our Beloved Dogs Angel And Starr, And All Other Blessings That You Alone Have Provided. May This Literary Creation That You Have Spoken Through Me Bring Glory And Honor To Your Name And Be A Blessing To Others As I Continue To Do Your Will Throughout The Ages. I Declare This With Eternal Gratitude And Love In The Name Of Jesus Christ Your Son, My Lord And Savior. Amen.

Immortality

Hollywood Legend, you know who you are…
You illuminate Heaven now…
With the Immortality that made you a star…
With just a few simple words…
To our faces, you brought many a smile…
Blessing us with your greatest humor…
As we laughed all of the while…
You gave us so very much…
Through living each role that became a way of life for us…
Many a heart you did touch…
As your memory lives on within us, we thank you from deep inside…
For all of the special moments…
Through which we loved, laughed, and cried…
Farewell Hollywood Legend, for now…
We will meet again in a short while…
We will never forget our cherished friend…
Who turned a human tear into a human smile…

For Walter Matthau

Chapter 1

Roy Dawson's heart soared with gratitude – in reflection upon *The Blessings Of Almighty God* that shined their brilliant glow upon him one year ago. Smiling, he closed his eyes. He was on his way back to the place where it all began – *The City Of Lights.*

In one flash of the slot machine lights, he had been blessed with the inspiration to reach for the star that he truly believed was his own at long last. Within the span of one year, he had gone from the resounding echo of that multi-million dollar jackpot to the melodious communication of multi-platinum songs.

Before then, no record company would sign him. No promoter would approach him. No one around him wanted to hear what he had to say. After all, songs without music – no matter how creative or enlightening – were unheard of in the music industry. However, in one silent instant of reaching for his dream, *The Power Of Almighty God* gave him the opportunity to fulfill the first two of his three dreams at long last. The first was financial security – in the name of releasing the songs that resounded from his loving heart with nothing but his powerful and melodious voice. The second was communication of them – which he realized through *A Glorious Blessing From Almighty God.*

At a young age, Roy's *Walk With The Lord* led him onto *Heaven's Paradise Christian Union* and the spiritual guidance of Pastor Clifford Mulholland. In dedication to his *Melodious Gift From The Lord,* he sang from his heart at services. Inspired by a few special words that *The Lord* had given him that remained a true source of strength for him throughout his pursuits within the music industry – Roy would never forget the inspirational truism: *"Whatever road you choose in discovery of the endless possibilities in life, you must love what you do. If not, then it is not worth doing."*

Instinct had given him the cautionary sense to never let his guard down. His personal ambition was reflected in his established routine of keeping his recordings with him at all times – and that one day *By Faith In Almighty God, In His Time*, his prayer would be answered in fulfillment of his melodious dream.

The day was October 1, 1976. It was Roy's 21st birthday. He was celebrating at *The Solid Gold Hotel And Casino* – the place that he had wanted to visit on this day ever since his childhood. Amidst the excitement of an unexpected victory on the *Lucky Seven* slot machine – in a far less comparison to **The Gift From The Lord** that would materialize only moments later – Roy found himself in need of a smaller cash denomination for his dinner at the famous *Jackpot Buffet* later in the evening. He stepped away from the machine – secure in the confidence that his recordings would be safe.

Upon his return, Roy felt his heart stop – the recordings had vanished. Amidst shock, Roy glanced at his previous path. Within the casino crowd, a search was both futile and impossible. Despite all of his personal setbacks in his travels throughout life, those few steps had led him onto devastation – or so he thought. Instead, he was about to realize **The Mysterious Ways In Which Almighty God Works** once more.

The next thing he knew, Roy heard an announcement from the prestigious radio station of *The City Of Lights – LUCK.7*. This announcement would come to change the course of his entire life. "This next song comes to us from the melodious talent of Roy Dawson on his 21st birthday. It is called *"With This One Voice…"*

Roy could not believe his ears – or eyes. As he listened, he could hear the familiar sound of the very first love song that he had ever written and recorded. From all around, fellow gamblers were clapping and raising their complimentary cocktails in recognition of his melodious masterpiece.

Bowing his head in confused acceptance, Roy placed a triple bet against his remaining cash value. With a rapid pull, he turned his head in silent hope that he would discover the source of his instantaneous encounter with center stage. Roy had forgotten that this was the playoff bet against his jackpot only moments ago.

Suddenly, he heard the sound of a rapid cash award. Uncertain as to its location, Roy did not have to look very far at all. Turning around, he saw the brilliant flash of victory on his own slot machine. Rubbing his eyes, his imagination elapsed into the reality of three sparkling red *Lucky Sevens* and more silver dollars than he could count – continuing to fall one at a time. In gratitude, he spoke:

"Almighty Father God, I Thank You With All Of My Mind, Body, Heart, And Soul For This Blessing That You Alone Have Provided. In The Holy Name Of Jesus Christ Your Son, My Lord And Savior, I Pledge To Do Everything Above And Beyond The Farthest Limitations Of My Power To Do Your Will In Communication Of The Gift Of Song That You Have Blessed Me With To Bring Your Message Of Love, Peace, Strength, Comfort, And Happiness To The World From This Day Forward In A Manner That Will Bring Glory And Honor To Your Holy Name. Amen"

As the crowd cheered once more, Roy did not even notice that the song had ended. Instead, he heard the closing statement "We here at *LUCK.7* would like to express our warmest birthday wishes to Roy Dawson once more. *May God Bless You.* Remember, *Lucky Seven* is with you always and forever." As Roy awaited the total jackpot, the mystery remained. This was only the beginning.

As the plane descended, Roy's visualization elapsed. In a final instant of reflection, Roy reached into his pocket – retrieving the golden envelope with the *LUCK.7* monogram upon it. The envelope was delivered to him with a payment receipt for the cost of his dinner at *The Jackpot Buffet*,

and a slice of yellow layer cake with vanilla ice cream. Inside, was a contract – stamped with the *LUCK.7* executive seal:
Greetings and Salutations Roy Dawson,

We here at LUCK.7 have never heard an artist with your powerful voice and natural talent – and are certain never to find one even in remote comparison ever again. It would be our genuine privilege to serve as your promoter. If you agree to record and release a minimum of one song each month for the duration of one year with LUCK.7 as your distributor, we will promote a compilation of songs from your previous work into your first album with a title of your choosing by a tour of our financing across the United States – also for the duration of one year. You will maintain complete legal and creative control over your work at all times. The tour will begin within one week after your acceptance of this proposal. Enclosed is an advance on your royalties for the first year. In the meantime, remember that Lucky Seven is with you always and forever.
Best Wishes And God Bless,
The Entire Staff Of LUCK.7 Radio

With a smile, Roy whispered the album title in sentimental reflection *"Some Dreams Really Do Come True."* In a final moment of spiritual reflection, Roy spoke a few words of gratitude for his safe return:

"Heavenly Father, In The Blessed Name Of Jesus Christ Your Son, My Lord And Savior, I Thank You For The Peace And Safety That You Have Always Sustained Throughout My Travels As I Have Sought To Do Your Will Every Step Of The Way. As I Return To The Place That You Have Given Me As My Home Throughout My Mortal Existence, I Look To You With Gratitude And Love And Declare Praise To Your Name Now And Forever. Amen!"

Suddenly, he remembered the one requirement that he had often forgotten when going out in public – he had to be aware of his adoring fans at all times. He truly wanted to spend time in their presence. After all, he would have never made it to this special point of return without them. However, this truth had a good and bad side to it.

The bad reality was that he was in a tremendous rush to get to his destination. Unfortunately, late travel opportunities had caused this inconvenience. Even so, he looked forward to the good side of these circumstances. The radio station had given special promotion to the triumphant return of the city's hometown hero. Thus, those who could not obtain tickets to his homecoming concert would be able to meet him during a general autograph session after the show. Amidst this resolve, Roy put his sunglasses on and proceeded into the airport. The day was October 1, 1977.

Without the slightest degree of difficulty, he made it to the secured parking garage. Amidst the excitement of anticipation, he retrieved his keys and watched as the sliding doors revealed his car. Last week, *LUCK.7* had informed him that this luxury vehicle would be his – as a bonus for completion of additional songs each month of the past year. For Roy, his sudden fortune and ***The Glory Of Almighty God*** had provided him with more confidence and inspiration than he ever knew to be possible.

Even so, he still marveled at the sight of this luxurious vehicle. After all, it was the car that he had wanted ever since its promotional release – and now, he had it. Before him, sat the sparkling brilliance of a 1977 Yellow Chevrolet Caprice. The car shined in the sparkling reflection of blazing red and orange flames and silver hubcaps. The yellow license plate declared *"Lucky 7"* in cherished sentimentality. He stepped in and closed his eyes - amidst mesmerized reflection upon the splendor of his good fortune once more. Upon starting the car, Roy chuckled as he tapped the red dice – hanging from the rearview mirror. Suddenly, he heard another promotional commercial from *LUCK.7*. "*LUCK.7* welcomes Roy Dawson back from his very successful U.S. tour and once again invites those of you who could not purchase tickets for his homecoming concert at *The Solid Gold Hotel And Casino* this evening to come for the general autograph session after the show. Roy, if you are listening, you will find your new contract proposal with us in your glove compartment. Until this evening, remember that *Lucky Seven* is with you always and forever."

Roy smiled. In a gesture of gratitude, he tapped the dashboard. With the famous *Landmark Of Lights* approaching, he breathed the fresh air and shouted "*City Of Lights*, by **The Glory Of Almighty God,** I have returned and it is great to be home!" Upon these words, Roy accelerated. This would be a night to remember.

Slipping through the crowd at *The Solid Gold*, Roy stopped in front of the familiar *Lucky Seven* slot machine. This seemed to be the ideal moment to reflect upon his final wish – to find *Everlasting Love. A True Romantic* at heart, Roy dreamed of a kindred spirit with whom he could share in the same heart to heart bond as those reflected in his tender melodies. Due to the fact that he believed in the sentiment of his melodious messages – which he knew throughout all of the days of his life were given to him by **Almighty God** and dedicated to solving the complex *Mystery Of Romance* – Roy had remained *A Hopeful Romantic.*

In a gesture that he had never done before, Roy removed his sunglasses and gazed at the flashing *Lucky Sevens.* Amidst deep reflection, he whispered:

"Almighty Father God, You Have Always Been There For Me. Since The Beginning Of Time, You Declared The Universal Truth That No One Should Be Alone. I Ask In The Cherished Name Of Jesus Christ Your Son, My Lord And Savior That You Shine The Powerful Glow Of One True And Everlasting Love Upon Me." Upon these words, Roy put his sunglasses back on and headed for the auditorium.

A short time later, Roy sat – calm in his final moments of anticipation. Softly, he sang a new song about his search for *Everlasting Love.*

Love is so distant…
But in time, I will find it…
One sweet day, it will come my way…
So close - yet so far…
Fallen star lost endlessly…
In heartache…
No chance to take…
I have had my share of pain and loss and deep heartbreak…
Hard living, suffering…
Through Faith In The Love Of Almighty God…
I know she is out there…
I will find her My Dream Come True…
Together… Forever…
Love, waiting for me – please give me some sort of sign…
Of love to be sweet and tender – forever mine…
Come to me and pick, Your Hopeful Romantic…

Closing his eyes, he repeated the warm truth of a sentiment from a short time ago. *"City Of Lights,* it is great to be home." Suddenly, there was a knock at the door. Confused, Roy arose and opened it. A silver box – wrapped in a gold bow – sat on the floor. With a smile, Roy searched the corridor. The source of its delivery was a mystery.

As he opened it, Roy could not believe his eyes. Inside, a solid gold heart sparkled before him. Touched, he noticed his name – engraved in letters of Old English. The heart had been divided into two. In the center of the division, Roy noticed a card with a beautiful inscription – written in golden ink. Smiling, he read: *"From Deep In My Heart, Everlasting Love Is Sent To You From Me. Now That You Have It, Let Us Unite By* **The Power Of Almighty God** *And Complete Our Romantic Journey."*

As he held the heart close to his own, the intimate mystery remained – the card was not signed. In his thoughts, Roy recalled the confusing mystery from one year ago – he never did find out who took his recordings. All that he knew was that he heard his songs playing throughout the *LUCK.7* radio station when he arrived to sign his contract. In his heart, he had a strong feeling that this might be the first clue in solving that unique mystery. Amidst deep reflection, Roy pledged *"Everlasting And True, If I Ever Find You!"* Upon these words, Roy proceeded onto his return in sentimental recognition of his *Dream Come True* that began one year ago – and would end on this night with yet another **Blessing From Almighty God** – amidst the sentiment of a few final words:

"Father God, I Thank You For The Blessing That The Gift Of Song That You Alone Have Blessed Me With Has Provided To The Multitudes That Have Given Of Themselves To Unite With Me In The Past And At This Time. I Ask In The Cherished Name Of Jesus Christ Your Son, My Lord And Savior, That You Continue To Bless Them In All That They Do. Amen!"

Upon these words, he stepped out and onto the stage. As the crowd cheered, Roy noticed a touching declaration displayed upon a billboard on the box seats platform. The sign read: *"Welcome Home Roy Dawson! You Are Our Number One Always And Forever!"* With a warm and sentimental smile, Roy waved and greeted the crowd. "Thank you very much! *City Of Lights*, it is great to be home! On the road, many people have written and approached me in acknowledgement of the misconception that I have made it to this moment on my own. This could not be any further from the truth. The fact of the matter is that I, Roy Dawson – as certain as I am standing before you right now – am back home to express my deepest love and gratitude to the true sources of my success, inspiration, and happiness – *The Gift Of Song* that **Almighty God** has blessed me with, **His True Blessing** that changed my life one year ago, the hometown in which I formulated my dream, the radio station that gave me the opportunity to reach it, and the greatest friends that have strengthened and fulfilled me through it all, each and every one of you. However, two mysteries have remained since that cherished day one year ago.

Someone was responsible for causing the words from my heart to be heard. Also, someone left a precious gift for me a few moments ago." With a smile of deep gratitude and sentiment, Roy paused for a moment of reflection and concluded "If these people are here this evening, please know and never forget that there is a place of warmth and cherished love in my heart for you for all of Eternity. Thank you very much and *May God Bless All Of You!* In the meantime, *City Of Lights,* this one is for you."

Upon these words, Roy began singing a special reflection of his melodious journey and homecoming.

The world is fine, I always have a great time...
Traveling from town to town...
Seeing places and new faces...
But you know, it is always great to come back home...
Born and raised in this great city, I return today – feeling better than ever...
City Of Lights, it is great to be home...
In this place that I will forget, never...
Thank you, my friends – from in my heart...
And deep inside, from you I will never part...
In The Name Of Almighty God...
Thank you so much...
My heart is full...
On that long and winding road, I looked back – and reflected on it all...
My gift is my song – and this one is for you...
Did you ever read about a poet who dreamed of singing a song?
And then he sang one...
Forget about name changes...
I admit that is true of me...
I give to you this one...
And I feel happiness deep inside...
In my heart, I truly believe...
That I am a man who travels wide...
But this is the warmest return I could ever receive...

Thank you, City Of Lights...
Wherever I may roam...
I will never forget you...
It is great to be home...

As the crowd proceeded with warm applause, Roy began his selection of words from his heart. In his thoughts, he felt the love of these special people that had guided and strengthened him onto this moment. However, the future held the promise of his final dream – that would materialize far sooner than he would have ever imagined.

Upon the completion of the concert, Roy stepped out to unite with his fans. With a refreshing gulp of his fruit juice cocktail, Roy felt his heart stop. He was mesmerized by *The Beautiful Angel* that stood right before his unsuspecting eyes.

Rebecca Davidson stood before him in sparkling reflection of the ethereal beauty of *The Golden Dream* that he had united with in his mind and resounded into his songs – but was yet to feel within his heart. Her gorgeous blue eyes reflected the ideal light for Roy to visualize the charming reality of this one moment in time. Her beautiful blonde hair shined with *The Golden Dream* that he had only sang about – now mesmerizing him in pure beauty before his very eyes. The brilliant glow of her smile provided Roy with a true sense of warmth that he had never known – until now. She was dressed in a bright golden bikini that sparkled in the glow of silver stars – which took the shape of the only word that could describe her ethereal presence before him – *"Lucky."*

"Hello! My name is Rebecca Davidson!" As they shook hands, Roy blinked his mesmerized eyes – gulping a nervous lump that had risen in his throat.

"Thank you very much for your support!" he declared.

"I have been waiting for the opportunity to meet you for quite some time!" Rebecca admitted.

"So have I!" Roy whispered – in unexpected communication of his personal reflection.

"Excuse me?" Rebecca inquired.

Embarrassed, Roy faced his nervous frame of mind – in silent gratitude that she had heard. "So have I!" he repeated – with a sudden confident smile.

In confused acceptance, Rebecca said "Your voice warms my heart. I feel as if you are singing to me – with no one else in the entire world! Would you sign my record album?"

"Absolutely!" Roy replied. As he took it, Roy felt the ability to communicate his deepest feelings at last. Fortunately, his heart guided his hand. After all, he could not take his eyes off of her. As his nervous smile remained, Roy wrote:

To Rebecca Davidson,
The Ethereal Sparkle Of Your Beauty Has Made My Dream Come True! In Your Eyes, I See The Brilliant Light Of A Beautiful Angel. Would You Care To Join Me This Evening So That My Heart Can Thank You?
With Silver Wishes And Golden Dreams,
Best Wishes And God Bless,
Roy Dawson

As he returned it to her, Rebecca closed her eyes and held the autograph to her heart. "May I ask one more thing of you?" she inquired.

"I would do anything for my fans!" Roy declared.

"Might I have the pleasure of a picture with you? No one at the radio station is going to believe that I met you!" Rebecca requested.

Amidst the hope that his own request would be granted, Roy made a mental note to ask her about the radio station of previous note. "Only if I can have one with you as well!" he concluded.

With a smile, Rebecca answered, "If you insist!"

Upon these words, Roy signaled to his friend, Steve Fitzsimmons – who was working security detail for Roy's homecoming concert. Placing his arm around Rebecca, Roy said, "Rebecca Davidson, this is Steve Fitzsimmons – my college roommate and a literary genius."

"It is very nice to meet you, Steve!" Rebecca declared as they shook hands.

"The pleasure is mine, Rebecca!" Steve asserted – retrieving Roy's instant camera. In sentimental capture of the special moment, Steve said "OK! Say *Golden Dreams!*" Upon these words, Roy and Rebecca chuckled as the flash bulb popped – crystallizing the moment within *The Eternal Capsule Of Time* for each of them. As Rebecca shook Steve's hand in gratitude, Roy said "Standby, Buddy! My public awaits!"

"You got it, Buddy!" Steve assured him – tipping his hat with the *LUCK.7* monogram upon it.

"One more thing!" Rebecca asserted – taking her own photograph. With a golden pen in her hand, she concealed her inclination.

Grinning, Roy signed his own picture with a formal inscription. This time, his nerves had gotten the better of him. Noticing that the crowd was heading toward him, Roy wrote *"To Rebecca Davidson, Best Wishes, Roy Dawson."*

As they shook hands once more, Roy and Rebecca whispered "Thank you!" in unison. Unexpectedly, Rebecca blew a kiss and departed. As she walked away, Roy watched the gentle glow of her hair and the sparkling beauty of her stride with intense excitement and anticipation. Although he did not know if she would be there, Roy knew that he had taken the first step in a very special direction. In his thoughts, Roy could not stop reflecting upon the unusual familiarity of Rebecca's soft voice. He knew that he had heard it before – somewhere.

With a smile, Roy glanced at Rebecca's photograph and read her secret sentiment:

To Roy Dawson,
A Sentimental Voice And Loving Heart
With Love,
Rebecca Davidson
A Lucky And Loving Fan

P.S. Remember, Lucky Seven Is With You Always And Forever!

A short time later, Roy stood before the familiar *Lucky Seven* slot machine with a restless frame of mind. Nervous, he called for another fruit juice cocktail. Unexpectedly, the drink was slipped right into his hand. Roy noticed a note written in red ink directly on the glass. Confused, he read, "Hey, My Marvelous Minstrel! Look behind you."

In an instant, he felt the soft caress of a smooth hand across the back of his neck. Turning around, he noticed Rebecca grinning. "Do you see what happens when you do not turn around fast enough?" she asked.

With a nervous gulp, Roy replied, "Yes! Thank you for meeting me!" Upon these words, he communicated a silent expression of gratitude to **Almighty God.**

"Ah, yes! It was your touching proposal! You are successful in another declaration of the fact that you truly do have a way with words!" She paused – touching his face. Mesmerized, she sighed "A face much cuter in person as well!" and proceeded with a drink. Roy marveled. She was drinking a fruit juice cocktail as well.

"Thank you very much!" Roy replied – blushing. "If you do not mind my saying this, your words on the picture were very touching. Where did you…" Roy began. Unable to finish, Roy could not understand Rebecca's rapid maneuver – she had silenced him with a finger upon his lips.

"Not now, My Marvelous Minstrel!" She paused – glancing at the slot machine. "Do you feel lucky?" she asked – raising her eyebrows.

Grinning, Roy took a refreshing gulp of his beverage. "If you only knew!" he responded. Upon these words, Rebecca reached into her shoe and retrieved two silver dollars. Closing her eyes, she kissed one of them. As she proceeded with a rapid thrust of it with her thumb, Rebecca laughed. "Catch!" she shouted. Upon his compliance, she suggested,

"Double bet, your pull! If you win, you have to listen to my life story tonight over dinner at my suite."

"What happens if I lose?" Roy asked.

"That is the best part! With me, you will never lose! In response to your question, you still win the same thing!" Rebecca declared.

"Interesting! A winning situation on all possible fronts! But, do you think that it is fair for me to win everything?" Roy challenged.

"Absolutely! However, you do not understand something. In the end, I will be the real winner. Now, bet!" Rebecca assured him – placing her end of the bargain into the slot machine.

With a confused smile, Roy complied. In his thoughts, he knew that she was wrong about one thing – he alone would be the true winner.

With his bet placed, Roy knew that he could never argue with the most beautiful woman that he had ever seen. However, he would have never believed that she would become far more than anything that he had ever dreamed of – very soon.

Upon execution of a rapid pull, Roy was mesmerized – Rebecca blew another kiss. Suddenly, a rapid cash award elapsed into her soft whisper *"Jackpot!"* Placing her arms around him, Rebecca caressed the back of Roy's neck once more – in gentle assurance that he was not dreaming. With a grin, she slipped the key to her suite into his pocket and whispered, "A bet is a bet! A deal is a deal! See you upstairs – I will make all of your dreams real!" As she walked away, Roy could hear her final request. "Do not forget your adorable charm or tender singing voice!" Amidst his mesmerized shock, Roy repeated her sentiment from a short time ago with a soft whisper *"Jackpot!"* – and thanked **Almighty God** once more.

A short time later, Roy stood in front of Rebecca's suite – in silent reflection upon its number, "7." Nervous once more, he held a solitary red rose to his heart. Roy smiled. Reminiscent of a familiar love song, he knocked three times – signaling his arrival. Opening the door – slowly - the moment of truth was upon him.

The room sparkled in yellow neon – dimmed to a gentle glow. Roy could hear *"With This One Voice…"* playing from the 8-track machine. Through the soft sound of effervescence, Roy heard a voice call to him. "Come on in! The water is great!" He followed the sound of Rebecca's charming laughter into a room that shed light through the dark living room. In an instant, his face flooded with sweat.

Rebecca glistened in aquatic glamour. Her beautiful blonde hair dripped in intimate unity with the steam from the spa. Around it, silver and gold candles were lit. A stationary bicycle was on the side of it. The entire room was absorbed in the intimate scent of her perfume. As he gulped a nervous lump that had risen in his throat, Roy noticed another unique feature – bubbles of heart formation were floating everywhere. As Rebecca kept her eyes closed, she continued to blow the bubbles from a golden container of heart formation – inscribed with the words *"Lovable Bubbles."*

As she arose with a refreshing gulp of her fruit juice cocktail, Rebecca noticed Roy's nervous glance. "Please forgive me, but I find my daily exercise routine so rewarding and fulfilling that I often lose track of time. However, your concert this afternoon and meeting you afterwards are two of the greatest changes to my schedule that I could have ever done."

"Thank you! Thank you very much!" Roy breathed in mesmerized reply.

Raising her eyebrows once more, she motioned him over to her. Roy's nervous frame of mind elapsed into a song.

I see Bubbles Of Love…
Carried from you to me…
As I look in your eyes, I see charming beauty…
As I look in your eyes, and you smile at me…

The Soft Bubbles Of Love float from here - up above…
Soft, pure, and sparkling…
A Creation Of God…
Sweet Rebecca, Thank You…
For your warmth and sweet kindness…
It is a pleasure to be here with you…
Hear me, Bubbles Of Love…
I know kindness exists…
I see it in the glow of your intimate mist…
As I stand before you, My Sweet And Charming Fan…
I now hear in your voice…
That I made the right choice…
To be with you right now…
With all of my heart, Thank you very much again…
For your warmth and support…
Take my hand, Rebecca…
And let this moment float soft and intimately…
On The Bubbles Of Love…

Shocked and charmed by his sentiment, Rebecca declared "Wow! Did I just have the genuine pleasure and privilege of hearing the latest melodious classic of Roy Dawson?"

Blushing, Roy replied, "Yes! I suppose so. If I may say so, you provided me with the first instantaneous inspiration that I have ever had! Thank you!"

"Well, thank you for the opportunity!" Rebecca declared - blushing

Embarrassed, Roy wiped the sweat from his forehead and presented the rose to her. "I hope that you do not mind this!" he asserted with mesmerized nerves.

"I never knew that roses could grow to be so beautiful. Thank you very much!" Rebecca sighed – caressing Roy's face. Lost in her tender charm, Roy was thankful for her helping hand onto a soft yellow armchair. "I hope that you brought your appetite! I ordered French onion soup, garden salad with Thousand Island Dressing, sourdough rolls with garlic butter,

Chicken Vesuvio with onion potatoes, and yellow layer cake with vanilla ice cream."

The culinary meeting of their minds surprised Roy. "You did all of this for me?" he asked.

As Rebecca mixed two fruit juice cocktails, she answered, "I only wish that I could have done more." As she looked up, he noticed an uncharacteristically nervous smile on her face. "After all, I have never felt this special in my entire life. I never dreamed that I would meet the face behind the most sentimental and loving voice that I have ever known. Your voice has been touched by *Almighty God!*"

Touched, Roy could not resist his sudden impulse. "Well, *He* has been very good to me!" he declared – smiling. As he rose, Roy brought Rebecca's face to his and gazed into her beautiful eyes. "Excuse me! Please forgive my brash audacity but I would never forgive myself if I let this opportunity slip by without telling you that you are the most beautiful woman that I have ever seen in my entire life."

Caressing his face, Rebecca smiled. "You are going to make me melt like sweet ice cream on your lips!" She sighed – touching his lips. "Come My Marvelous Minstrel! Good food is best when it is eaten in good company!"

"Ah, yes! But, you are the best company that anyone could ever hope for!" Roy answered. As he opened his mouth to speak once more, Rebecca reclined him into his chair with a slight push motion. With a deep breath, Roy raised his glass and proposed a toast. "Here's to dreams to come true!"

"If you only knew!" Rebecca replied in acceptance. Upon these words, Roy and Rebecca closed their eyes in declaration of a blessing before their meal.

"May I?" Roy asked.

"Absolutely!" Rebecca responded.

"Heavenly Father, We Thank You In Mind, Body, Heart, And Soul In The Beloved Name Of Our Lord And Savior, Your Son Jesus Christ For This Food And Time Together. We Declare Blessings To Your Name And

Look To You With Gratitude And Love As We Continue To Do Your Will Throughout The Ages."

As they united in the words *"All God's People Said, Amen!"* they began to eat. As Rebecca placed her knife into the butter, Roy felt his heart melt once more.

Confused, Rebecca asked, "Is everything OK?"

With a nervous gulp, he spoke. "Please forgive me, but I have been waiting to hear the life story of a truly beautiful woman. You might know her – she is sitting right in front of me. Please do not keep me in suspense!"

Upon these words, Rebecca's hands began to shake. Noticing this, Roy said, "I apologize! That was far too direct!"

Touched but still nervous, Rebecca replied "Absolutely not! I am still trying to compose myself from the shock of meeting you at long last. I realize that you have so many fans that would just as easily say the exact same thing…"

Before she could finish, Roy interrupted her with a rapid declaration. "That is very true. However, I have never come into contact with anyone as beautiful as you. Also, I was very touched by your kindness in inviting me here. No one has ever done that before."

"Perhaps, they were far too nervous!" Rebecca suggested.

"No! Please understand that ever since the first moment that I saw you, I have had a sense that there is a far greater connection between us than a singer reaching out to one of his fans," Roy replied.

"I quite agree!" Rebecca affirmed. Upon these words, she looked at Roy with a futile gulp of her drink to steady her into the reality of this moment. "Roy, please understand that I am far too nervous to tell you what I must!"

"I understand! However, I am afraid that we will never have this chance again," Roy admitted.

Upon these words, Rebecca appeared troubled. Blinded with tears, she whispered, "I have no intention of going anywhere – much less asking you to leave! But, I cannot force you to stay!"

Confused and relieved, Roy smiled at this unusual misunderstanding. "Let me assure you that if you want me here, there is nowhere in this universe that I would rather be! However, I would never force you into anything or do anything to make you uncomfortable." Offering a nervous hand to her, Roy suggested "A story for another time?"

With a smile, Rebecca accepted "A story for another time." As they ate, Roy and Rebecca began to connect in a way that neither of them had ever thought possible. This was only the beginning.

Chapter 2

The next day, Roy found himself struggling with a complex dilemma – one that he had never known before. In his thoughts, he wanted to thank Rebecca for their very special evening together. Even so, he knew that he could not go against his word and had to be conscientious of any potential means of making her uncomfortable.

Despite this intense conflict, he was instilled with a sense of confidence that he never had before. As he signed the card, he whispered:

"Lord, I Thank You In The Name Of Your Son, My Beloved Lord And Savior Jesus Christ For The Ethereal Blessing That Brought Us Together!"

Upon these words, Roy smiled – he had placed an order for one dozen red and yellow roses. In soft reflection, he read:

Rebecca,
I Thank You For Blessing Me With Your Beauty, Warmth, And Kindness.
The Blessing Of Meeting You Has Touched Me In Truly Special Way That I Never Knew To Be Possible.
With Gratitude And Hope, I Seek One Goal...
Only To See You Again And Show You The Happiness Of A Hopeful Romantic Who Has Witnessed The Ethereal Presence Of His Angel.
With Melodious Inspiration And Songs From The Heart,
Love,
Roy

Secure in his resolve, he returned to his room. Intent on easing his restless frame of mind, Roy sang a song in reflection upon his deepest feelings.

With this strange mood I am in...
Will the best days begin?
Is this how it feels to love?
There is a smile – bright and true...

Sweet Rebecca, it is for you…
Is this how it feels to love?
At long last, the future seems to be…
Bright and warm – since you came to me…
By The Power Of Almighty God, I declare…
From the way that I feel…
This is true, right, and real…
This Is How It Feels To Love…

A short time later, Roy heard a knock at the door. Not expecting anyone, he asked "Who is it?"

"Someone with a problem that only a singer can solve!"

Grinning, Roy recognized Rebecca's voice. Opening the door, he was lost in her ethereal beauty once more.

Rebecca was dressed in a yellow hooded sweatshirt – opened to reveal a white sports bra – silver shorts, and yellow shoes. Beneath a silver bandana, sweat dripped from her forehead and gorgeous blonde hair. She was running in place. Through rapid breaths, she asked, "Do you know of someone who can help me?"

Smiling, Roy answered, "You are in luck! I happen to know someone who has a great mind for solving problems. However, he always likes to know the nature of them before he can do anything."

"I see! Well, tell him that someone sent beautiful flowers to my room and I want that person to race me to the bowling alley for a special reward!" Rebecca replied.

"Interesting! Would you care to reveal the nature of the reward as well?" Roy asked.

Upon these words, Rebecca pulled him close to her and raised her eyebrows. "A great big kiss! Come on! Move it out!" Upon these words, she was off and running. Mesmerized, Roy raced after her.

Moments later, they stood in front of *Lucky Strike Bowling Lanes*. Rebecca had won the race. Roy was out of breath. Even so, he was quick to deliver an amusing declaration of unfair tactics. "Foul! Foul! You were at an unfair advantage the entire time!" Wiping sweat from his forehead, he grinned at the knowledge that his sweat was not from exhaustion – but mesmerized nerves.

"Really? How did you arrive at that cute conclusion?" Rebecca asked. Grinning, she turned to him. Placing her hands upon her hips, she stretched – releasing her navel from the constraint of her shorts. As his nerves grew more intense, Roy knew that he could not and would not stop himself now.

"You are so beautiful, that you had me exhausted and defeated by simply looking at me!" he answered.

Touched, Rebecca reached for him. "Aw! My Marvelous Minstrel wishes victory. What he does not know is…" She paused – raising her eyebrows. "It was right here waiting all of the time!" she concluded.

As their eyes met, Roy knew that he had waited throughout his entire life for this one moment in time. With his hands shaking, Roy turned away from her with a rapid maneuver. In his thoughts, Roy was in intense conflict with his true feelings at this moment because he did not know how she would respond.

Softly, Rebecca caressed his back. In an instant, a warm sense of relief allowed him to face the darkest fear that had plagued him throughout his entire life. "I am terrified of being alone!" Roy admitted.

Softly, Rebecca caressed his back. "Roy, please look at me!"

Upon turning around, he was still unable to look at her. At a loss for words, he fell into her arms. "This is too good to be true! I must be dreaming! I love my fans and my career, but no one has ever reached out to me in a genuine love for my strongest and greatest gift – my heart!" he declared.

Able to look at her at last, Roy caressed Rebecca's face. "Rebecca, I know that we just met. However, I feel that **Almighty God** has touched my life with the ethereal presence of an *Angel* – through the gentle glow of your presence upon me. I have spent my entire existence in search of someone to share in my dreams, trials, and triumphs. In my heart, I feel that *The Power Of Almighty God* brought us together when I saw you in that first sweet moment yesterday. I must know do you feel the same way?"

Rebecca's eyes blinded with tears. "We both know that *The Good Lord* has always shown that it is not good for people to be alone. When I heard your voice for the very first time, I knew that you were someone kind, understanding, and loving. You possess a special nature that is truly one of a kind. You have achieved your success by the guiding light of *Everlasting Love* – the same of which I remain in intense search. So, I am asking you, Roy Dawson, guide me in my search for *Everlasting Love.* Perhaps, with the union of your melodious magic and my ethereal vision, we will discover *The One True And Everlasting Love* that we have always dreamed of together as one. Will you help me, My Marvelous Minstrel?"

Smiling amidst the idealistic meeting of their minds, Roy answered "Absolutely! But, I believe that if you agree with what I am about to say, we can do even better than that!" As he gazed into her beautiful eyes, Roy caressed her face and declared "Rebecca, aside from my aspirations of a singing career, I have spent my entire existence in intense pursuit of a very special dream. This dream came true when I gazed into the eyes of the most beautiful woman that I have ever seen in my entire life. In my heart, I knew that the tenderness of that *Beautiful Angel* would shine within my heart from that moment onward and into Eternity. I believe that the search for *Everlasting Love* has brought us together because this dream is the discovery of *One True And Everlasting Love* that I will now cherish from this moment onward in a true feeling of *Spiritual Blessing* that only *The Power Of Almighty God* can provide. My journey in pursuit of *Everlasting Love* has come to an end at long last. I am in love with you!"

Rebecca slipped out of her sweatshirt. Softly, Roy began to caress her back. As she caressed his face once more, a tear fell from her eye.

Concerned, Roy asked, "Rebecca, are you…"

Before he could finish, she concluded, "Yes, I am fine! I am very fine! I am in love with you too, Roy."

Amidst shock, Roy felt his heart stop. For the first time in his life, he realized the cherished reality behind the universal absolute of *Everlasting Love*. Taking her hand, he placed it upon his heart. "From this moment onward and into Eternity, I will dedicate the remainder of my existence to your realization of my love!" Roy pledged.

"In return, I will dedicate my existence to the same – fulfilled onto your loving heart alone!" Rebecca proclaimed.

As he looked into her gorgeous eyes, Roy noticed a flashing glow within them. At the same time, he felt a soft moisture within his own eyes. As the wave of love swept over them, they cried silent tears – but the smiles of love and happiness remained. Roy and Rebecca whispered the tender words that Roy spoke from his heart a short time ago.

"This is how it feels to love!" Lost in the moment of dreams so far away for so long, Roy and Rebecca became one through the unified whisper *"To Almighty God Be The Glory."* Roy knew that he was dreaming no longer.

Roy and Rebecca united in a prayer of spiritual blessing upon their cherished union. *"Father God In Heaven, We Thank You In Mind, Body, Heart, And Soul For Uniting Us In Your Spiritual Blessing Of One True And Everlasting Love That You Know We Have Searched For Throughout Our Entire Lives And Pledge In The Precious Name Of Jesus Christ Your Son, Our Lord And Savior To Love One Another As You Love Us!"*

As they sealed one another into a warm embrace, *"With This One Voice…"* began playing. "Dance with me?" Roy asked.

Rebecca began to sway in acceptance. "Only if I can stay in your arms forever. I love you, Roy."

"I know. I love you too, Rebecca!" Roy declared once more.

"I know. I just wanted to say it and hear it again!" Rebecca replied.

"Well, I can assure you that you will be hearing it very often now. In fact, you would have heard it in the first sweet moment that I saw you!" Roy asserted.

Softly, Rebecca whispered "You would have too!"

"I held back out of fear of scaring you!" Roy confessed. "How about you?"

Upon these words, Rebecca still could not tell him. Instead, she held him even closer. "A story for another time!" she whispered. "However, I have one request. Will you sing the words upon which I fell in love with you?"

With a mesmerized gaze into her eyes, Roy replied "Yes, on one condition. All that I ask of you is that you continue to look at me just as you are right now – so that I may pledge my love while gazing into *The Eyes Of My Dream Come True* – and speak the truth behind the words at long last."

"These eyes have dreamed of *One True And Everlasting Love*. But, never again will they have to look any further than the one that they see in you!" Rebecca asserted – gazing into his eyes and mesmerized by his love. Upon these words, Roy began to sing.

With This One Voice...
I send love from my heart to yours...
I have dreamed of this moment, since very early days...
With endless searching down many pathways...
Dedicated to finding My Dream Come True in love's gaze...
When I looked into your bright eyes, I knew...
I would never see another vision of such beautiful charm...
*Then **God** told me it was meant to be...*
Forever you and me...
I am the luckiest man in all of the universe...
I declare Everlasting Love...
With This One Voice in sweet verse...

As the song ended, Roy Dawson and Rebecca Davidson gazed into *The Eyes Of One True And Everlasting Love.* Roy began to caress Rebecca's body with a soft and gentle touch. He ran his fingers through her sparkling blonde hair – onto the smooth beauty of her face and neck. Roy noticed that Rebecca was closing her eyes.

Mesmerized, he did the same and proceeded with a passionate kiss upon her soft, sweet lips. The wave of love swept over them and into *The First Kiss Of One True And Everlasting Love.* As they kissed, Roy and Rebecca sealed one another into a loving embrace once more.

"I love you, Rebecca Davidson!" Roy whispered.

"I love you too, Roy Dawson!" Rebecca sighed.

Softly, they issued a unified challenge "Bowling, My Love?"

As they selected shoes and bowling balls – Rebecca's in red and Roy's in yellow – Roy had a suggestion to raise their competitive spirits. "The winner of each frame can ask the loser anything about love. The questions can be identical. Anything goes!"

"I accept!" Rebecca answered.

"*Beautiful Angels* first!" Roy declared. As Rebecca stepped up to the lane, she and Roy whispered in cherished unison, "Thank you, **Almighty Father God!**" With a rapid throw, Rebecca scored a strike.

"Like I always say, a beautiful woman is impossible to beat!" Roy laughed.

Grinning, Rebecca turned to him. "Remember, *Lucky Seven!*" she said as their hands met and slid apart – slowly.

"Here goes nothing!" Roy sighed with a swift throw. He scored a strike as well.

"It seems that I am unaware of the competitive edge of my adorable opponent!" Rebecca snickered.

"Give me a chance! I have been known to buckle under the pressure on far too many occasions!" Roy admitted – as their hands touched once more.

"How do we handle this one?" Rebecca inquired.

"How about a change of plans?" Roy suggested.

"Those are fun!" Rebecca answered. "What are you thinking?"

"Let the game continue and I will explain!" As they resumed their frames of fun, Roy began once more. "I suggest playing the best of ten – keeping five questions in mind. Again, they can be identical. The winner can ask all questions first – and another for each one that is identical. If the game is a draw, all questions get asked one at a time. Any identical ones must be resolved in a different game."

Roy paused. By now, they were on the fourth frame with their scores still at an exact tie. Rebecca paused. Turning around, she was confused over Roy's grin – he was raising his eyebrows. "I see! You want me to pick the game!" she asserted.

Uncharacteristically, they were not prepared for the amusing meeting of their minds. As their eyes met, they shouted in unison *"Truth Or Dare!"*

"There must be an echo in here!" Roy concluded.

"There must be!" Rebecca replied – shaking her head in amused sarcasm. By now, they were on the seventh frame. *"Lucky Seven* stands before us, My Love!"

"What do we do?" Roy asked.

"I propose something fun and interesting!" Rebecca replied – stepping forward. "Let us see who can score higher amidst distraction!"

"Interesting!" Roy agreed – formulating an amusing plan in silence. Nervously, Rebecca tried to keep one eye on Roy. "Keep your eye on the ball, My Beautiful!" Roy instructed. With that, he pinched Rebecca's tummy. No sooner did she release the ball than grab the back of Roy's neck. Giggling, she shouted, "You are going to pay for that!" She did not even notice that she had scored another strike.

As Roy stepped up, Rebecca gazed into his eyes and kissed him with such unexpected intensity, that Roy lost his

36

grip on the bowling ball. "Point taken!" Roy breathed – mesmerized and thankful that the ball had fallen into the retrieval.

As the score remained equal, Rebecca caressed his back. "You have not seen anything yet!" As she prepared for the eighth shot, Rebecca giggled "You have made me melt – yet again!"

"Trust me! The mere thought of you makes me melt as well – lost in the warmth of your tender beauty and gentle touch." Upon his shot, Roy challenged, "I think we should begin *"Truth Or Dare"* with the flip of a coin!" – in charming reflection upon their amusing victory a short time ago.

"How about a kiss instead?" Rebecca inquired.

"Interesting! However, do we really have to wait?" Roy asked - blushing.

The ninth frame ended with Rebecca's gentle sigh "Patience, My Love! Patience! Remember that there is a time and a place for everything!"

With an amused chuckle, Roy raised his eyebrows once more. "I could not have said it better myself!" he sighed.

"You certainly could have! After all, you are the singer!" Rebecca finished.

"OK! *"Rock, Scissors, Paper"* will decide who starts!" Roy resolved.

"Wise choice, Roy! Last shot!" Rebecca accepted. In an instant, she had scored a perfect game.

As Roy stepped up to the lane, he whispered, *"Lucky Seven,* this one is for you!" As he took his final shot, she flew into his arms – sealing their mutual victory with a flood of tender kisses.

Suddenly, Rebecca lowered her arms – slipping out of her hooded sweatshirt once more. As Roy stood there holding it, his face flooded with sweat. Rebecca grinned. "Well, I guess I will not be needing that anymore. But, I am so tired. Would you be willing to…" she paused – reaching out to him – "lend a helping hand?" she concluded.

"I thought that you would never ask me!" Roy answered. Upon these words, Roy took Rebecca into his arms and carried her to the elevator. Softly, they began to kiss once more. "My place or yours?" he asked through rapid breaths.

"Start with this kiss…" she paused – caressing his face – "and let your heart follow!" she concluded. As the elevator doors closed in front of them, Roy and Rebecca elapsed into a flood of sweet kisses.

Upon reaching his suite, Roy whispered what would come to be his first question "Where have you been all of my life?"

Through rapid breaths, she whispered "Waiting for you!"

As he reclined her onto the bed – slowly - Roy whispered, "Tell me your dreams!" Kissing her once more, he breathed, "Tell me your desires. Tell me the story that has led you to this moment to touch my restless heart with a love that I have only dreamed about – until now!"

Uncharacteristically, Rebecca giggled "It sure is getting hot in here!"

Overcome by embarrassment, Roy confessed, "I apologize! You are so beautiful! I became lost in the heat of the moment!"

Grinning, Rebecca raised her eyebrows. "Did you have to stop kissing me to tell me that?"

As Roy opened his mouth to speak, Rebecca placed her finger to his lips – silencing him. As she smiled, his face flooded with sweat. Roy could not believe his eyes. With just one look, he knew that it was true – Rebecca defined and personified the most beautiful woman that he had ever seen in his entire life.

Roy whispered, "I love you!"

Rebecca giggled, "I love you too!" – caressing the back of his neck.

As they proceeded to kiss once more, Roy and Rebecca closed their eyes. Rebecca began to caress Roy's face - onto his neck and down his back. Slightly, they opened their eyes to cherish the tenderness of the other's kiss. As the wave of love swept over them in cherished intimacy, Rebecca whispered a tender expression of her love - Roy was caressing her tummy. For Roy, the sweetness of the moments to follow would come to represent the deepest and most intimate senses of warmth and tenderness that he had ever known.

With a gentle sigh, Rebecca spoke his name. Roy knew that she was at peace. Removing his hand for a brief moment, Rebecca kissed it – placing it upon her face. Descending his tender touch down her neck, and upon her tummy once again, Rebecca caressed it. Roy's hand rested upon her navel. As Roy kissed her lips, Rebecca arose – slowly. Amused, she raised her eyebrows and whispered a sentiment from a short time ago, "You sure do know how to make me melt!" Upon these words, Rebecca reclined her body once more.

As he looked into Rebecca's eyes, nothing could have ever prepared Roy for what she was about to say. "I have dreamed of having you all to myself – and making you as happy as you have made me through your thoughts, words, and all that you are. My desire is to achieve all of this and make you my own. You see, I believe that our hearts can join in more than just a bond of *Everlasting Love*."

"Well, I do believe that we are off to a great start! I love you so much!" Roy whispered.

"I love you too! You do not know how glad I am to hear you say that. *The Power Of Song* is a part of me as well," Rebecca replied – caressing Roy's face. "I work for *LUCK.7* – so I have had the genuine privilege of hearing your melodious voice up close and personal. However, I never dreamed that I would get as up close and personal with you as I am right now!"

Smiling, Roy was interested and confused at the same time. "So, that is the radio station that you mentioned yesterday?" he inquired.

"But of course!" Rebecca replied amidst a sentiment of common sense. "What other radio station could I possibly work for with such an idealistic reputation in this fair city?"

"True! Very True!" Roy replied – amidst his own sentiment of gratitude for all that the radio station had done for him. "However, I have taken many trips there. Unfortunately, I have never had the genuine privilege of seeing your tender beauty before. What department do you work for?"

Reclining into his arms, Rebecca confessed, "I do not do anything important! I am a glorified Go-'fer!" She paused in embarrassment. "Go-'fer this, Rebecca! Go-'fer that, Rebecca!" she concluded – in silent suppression of the truth that must remain untold for now.

"Well, at least you have been close to the action. Unfortunately, I used to make recordings in my basement and carry them everywhere I went – dedicating my very existence to the mere hope that I might get noticed – somehow, somewhere, someday. Guided by **The Power Of Almighty God** and the spiritual guidance of my minister, Pastor Clifford Mulholland at *Heaven's Paradise Christian Union*, I developed a strong passion for singing at a very young age and have been singing at services for many years." He paused for a tender kiss.

As Roy spoke, Rebecca listened with sentimental and mesmerized interest – finding herself in intense conflict with her deepest secret. "Please, continue!" she sighed.

"It all began right here last year. I was playing the same *Lucky Seven* slot machine where we sealed our intimate victory last night – about to play off a win. In an instant, it happened..." He paused – nervous and excited. "No sooner did I step away for a brief moment, then my recordings were gone – vanished without a trace – until..."

As Roy paused once more, Rebecca blushed – in deep hope that he would not notice. "Until???" she inquired.

Lost in his moment of reflection, Roy said, "I apologize! I am still confused as to how what happened next could remain a mystery to this very moment. The next thing I knew, my very first song was playing over the *LUCK.7* airwaves – *"With This One Voice…"* I was so surprised, that I did not even notice **The Blessing From Almighty God** that would come to aide me in the discovery of my dream of becoming a singer – right before my unsuspecting eyes. In an instant, I had enough money to realize my dream. Ever since that day, I have never stopped thinking about how special it would be to meet the person who was responsible for that very special moment. Words could never hope to express the gratitude that I will always feel for him or her. But, you know Rebecca, it is very strange because I found you exactly one year to the day upon which my life was touched by **Almighty God** in that special way…" He paused – for a soft kiss. "Now, I have you – *My Everlasting Love And Dream Come True.* Now, not only do I believe in you and me. I believe that **The Power Of Almighty God** has united us!" I love you, Rebecca!"

"**To Almighty God Be The Glory!**" I love you too, Roy!" Rebecca replied. "I love you too!"

Upon these words, Roy had an idea. "The hotel is hosting a dance competition tonight!" he mentioned.

Amused, Rebecca sighed, "Do you really think that it is fair to step out onto the dance floor with the unfair advantage of the rhythm of a love as strong as ours?" As they gazed into *The Eyes Of Everlasting Love,* they shouted in amused declaration "Let's Go-'fer it!"

A short time later, Rebecca appeared before Roy in all of her splendor. She was dressed in a golden jumpsuit – sparkling in the silver reflection of playing cards, poker chips, dice, and *Lucky Sevens* - and boots. As his eyes blinded with her beauty, Roy sighed "I have something for you!" Upon these words, he retrieved a box of silver velvet. "**My Faith In Almighty God** has always been a true source of strength, comfort, and peace. However, I realize yet again that

He fulfills every desire and need of the heart. In that first sweet moment of our union, I saw *My Dream Come True*. Ethereal and beautiful, you seemed so close and yet so far. When I signed your record album, I signed my name in declaration of a pledge of *Everlasting Love* – even if I never saw your precious face ever again. In the few moments that I had before I would solve that intimate mystery, I bought this," Roy said – placing it into her hands.

Upon opening it, Rebecca could not believe her eyes. Inside, was a solid gold locket – engraved with a beautiful angel with a touching inscription around its ethereal image. *"To Rebecca, My Beloved Angel, Love, Roy."* Opening it, Rebecca marveled. Their faces were inscribed in sparkling beauty – forever side by side. "I hope that you do not mind my making such a definite investment in the strength of my initial feelings. I knew that we were meant to be together. I love you so much!" Roy said.

Closing her eyes, Rebecca held the locket to her heart – placing her hand into Roy's. Rebecca could not find the words to communicate her deepest feelings. "If you only knew, Roy!" she sighed.

"Knew what?" Roy inquired.

Lost in the intimacy of his love, Rebecca could not speak. Caressing his face, she silenced him with a sweet kiss. In a soft breath, she pledged, "I love you, Roy! I always have and always will. Please take that to heart and never forget it!" As they joined hands, Roy and Rebecca proceeded onto the dance competition.

The room sparkled in lights of red and yellow neon. A festive crystal ball began rotating in illumination of its sparkling light within the shadows. As Roy and Rebecca stepped forward, applause proceeded. In an instant, a selection of Roy's tender love songs began playing.

As the dance competition began, Roy and Rebecca united in complete rhythm with their every move. All of the while, their eyes never left one another. As they danced, they cherished the tender love between them and became one in truly special connection that they had never known before – and would cherish from this moment onward together as one. They moved on the wave of love as their deepest thoughts traveled in gratitude and praise to **Almighty God.** Roy and Rebecca knew that they were meant to be together.

A short time later, the past few moments ended just as they began – with a mesmerized gaze into *The Eyes Of Everlasting Love.* The next thing they knew, they had won *"The Solid Gold Hotel And Casino Movers And Shakers Award."* As applause proceeded, Roy and Rebecca began waving and bowing their heads in acceptance of their spectators.

They were presented with frosted crystal globes with silver and gold musical notes around them. A solid gold inscription sparkled upon them:

The Solid Gold Hotel And Casino
Movers And Shakers Award
October 2, 1977

Also, they received satin jackets – Roy's in gold and Rebecca's in silver. Each was inscribed with *The Solid Gold Hotel And Casino* monogram on the back, a slot machine on the front, and the year '77 representation on each shoulder – a gesture that Roy would come to reflect upon as *The Year Of His Heart.* After all was said and done, Roy and Rebecca sealed their special victory with a tender kiss.

As Roy and Rebecca joined hands, the crowd of spectators began clapping and spreading itself in their path. Slowly, they ventured onto the area of ceremonial photography. After slipping into his jacket, Roy helped Rebecca with hers. They held the awards close to their hearts. Rebecca appeared in all of her splendor. As Roy gazed into her gorgeous eyes, they stood amidst the enchantment of this *One True And Everlasting Love.* With a unified expression of their love, the flash bulb popped.

Joining hands once more, Roy and Rebecca kissed and stepped out into the sparkling darkness of *The City Of Lights*. As they stood mesmerized by the cherished beauty of their hometown – in sentimental union with the intimacy of their love – Roy and Rebecca gazed at the brilliant glow of fireworks in resounding blast above them. With their hearts together as one, Roy and Rebecca wished upon every star – in deep reflection of any dreams that they would have from this moment onward and would find in the hearts of one another. Only love remained.

Chapter 3

The next morning, Roy met Rebecca at her suite. As she opened the door, he was mesmerized by her gorgeous appearance in the familiar beauty of the bikini that she had worn in their first cherished meeting – sealing the moment with a tender kiss. Caressing his face, she asserted, "OK, My Marvelous Minstrel – now it is my turn!"

Lost in her tender beauty, Roy sighed "For what?"

Upon these words, Rebecca placed her finger to his lips – silencing him. "Sorry! That question goes against the rules – the same of which we agreed upon yesterday, I might add! Now, it is time for you to tell the truth! Do you think that breakfast is the most important meal of the day?" Upon these words, she pointed.

Roy smiled. On a room service cart, was a tray with a yellow pound cake, a carton of "Sweet Treats Vanilla Ice Cream," and a bottle of "Dream Dairy Milk." As Roy looked into Rebecca's beautiful eyes and kissed her, he sighed "Very interesting and charming! However, I must be honest. I have never had a sweet - and at the same time nutritious - breakfast before. Even so, if the food is half as good as the company, I can get used to it! But, before we eat, I want to share a new song that came to me in my dreams last night."

As he took Rebecca into his arms, Roy rested her head upon his shoulder and began to sing.

Love, as I hold you in my arms…
I will keep you safe from harm…
And see the glow of your tender charms…
Sweet Love, you are My Tender Dream Come True…
And now here with you, together we two…
This Is True Love to last through now until the end of time…
This Is True Love…
Always and forever, I will love you…
This Is True Love…
And now, I dedicate myself to making your dreams come true…

True Love, as I look into your eyes...
From my heart, I realize...
The future seems so bright because of you...
God's Love *– united our two hearts as one...*
The best days are ahead – and have just begun...
As I stand hand in hand with you...
I will live through each new day...
Love, sent from **Heaven...**
You showed me the way...
Into my heart, you came – with a tender love so true...
Within my heart, I love you and only you...
Rebecca, let us be together forever – we two...

Rebecca sighed in tender sentiment. "Thank you, Roy! Now that we have found one another, we will be just that – together forever, we two." With a passionate kiss, Roy turned to prepare their breakfast. Rebecca stepped toward the closet and retrieved something from her hooded sweatshirt. However, she knew that it must be kept from Roy – for now. As she reclined into a familiar armchair to wait for him, she could not stop smiling.

Upon his return, Roy and Rebecca prepared themselves to pray. This time, Rebecca spoke.

"Heavenly Father, We Thank You In Mind, Body, Heart, And Soul In The Blessed Name Of Your Son, Our Lord And Savior Jesus Christ For This Food And Time Together. We Thank You For The Blessing Of One True And Everlasting Love That We Would Never Have Discovered Without Your Spiritual Guidance. Blessed Be Your Holy Name, As We Look To You With Gratitude And Love And Continue To Do Your Will Throughout The Ages."

As they united once more in the words **"All God's People Said, Amen!"** they began to eat.

As they ate, Rebecca asked, "How is it that a one of a kind heart as loving as yours could possibly stay lonely for so long?"

46

Roy sighed. "If you only knew. You see, singing has been a cherished part of my life for as long as I can remember. Aside from my spiritual focus at church, I have been inspired by many sentimental and melodious voices of past decades and have always felt that I could turn to them - just to reflect upon the love that I have always dreamed about. Even though they were distant voices that I always wanted to meet and thank for their melodious inspiration and understanding of my fear in discovering the strength from within to take a chance on finding *One True And Everlasting Love*, I have always had this fear deep inside of me that I feel claimed the life of one of my favorite entertainers. Do you remember Andrew Manchester?"

"Yes, of course! He was a great entertainer!" Rebecca replied. "You knew him?"

"Yes. Very well!" Roy asserted. "Anyway, he became famous at a young age as well. I came to identify with him because he sang from his heart as well. Unfortunately, he soon became absorbed into the dark side of fame. Much like myself, all that he ever wanted – aside from melodious success - was to find *True Love*. Unfortunately, a rather self-centered, egotistical, and manipulative person appeared out of nowhere wanting to take advantage of him. What this self-centered individual did not understand was that although he was famous, he was a human being with a lonely heart in endless search." Upon these words, Roy's eyes blinded with tears. As Rebecca caressed his face, he found the strength to continue.

"One day, at a music store autograph session, he met this fan who – through bold and extreme methods to approach him – secured his feelings for her by taking advantage of his feelings. She claimed to love him too. Unfortunately, as with many struggling artists, he became a victim of the universal and constant shift in the name of changing his style. However, he knew that his true purpose in life was only to sing. After all, his gift was his song – he was not about to begin singing a different tune. Even though his true fans continued to support him in the name of his one true passion, his love abandoned

47

him – merely because his songs were no longer Number One on the music industry charts. This loss left him with the deepest sense of sadness that he had ever known. In his heart, he knew that his one true happiness had always been and would always be the sole foundation of his success and fulfillment – his true fans. Even so, he never truly came to terms with his loss. Tragically, one night he collapsed on stage and died. Even though there were many rumors surrounding the cause of his untimely death, the truth that no one will ever know or understand is that he died of a broken heart," Roy asserted.

Rebecca took Roy's hand. "How did you discover all of this?" she asked.

Upon these words, Roy's hands began to shake. Releasing a deep sob, Roy whispered, "I was there! We had become friends and he understood my own message from the heart better than anyone I had ever known. In fact, he asked me to sing in his opening performance at a few of his concerts throughout this great city. Also, he had always stayed in contact with me when he was on the road. That night, he was performing at his homecoming concert. I will never forget it. He invited me to a front row seat and I could see the pain in his eyes. As he collapsed, I ran to his side. With powerful hope that I could somehow bring him some comfort and peace of mind, I whispered 'Your heart has shined your love upon others through your songs. It is out there waiting for you as well – as it is for all of us. Hold on! Just, hold on!' Unfortunately, he was already slipping away. As he looked into my eyes, he smiled and said 'Love has abandoned me – but must live on in you. I was misguided and weak. You must find it.' Upon these words, he touched my heart. 'Because your heart has the strength to make the most beautiful songs to ever be heard and *The Power Of Love* to last for all time. Believe in yourself. Never give up. Remember, I will always be with you.'"

As Roy became lost in his thoughts, Rebecca finished them for him. "His last words?" she asked.

"Yes!" Roy whispered. "Since that day, I have been terrified by the belief that if I was ever fortunate enough to become famous through *The Gift Of Song* that I love and cherish so much, the same thing would happen to me!"

As Roy wiped his eyes, Rebecca inquired "Did he ever mention her name?"

"Reese was her name," Roy replied.

Overcome by fear, Rebecca began to sweat. In deep hope that he did not notice, she gripped Roy's hand even tighter and held him close to her. Softly, she began to cry silent tears – knowing that her thoughts must remain silent – for now.

In the comfort of Rebecca's arms, Roy kissed her and whispered "When I saw you for the very first time, I knew that your beauty was a vision that I had never known before – and would cherish from that moment onward - always and forever. I have dreamed of you throughout my entire life. Now that I have you, I know that *The Power Of Love* does exist. Let it be said that Andrew Manchester was right!"

"Always and forever!" Rebecca replied. Upon these words, Rebecca reached into her pocket. As Roy watched, she opened a golden box. Inside, two rings sparkled in a charming and brilliant prophesy. A silver one declared *"Lucky."* The other – a golden one – declared *"Seven."* As her eyes blinded with tears, Rebecca reached for the silver ring and spoke. "I wore this word upon my heart on the day that I met you to show you that by **The Blessing Of Almighty God,** I am yours now and forever – for the rest of my life." Upon these words, Rebecca placed the gold ring upon Roy's finger and the silver one upon her own.

Lost in the intimacy of her declaration of love, he cried silent tears and whispered "As I am yours! ***To Almighty God Be The Glory!*** Come to me, *My Everlasting Love And Dream Come True.*"

Before Roy could finish, Rebecca fell into his arms and concluded, "Through now and forever, I will love only you!" The tenderness of the moment elapsed into a flood of passionate kisses. As they rested in *The Arms Of Everlasting Love*, Roy and Rebecca whispered a unified expression of love.

Suddenly, something occurred to Roy. "I forgot to tell you! The radio station has a birthday gift for me!" he explained with excitement.

"What might that be?" Rebecca asked.

"It is going to be as much of a surprise for me as it will be for you. You see, I have not seen it yet. All that I know is that it is downstairs waiting for me!" Roy replied.

"Sneaky! Very Sneaky!" Rebecca snickered. "So, what would you like to do today, My Marvelous Minstrel?" she asked.

Smiling in reflection of a silent mystery, Roy replied, "I am quite certain that we can find some mischief to get into!"

Intrigued, Rebecca said "Really? Do tell! I am very anxious to know!"

"OK! The only way to settle this is a friendly game of *"Rock, Scissors, Paper!""* Roy resolved. "You call it!"

"OK! *"Rock, Scissors, Paper!""* Rebecca shouted. He drew *"Scissors"* and she drew *"Paper."*

"Ha! Ha! *"Scissors"* cut *"Paper!""* he declared in laughter – sliding his fingers in a cutting motion all of the way up to her face – ending with a gentle caress. With a kiss, Roy declared, "I am going out to check on something. Please, stay here until I return! If you do not..." He paused. In a rapid maneuver, Roy slid his fingers in a cutting motion across Rebecca's tummy and concluded with "Beware of the *"Scissors!""*

Upon these words, Rebecca giggled and sighed, "I have no need to fear them! Trust me!"

As they arose, Roy held Rebecca close to him and gently kissed her as she walked toward the door – holding onto him in a tender embrace in their stride.

With a mesmerized gaze into Rebecca's eyes, Roy sealed her into a warm embrace. As she looked at him with an anxious smile, Rebecca asked "Are you willing to give me a hint as to what is in that devious mind of yours?"

Chuckling, Roy replied "My Beloved Rebecca! I want to take this opportunity to inform you of something right now!" He paused for a passionate kiss upon her unsuspecting lips and concluded with "I am full of surprises!" Raising his eyebrows, Roy said, "I love you!" and departed.

Blushing and mesmerized by his charming sentiment, Rebecca stood at the door watching him. "I love you too!" she shouted. Giggling, she closed the door.

Later that day, Roy appeared at Rebecca's suite once more. As she opened the door, he could not believe his eyes. Rebecca was dressed in a yellow sports bra – envisioned by a transparent shirt of sparkling silver and golden stars that was tied in tender accentuation of her navel – silver denim jeans, and white shoes. As she greeted Roy with a warm smile, Rebecca raised her eyebrows. "Hello!" she sighed.

Nervously, he whispered "Hello!" In an instant, each of them knew what the other was thinking. In rapid declaration, they shouted "*Rock, Scissors, Paper!*" and Rebecca flew into his arms. Rapidly, the door closed. Roy and Rebecca began to kiss.

Gently, he reclined her delicate body onto the bed. The intense love and passion within her eyes caused Roy to become lost in the intimacy of the moment. Suddenly, Roy sensed a deep and passionate desire that he could no longer control. Blushing, he declared "I have dreamed of this moment ever since the first glance into your eyes. Your ethereal charm was gorgeous and glamorous – so close and yet so far. I can no longer resist this moment of tender touch. *My Beautiful Angel,* I love you very much!" Slowly, Roy began to cover Rebecca's tummy with soft kisses. Amused, Rebecca closed her eyes and caressed his back. She began to sigh and speak his name. Only by his discovery of a sensitive area did he excite Rebecca's peaceful comfort. All at once, he knew that his senses would never be the same again.

With a mesmerized gaze into Rebecca's eyes, Roy sighed, "Would you grant me the pleasure of a favor?"

"Anything, My Love!" Rebecca whispered in comfort. Upon these words, Roy reached into his pocket in revelation of his surprise. He retrieved two tickets to the famous theme park of *The City Of Lights – Pleasure Paradise*. Smiling in acceptance, Rebecca said, "I have only been there once before – for a particular purpose!"

"What purpose was that, *My Beloved Angel?*" Roy inquired.

"To see one of your first concerts, My Marvelous Minstrel!" Rebecca asserted. "I will go with you, but only on one condition – I want you to sing *"One Love… One Heart…"* for me!" Blushing amidst compliance, Roy gazed into *The Eyes Of Everlasting Love* and whispered, "Now that I have realized the truth behind the words at long last…" He paused – concluding his sentiment in song.

You are My Angel…
I am lost in your charm…
With one tender look, you took my heart on your wings and flew…
You whispered true 'I love you…'
After lonely days of endless searching…
I found a love – tender, sweet, and true…
Joining we two…
I love you…
You Are The Love…
I Am The Heart…
From here on out, we will never part – My Love…
Forever Blessed By The Love Of Almighty God…
Every future day will show us the way…
In your arms, I will stay - never go away…
Day and night feels so right forever…
From down the road of chance that life takes…

Our two hearts found True Love in just the right place…
At the right time…
Forever mine, you and me…

The tender words elapsed into a warm embrace. Amidst amused unison, Roy and Rebecca shouted "Let's Go-'fer it!"

They raced to the parking garage. Before reaching his car, Roy asked Rebecca to close her eyes and said "You are well aware of how generous *LUCK.7 Radio* is. Would you like to see how *they* fulfill my dreams?"

"But of course!" Rebecca replied.

"OK! Say *Golden Dreams*! Roy declared in a familiar sentiment from a short time ago.

As Rebecca chuckled, she could not believe her eyes. "Wow! A 1977 Yellow Chevrolet Caprice! Very nice!" Rebecca asserted. Upon kissing her, Roy opened the door and held Rebecca's hand in entrance. Entering the driver's side, he took her hand once more and they closed their eyes in deep reflection of the moment. Roy spoke:

"Heavenly Father, We Thank You For The Peace And Safety That You Have Always Sustained Throughout Our Daily Lives As We Seek To Do Your Will Every Step Of The Way. We Ask For The Same In Our Travels At This Time, In The Cherished Name Of Jesus Christ Your Son, Our Lord And Savior…"

Upon these words, they concluded in spiritual unison, ***"Amen!"***

As they rode through the sparkling scenery of *The City Of Lights*, Rebecca rested her head upon Roy's shoulder and closed her eyes. In their travels, a familiar song that they had cherished from their childhood began to project its nostalgic melody into their hearts – *"Hand In Hand."* In content reminiscence, Rebecca kissed Roy and said "I have not heard this song in years."

Upon their arrival, Roy took Rebecca into his arms and carried her a short distance. As Roy reclined her body onto a cool surface, Rebecca laughed at the sensation of water dripping across her back. Behind her, was a large brilliant globe of frosted yellow crystal that featured the *Pleasure Paradise* monogram in red neon. From all around it, a circular formation of sparkling globes splashed their aquatic flow. Red crystal stars sparkled on each side of it.

As Roy took her into his arms once more, a passage of soft kisses led them onto the legendary roller coaster, *"Surfin' Suspense."* Upon ascension of a great spiral staircase, Roy and Rebecca seated themselves into a coaster in the unique formation of a space shuttle with red and blue stripes and silver stars. Fastening the safety guard around them, Roy kissed Rebecca and whispered a mischievous intention. "See you at the bottom, My Love!" he snickered. He could feel a silent giggle of laughter in her tummy.

In an instant, they were gliding upon the wings of excitement through the cool breeze of water whirls and loops of gravity defiance. At the last possible second in the air, Roy declared, "Rebecca, you make me feel so free!"

As they descended, she replied "Ah, yes! But let us now put both feet on the ground – and forever in love we will be!"

In the end, the hearts of Roy and Rebecca continued to soar upon the altitude of *Everlasting Love.* An escalator transport guided them onto the ethereal travels of *"Shooting Star."* Their flight cabin was of a unique silver star formation – sparkling in the glow of minute golden stars and illuminating in yellow neon lights. Roy and Rebecca reclined into *The Arms Of Everlasting Love* and relaxed for a ride across the sky. As they gazed into *The Eyes Of One True And Everlasting Love, The Light Of Love* reflected upon their fingers. Only love remained.

The wave of love guided them onto the dynamic destination of *"Cosmo Town."*

Astride a bicycle built for two, Roy and Rebecca rode through a futuristic city. A great population of animated yellow Martians inhabited the metropolis – drifting through the unique atmosphere of gummy bears and lemon drops upon the sparkling flight of marshmallow stars. With a smile, Roy and Rebecca caught a few of the luscious candies in their mouths.

As the bicycle soared through the world of Outer Space, they found themselves on a crimson path through an enchanted forest where animated red Martians frolicked in the bright world of licorice powder and gumdrops. Once again, Roy and Rebecca were fortunate in their catch of a small snack. A final view on the galactic horizon found Roy and Rebecca inside of *"The Pleasure Paradise Power Play Casino."* Rebecca pointed at an advertisement for *"The Super Sevens Slots Tournament."* Raising her eyebrows, she giggled, "Let's see how hot you are, Hot Stuff!"

Grinning in sentimental recollection of a similar challenge, Roy replied "Game on!"

With a tender kiss, Roy and Rebecca launched into the amusing competitive spirit of fun. Upon Rebecca's declaration, the stakes would raise higher than Roy could have ever imagined. "The winner loves the loser more!" Rebecca added with a rapid pull.

"I will win for sure!" Roy declared - grinning.

"Ah! My Marvelous Minstrel has such determination! A dream made possible by **The Power Of Almighty God** brought us together. But, you must keep dreaming if you want to win this one!" Rebecca challenged. Upon these words, Roy grinned and raised his eyebrows. Lost in the moment, they neglected to keep track of their scores. As the end of the game resounded in bright lights, Roy and Rebecca's match was declared a draw. They had identical scores of 777.

Sealing their mutual victory with a warm embrace, Roy whispered, "How do we handle this one?"

"Fear not, My Marvelous Minstrel! We will settle this cute competition tonight!" Rebecca snickered.

"Ah! The isolated approach! I admire that in a one of a kind and gorgeous woman. Then again, I admire everything about you!" Roy replied.

A flood of sweet kisses led them through a dark escalator transport and found them in front of the virtual simulation of *"City Of Lights: Lazer Land."* "The competitive edge! You have to love it!" Roy observed. Stepping into two neon doors – Roy's reading *"Lucky"* and Rebecca's *"Charm"* – they planned their costumes and strategies.

Roy wore a helmet with yellow visionary scopes, a utility belt with projectile clubs, diamonds, dice, hearts, and poker chips – glowing in yellow neon - and censors. Activating a gold laser gun, he entered the battlefield of *Everlasting Love* – astride a sparkling golden skateboard.

Rebecca slipped into a helmet with red visionary scopes, a utility belt with projectile clubs, diamonds, dice, hearts, and poker chips – glowing in red neon - and censors. Astride a sparkling silver skateboard, she activated a silver laser gun and whispered, "I do love the competitive edge. But, I love you more, Roy!"

As the contest began, their only light was a brilliant crystal ball above them – flashing in alternating intervals of red and yellow. Suddenly, Roy emerged from behind a large slot machine display on the course and threw a heart. "Looking for me?" he asked.

Rebecca raced after him in resounding blasts. In rapid sequence, they flipped as their skateboards passed each other. Landing upon them in constant motion, Roy and Rebecca discovered that they had each gained seven points. Slowly emerging from passing dice and cherry displays, Roy connected with one of Rebecca's glowing projectiles. "I found you!" she answered.

Their battle proceeded onward through twisting tunnels and pathways – illuminating in virtual neon images of *The City Of Lights.* The strategic advantage remained in constant shift. "Give up! Victory is mine!" Rebecca asserted with seven additional points scored.

"Never! It makes this pursuit much more fun!" Roy laughed with a successful throw of his dice.

In an instant, Rebecca knew how to ensure victory. "Roy, check this out!" Upon these words, she lowered her gun to her utility belt – as if to surrender. In an instant, Roy fell from his skateboard in mesmerized distraction. Slowly, Rebecca stepped over him – removing her helmet. Raising her eyebrows, she removed her utility belt – revealing her navel. "Do you give up?" she breathed.

"Take me, I am yours!" Roy whispered in sweet surrender. As they kissed, Roy and Rebecca declared in soft unison, "In the end, we are both winners!" These words elapsed into the tenderness of the moment. Only love remained.

Standing before *"Little Links Putting Green,"* miniature golf was their next inclination. "Best of six?" Roy offered.

"You're on!" Rebecca accepted.

The first hole was called *"Bowling Ball Blast."* Roy and Rebecca laughed at the amusing sentiment of their own bowling experience. With a powerful swing, Roy heard the electronic sound of falling pins. With that, an animated bowling ball knocked nine pins down in front of them. The ball rotated into the hole – slowly. Grinning, Roy turned to Rebecca. "Beat that, Laser Woman!" he challenged.

Caressing his face, Rebecca replied "I would be glad to!" Tossing her hips into position, Rebecca raised her eyebrows. "Observe!" she asserted. With a swing, Rebecca watched the scoreboard flash in its yellow neon declaration of "STRIKE!!!" – sinking the putt, and all ten pins. "Golf claps only, please!" Rebecca requested. Upon Roy's compliance, she said, "Kiss me!"

"Not now, Old Golf Pro! Five holes to go!" Roy said – raising his eyebrows. Upon these words, they stepped forward – joining hands. At the last possible second, he kissed her unsuspecting lips. Rebecca blushed. Lost in the tenderness of the moment, they proceeded onto the second hole – called *"Hoops."*

Near the hole, Roy putted. An animated basketball rolled onto the platform and flew into the basket. The buzzer sounded with a triple point dunk. Roy's ball made a swift roll and scored. "Come, your shot awaits!" he said. Rebecca stepped forward. A rapid swing resulted in a mere score of 1. As the buzzer sounded, Roy concluded "Beautiful, you are! Basketball Great, you are not!" They laughed in amused unison. *"Galloping Goal"* was next in line. Before the horserace simulation, Roy putted. His animated horse reached victory in 10 seconds. "Call the bets in!" he declared - smiling.

Rebecca managed to cross the finish line in 5 seconds. "Luckily, my money was on me!" she answered.

"Electric Eruption" followed. Roy advanced with a simple swing. His ball shot out of the effervescent volcano – shooting straight into the hole.

"OK! Once Hot Stuff, always Hot Stuff!" Rebecca giggled. Upon her shot, Rebecca's ball cast upward – only to fall back into the volcano. In a path of red liquid, it slipped into the hole - slowly.

"Power Puck" was the fifth hole in succession. Roy's forward swing resulted in the virtual hockey stick's thrust – with the puck slamming into the top of the goal. The golf ball traveled steadily to its score. "Slippery! Very Slippery!" Rebecca responded – stepping forward. With a hit, the puck spun into a quick goal.

"The next one is for all of the marbles!" Roy announced.

"Knockout Punch" was par for the course. Taking his shot, Roy watched the animated boxing glove slam into the speed bag. As the ball rolled forward, the bell signaled victory. Roy scored a "Knockout!!!" "May the best player win!" he proclaimed. In Rebecca's final swing, the swift punch delivered a "Technical Knockout!!!"

"Good game!" Roy and Rebecca declared in unison. Upon these words, they sealed one another into a warm embrace. In an instant, the sweet melody of a familiar song began to echo in the distance. Amidst silent laughter, they joined hands and proceeded toward the musical cruise of *"Hand In Hand."*

"I did not know that this place had a feature ride for this song!" Rebecca admitted.

"Neither did I! I did not get to see the entire park when I came here for that concert. Although, I wish I could have seen you on that day! Just think! Maybe, you could have gone on tour with me!" Roy suggested.

Blushing in the name of keeping her deepest thoughts a secret for now, Rebecca sighed, "You know that I would have!" As they reclined into a boat that featured a unique mixture of beautiful rainbow colors, the voyage began with a passage through an effervescent window with a mural of the world upon it.

In the beginning of the journey, the animated world of Outer Space featured the chorus of the animated sun, moon, stars, and planets – united in the ethereal melody. Soon, the animation divided into a rural landscape to its left and an urban landscape to its right. From all around, animated children sang the song in melodious harmony. A musical view of the aquatic world came to follow with the sound of animated fish, amphibians, reptiles, and coral shells in their pacific proclamation. Passage onto a tropical rainforest could be heard through the virtual vocals of exotic wildlife. In the end, the song soared upon the wings of animated angels through the ethereal spectacle.

Having spent an afternoon of mirth in the intimate presence of *Everlasting Love,* Roy and Rebecca returned to *The Solid Gold Hotel And Casino* – traveling amidst tender kisses and the unified words:

"*Almighty God, We Thank You For The Times Of Recreation That We Share In The Cherished Unity Of One True And Everlasting Love And For The Many Gifts That You Continue To Bless Us With Throughout Our*

Days In The Beloved Name Of Jesus Christ Your Son, Our Lord And Savior. Amen!"

The early evening hours found Roy and Rebecca inside of the hotel's secured parking garage once more – in intense anticipation of Roy's belated birthday gift. Earlier that day, their curiosity had been furthered by being told that Rebecca would be receiving a gift as well – in recognition of her dedicated service to the radio station. As the door opened, Roy could not believe his eyes – neither could Rebecca. Before them, stood two motorcycles. Each was inscribed with one of their names – Roy's was gold and Rebecca's was silver.

Amidst the laughter of surprise, Roy issued a challenge. "I dare you to race me!" he declared.

"Ah, yes!   But, the truth is that I will beat you!" Rebecca resolved.

" *"Truth Or Dare"* at its very best!" they shouted in unison. Upon these words, they ran to the vehicles and were out of the garage in a matter of seven seconds.

As they rode aside one another through the sparkling spectacle of *The Landmark Of Lights,* Roy shouted, "Follow me! I know of a very interesting detour!"   Within a matter of seconds, they were racing up a large ramp that seemed to be leading to somewhere very familiar to Rebecca – although she could not identify the reason at first.   With a smile of acceptance, she followed Roy. They were headed for the roof of *The Solid Gold Hotel And Casino.*

Upon parking the motorcycles, Roy stepped over to Rebecca. With a kiss, he proceeded to shield her vision and whispered "I wanted to show you in some small way a small portion of the height upon which my love for you soars." In an instant, Rebecca could not believe the marvelous spectacle before her unsuspecting eyes.   Below, *The City Of Lights* sparkled in its rich essence – reflecting in the glow of *The Landmark Of Lights.* As he held Rebecca's waist in a tender embrace, Roy's declaration of *Everlasting Love* would come to serve as a brilliant reflection of loving intimacy that would be the source of strength   that   the tender love between them would need – in triumph over the sudden and painful moment that was about to occur.

Softly, Roy whispered, "Perhaps, one day we can sing together and unite our voices in melodious declaration of our *Everlasting Love*." Upon these words, Rebecca's hands began to shake. With pain in her voice, she whispered "I would love to, but…"

"But, what?" Roy inquired.

Suddenly, Rebecca's head fell into her hand. With a rapid withdrawal from Roy's loving embrace, she stepped toward the edge of the roof. Stretching her trembling hands out, she screamed "No!!!"

Shocked by this confusing instant of pain, Roy grabbed her – in fear that she might fall. "Rebecca, what is wrong, My Love?"

Turning around, she caressed Roy's face in a tender instant of reaching out for the love in his heart – reflected in his terrified eyes that were flooded with silent tears. Falling into his arms, she whispered through deep sobs "I have something to tell you!"

Placing her hand upon his heart, Roy sighed "Of course, My Love!" As they sat, Roy held her close to him. Despite the pain in her eyes, Rebecca was at ease and ready to face the ghost from her past.

"Not long ago, something happened that changed the course of my entire life. Before that time, I was an aspiring singer. Much like you, I developed a passion for singing at a young age. Fortunately for me, *LUCK.7 Radio* was there to help me in the same way that it helped you. While working there, my fellow workers would stand silent and listen as I sang throughout the building and encouraged me with friendly applause and warm sentiments. Looking back, it seems now that they knew in their hearts of the reality that had remained uncertain for far too long for me – the singing opportunity that I had always dreamed about was about to happen.

Unfortunately, someone very close to me wanted to ruin it for me – my sister who worked with me at the radio station. She wanted to become a singer as well. Unfortunately for her, she never truly had the voice or talent that I had. Consequently, she grew jealous. One day, one of the greatest things ever happened to me. I was called into the office of the same executive that drafted your contract – I know, because I did it for him. Anyway, he said something that I will never forget. 'Rebecca, you have the voice of an *Angel* that will bring happiness to the hearts of many people in search of an inspirational voice from the heart.'" As she wiped a sentimental tear from her eye, Rebecca concluded with "The next thing I knew, he said 'I did not want to say anything while your sister was around, but would you be interested in a recording session?' Overcome by excitement, I knew that my moment to shine was upon me – or so I thought. We began the next day. I sang from my heart – drawing inspiration from a picture of you that I kept with me everywhere I went." Upon these words, Roy kissed her in sentimental appreciation.

"Upon completion of the session, my sister came from the next room and said, 'Congratulations on your big break. I am sure that you will be a great success. You must be tired. If you would like, I will carry this down to the editing room for you.' Confused by her change of heart as an uncharacteristic contrast to an argument that we had only hours before, I allowed her to do it because I was in a rush to hear the debut of your most recent song at the time – "*One Love... One Heart...*"" In his thoughts, Roy blushed at her kind words as a loving fan. Gently, he kissed her once more – holding her closer.

"The next day, the radio station began to echo in the melody of my recordings. Unfortunately, there was something very peculiar and unfamiliar in absolutely every aspect of the sound. Clearly, I knew that my songs would sound different "on the other end of the microphone" so to speak. Even so, this was far too much of a difference. Immediately, I called the editing room and asked them when they received the tapes. I was told that they were received and edited earlier that morning. To make matters even worse, they mentioned being at a deadline – and distributed them in a rapid fashion. Lastly, I was told that the person that delivered them had a *LUCK.7* shirt on and dark sunglasses – she seemed to be in quite a rush. Investigating further, I discovered that a few of my fellow workers had heard someone in the recording studio – hours after I left. Every one of them said that the songs that they heard were exactly the same as my own. However, the voice and melodious impact behind them were not. One even said that she saw the silhouette of a woman through the frosted glass window. She pounded on the locked door – but no one answered. After searching for a key, she discovered that the room was empty – with no trace of any recordings. All that remained was a note with my name on it. Amidst deep shock, I read "R: Your star has already fallen!" Even though the writing had been disguised, I knew at once whom it belonged to. This scheme had been carried out by one person – the same that I saw sneaking around the room and out the door at that very moment with a *LUCK.7* shirt and dark sunglasses on with a sinister look on her face. Quickly, I raced after her – it was my sister. As I chased her throughout the building, we ended up on this very roof in a matter of seconds. Through painful tears, I demanded 'How could you do this to me?' Keeping a mysterious distance between us, her reply was 'Poor Rebecca! How could you miss the one constant in this business? This business is built on beauty, brains, and the occasional need to stay one step ahead. Unfortunately for you, I have them all.' These harsh words gave me the strength to match them and bring her back to reality. Although I was very angry, I asserted myself with some very true words. 'You have always been jealous of me. You have forgotten one thing – rights are always greater than wrongs in this business. Sooner or later, every scandal is uncovered. However, this will never come to that. Instead, I hold the key to the truth behind this mystery.' These words made her shake with fear. 'Stop! You have no idea what you are talking about!' she shouted. Triumphantly, I replied 'I certainly do! I will go public and show the entire world that not only did you steal my greatest gift, but also that my voice and talent are far greater than yours will ever be. Aside from that, *The Love And Guidance Of Almighty God* are on my side' Despite the smile of vindication upon my face, nothing could have ever prepared me for what was about to occur. With an evil grin, she declared 'This will never come to that. I will kill you first!' Before I knew what was happening, she lunged at me. By pure instinct, I moved out of harm's way – forgetting where we were. Immediately, I saw her stumbling at the edge – desperate to regain her balance. Despite my rapid maneuver to save her, it was already too late. My sister fell to her death with a horrible crash." By now, Rebecca was unable to control her sobs. Fortunately, Roy's warm touch and gentle words would become her source of strength in this moment of deep pain.

"Everything is going to be fine, My Precious Love! However, there is one thing that I need to know. What was your sister's name?" Roy asked with a tender kiss.

Still unable to gain full composure, Rebecca continued to speak her mind. "She was always self-centered, egotistical, and manipulative. Everyone in my family knew that she was going to be trouble. In fact, they asked me to look out for her and try to straighten her out! I even helped her get a job at *LUCK.7*." Closing her eyes in a moment of reflection upon her lost cause, she concluded with "I did not mean for you to die, but thank you for ruining my career, Reese!"

Suddenly, Rebecca froze. As she looked into Roy's eyes, they both were shocked by the name that just escaped her trembling lips. As Rebecca fell into his warm embrace, Roy asked "Rebecca, do you think that she was the one who…" Before he could finish, Rebecca affirmed his suspicion "I know she was! She always bragged about how her boyfriend – who was an entertainer – died on stage because he could not live without her – even though she never once told me his name. Now, there is no doubt in my mind! My sister was the self-centered, egotistical, and manipulative force behind the tragic death of Andrew Manchester."

With the dark truth revealed, Rebecca understood the source of Roy's fear – after all, she was related to the cause of it. Gently, she spoke. "Roy, ever since I met you, I knew that I would do everything above and beyond the farthest limitations of my power to show you the same tender feelings of warmth and happiness that you have shown me. I assure you by the strength of these very same feelings that now that I have you, you will never have to be afraid ever again."

"In return, I have pledged to do the same for you, Rebecca!" Roy asserted. "People should look out for one another. Sometimes, we get lost. If only there had been someone looking out for us to help us understand, many of the sad and painful things that happen to us could be avoided. I am here for you always and forever!"

"Promise?" Rebecca asked.

"Promise!" Roy asserted – taking her into his arms. Knowing of the pain that she was in, Roy spoke a blessing upon the moment.

"Father God, In The Precious Name Of Our Lord And Savior, Your Son Jesus Christ, I Speak Peace, Healing, Comfort, Strength, And Love Upon Your Loving Daughter And The Woman That I Love, Rebecca Davidson. You Know Of Her Pain, Father God. However, You Know Her Heart As Well. I Speak To The Painful Moment Of Her Past And Cast Out The Spirit Of Evil And Declare Here And Now That She Is Free With A Powerful Sense Of Spiritual Renewal To Continue To Love You As She Always Has And Always Will! Amen!"

Gaining composure as her peace of mind began to restore once more, Rebecca declared *"Amen!"* and Thank you..." Before she could finish, he placed a finger to her lips – silencing her. Softly, Roy began to sing.

Life is hard...
Too often, you cannot let down your guard...
But, look into my eyes and you will see...
True Love in me...
Right Here waiting for you...
Times do get rough...
And you can reach the point where you have had enough...
I will look out for you...
Keeping you safe from harm and pain...
To you, this is my pledge...
Be not afraid...
In The Name Of God's Love...
I will protect and strengthen...
Restore your peace of mind...
Just please take the hand of the love that you will have until the end...

Upon these words, Roy held Rebecca's head to his heart – caressing her hair. "Do you hear that?" he asked.

"Yes," Rebecca breathed.

Amidst the cherished love within his heart, Roy spoke. "That is the sound of my heart. It beats to the rhythm of a tender melody – sung with *The Power Of Love*. This rhythm and this song resounded from my heart to yours upon the first sweet moment of my union with you, *My Beloved Angel*. Listen, and you shall hear the song of my *Everlasting Love* for you."

Roy placed her hand upon his heart and spoke. "With your hand upon the heart that beats in declaration of **The Powerful Love Of Almighty God** that brought us together, I would like to correct you on one simple word. In the name of my life, everything that I have ever believed in, and my love for you itself, I pledge to you that *we* will never have to be afraid again. I love you, Rebecca!"

"I love you too, Roy!" Rebecca replied.

Secure that the moment of pain had passed, Roy listened as Rebecca spoke of her personal resolution to the tragedy. In his thoughts, he already knew of a way to make it even better – for both of them. "After she died, I blamed myself – although I was not guilty of anything. For a very long time, I could not face the radio station. To make matters worse, I felt that I could never sing again. However, through it all, my two sources of comfort and strength were then and are now **The Love Of Almighty God** and the cherished sentiment of your beautiful love songs." These were the words that Roy had been waiting for.

Placing his finger to her lips – silencing her with a warm smile of cherished sentiment – Roy spoke of something that he had been reflecting upon ever since his friend's death. However, it took on a whole new dimension in these last few moments. "Rebecca, you do not know how glad I am to hear you say that. Listen, and I guarantee you that you will never feel that way ever again."

Upon these words, Rebecca accepted - with one condition. "Speak away – but one more thing!" As she looked into his eyes, Rebecca cherished his love once more through a passionate kiss and soothing declaration "I love you!"

Amused and charmed by her sentiment, Roy replied, "I love you too!" Kissing her once more, Roy continued. "Ever since Andrew Manchester died, I have wanted to record a song in tribute to him. Since that time, I have only dreamed of the additional hope that I now ask of you. You see, although I never truly knew when or even if my dream of your ethereal beauty and *One True And Everlasting Love* would ever materialize, I told myself that I would wait on recording it until I knew for sure that his final words were correct. So, I am asking you, Rebecca, as *My Beautiful Angel, Everlasting Love,* and a loving spirit searching for the brilliant glow of her own rightful star to brighten the music industry once again and to right the wrong that was done to you, would you be willing to pursue a new recording venture with me?"

Suddenly, Rebecca flashed a warm smile and raised her eyebrows. Taking Roy's hand, she said, "Come with me! I have something to show you!" Confused, Roy complied. He was further confused because Rebecca was shielding his vision. To strengthen his curiosity, Rebecca declared, "I am going to show you where real songs come from!" A short time later, they were in an unfamiliar area. With a kiss, Rebecca placed her hand upon the door. With the words "OK! Rock on!" she pushed the door open. Roy could not believe his eyes. They were inside a recording studio that appeared to have been abandoned for some time. Even so, it possessed the essence of true melodious magic. From behind him, Rebecca pressed a button – activating a sign of gold neon above the console. Roy was surprised once more – *LUCK.7* flashed in all of its melodious splendor. As Rebecca held him in a tender embrace, Roy asked, "What is this place?"

Rebecca smiled and began to explain. "This, My Marvelous Minstrel is the original *LUCK.7* radio station. When Reese stole my recordings from me, the police shut it down because it was declared the scene of a crime. When I left *LUCK.7*, my agent informed me that the listening public had been expanding at a rate so constant, that the radio station could no longer operate in such a limited facility. For these reasons, it would be moving. Due to their belief in my singing ability, the owners decided that I could open and use this facility anytime I want – once I decide to pursue my singing aspirations again. This is the first time that I have been in this room since it happened."

"See? They continue to believe in you – and now, I do as well. It is time for us to unite into melodious magic – amidst *The Gift Of Song* that **Almighty God** has blessed both of us with. But, you still have not answered my question," Roy reasoned.

Upon these words, Rebecca appeared nervous. "Roy, I am not sure that I could…" she stammered in hesitation.

Silencing her with a kiss, Roy said "If I have to turn this room up-side-down and back again, I will find something to convince you to do it."

With a smile, Rebecca inquired, "You never give up, do you?"

Fortunately, Roy did not have to look very far at all. As he retrieved two recording reels from a box on the floor, he brought them to her and replied "Never!"

As Rebecca looked, her eyes blinded with tears. The reels were labeled *"Rebecca Davidson: "The Tie That Binds Us...""* "That was my very first recording," she sighed with a smile. Upon these words, she fell into Roy's arms and looked into his eyes. "I wrote that the day after your debut album came out. From the first sound of your melodious voice, I knew that I was in love with you. After I wrote the song, I always dreamed of performing it in a duet with you. Unfortunately, those terrible events happened and I did not know if I would ever sing again – let alone, meet you."

"Well, I am here right now – and will always be. Will you grant me the pleasure of hearing it and dancing with you?" Roy asked.

"At this moment, there is nothing that I could want more!" Rebecca accepted. As she activated the recording, Roy stared at his *Beautiful Angel*. As the sparkling lights reflected about her, Rebecca was his melodious inspiration – a vision of *Everlasting Love* sent from **The Ethereal Essence Of Heaven.** Rebecca grinned at the sparkling essence of the one word that defined and personified this moment. Softly, she sighed, "Roy Dawson, I want you to know here and now that I am the luckiest woman in the entire world!" As the distant memory of her melodious magic began, she motioned him over to her. As they gazed into *"The Eyes Of Everlasting Love,"* they danced to the rhythm of Rebecca's soft voice.

> *In your arms, soft and warm...*
> *I feel safe from harm - because of you...*
> *The Tie That Binds Us...*
> *Is full of dreams that will come true...*
> *In the warm and gentle light...*
> *The Tie That Binds me and you...*

Time is on our side…
In love with you…
No need to hide…
We will face the trials and triumphs of Everlasting Love…
Take my hand…
The Tie That Binds Us…
Will give us strength each new day…
Because of you, I have found my way…
To The Tie That Binds Us, we two…
True and lasting love…
Sent from **Heaven***…*
In God's Love*…*
I always will want to be here by your side…
In the light of your love – sweet, tender, true…
Because of you, the future is so bright…
Feels so right…
Until time does end…
The Tie That Binds Us…
Is always and forever…
Let us join together and become one…
The Tie That Binds Us in love…
Precious Love, it is true…
In all that we say and do…
The Tie That Binds Us Is Love From Me To You…

As they sealed one another into a warm embrace, there were no words left to speak – except one. Softly, Rebecca answered Roy's melodious inquiry with a solitary "Yes!"

Amidst powerful gratitude, Roy smiled and replied "Thank you, *My Beautiful And Melodious Angel.* Together, we will make cherished memories in the melodious echo of *Everlasting Love!*"

"Of course we will!" Rebecca replied with a kiss. "Just the two of us!" Amidst the mesmerized gaze of *Everlasting Love,* she stopped for one final look at the room that would make melodious history once more – this time, with their hearts together as one.

As Roy and Rebecca joined hands, they united their voices in a prayer of blessing upon their melodious challenge ahead:

"Heavenly Father, We Thank You In Mind, Body, Heart, And Soul For This Blessed Opportunity To Unite Our Voices In Communication Of The Gift Of Song That You Alone Have Provided Us With, And We Ask You, In The Blessed Name Of Jesus Christ Your Son, Our Lord And Savior, To Strengthen Our Voices And Guide Our Hearts As We Seek To Continue To Do Your Will In A Manner That Will Bring Glory And Honor To Your Name. Amen."

Sealing the moment with a smile and tender kiss, Roy turned the lights off. As he took Rebecca into his arms and carried her to the elevator, Roy had a very important question. "By the way, when is your birthday?" he inquired.

As the door closed, Rebecca whispered with a smile "October 4th!" In silent surprise, Roy sent the elevator to the 7th floor and checked his watch. Fortunately, Rebecca's eyes remained closed as her head rested upon his shoulder – unaware of his development of a silent mystery.

With every intention of maintaining the tenderness of the moment, Roy declared in the same whisper "That is tomorrow!"

In nervous acceptance of the reality, Rebecca sighed, "Please, do not remind me! Another year older! What else is new?"

Upon these words, Roy released her to her feet and spoke in a louder amused tone. "What else is new?" Without any difficulty, he located the sensitive area of Rebecca's tummy and began to tickle her. As she began to laugh, he repeated, "What else is new? I will tell you what else is new! This new year found *Everlasting Love* for both of us!"

As she continued to laugh, Rebecca breathed, "Why must you always be so…" She paused with a futile attempt to

71

regain composure. In an instant, she found the ability to conclude with "truthful?"

"Another year of truthfulness! The horror of it!" Roy sighed – continuing his charming torture.

"Yes, I know! Especially since you know my most ticklish spot!" Rebecca replied – playing along.

"But, you love it!" Roy replied – raising his eyebrows.

As they entered Rebecca's suite, she replied "Ah! More truth!"

Roy laughed with another challenge. "How much of this can you take?" he asked.

"As much as you can dish out!" Rebecca sighed in laughter. Upon these words, the wave of love swept over them. Roy knew that he was dreaming no longer.

Soon, Roy arose in silent reflection upon a matter of paramount importance. "Rest now, *My Beloved Angel*. I have to go and check on something. When you wake up, I will be right beside you with a very special surprise for you!" he whispered.

As he looked into *The Eyes Of Everlasting Love* once more, Roy sighed, "*The Power Of Almighty God* brought us together. Now, we will sing from our hearts together as one in melodious declaration of *His Spiritual Blessings. My Sweet Angel And Precious Dream Come True*, our love has just begun." With a soft kiss, Roy concluded with "I love you, Rebecca."

In a soft breath, Rebecca replied, "I love you too, Roy. I have waited throughout my entire life for someone with your loving vision to come into my life. Now that I have you, I can look forward to your return from a moment of departure – with your gentle and loving heart."

Upon these words, Roy began to sing the melodious echo of sweet dreams to come in the cool darkness of night with the promise of a new day and *Everlasting Love*.

Sleep now, My Loving Angel…
*Rest In **The Peace Of God's Love…***
In your dreams, I will watch over you…
And give you tender love – so true…

And love you until forever...
Find me in the gentle light...
In my arms, you will be all right...
Sleep tight, My Love...
Trust this promise – I will guide and protect you...
Kisses – sweet, pure, tender, soft, and true...
As from deep in my heart, I give love to you...
In everything that I say and do...
True Love...

As Rebecca drifted onto the peaceful comfort of Dreamland, Roy was mesmerized by the unified declaration from their hearts *"**Thank You, Lord!**"*

A short time later, Roy emerged from the only place that could provide a birthday present to last for a lifetime – *Sparkling Sentiment Jewelers*. As he closed the box of silver and gold velvet, Roy closed his eyes in an instant of reflection upon the moment that had changed the course of his entire life – on his own birthday three days ago. As he heard that cherished knock at his dressing room door once more, he knew that he would stand firm in his resolve not to take anything for granted. Even so, the wish remained deep within his heart through a few simple words. In a soft whisper, he asserted, "It had to be you!" Mesmerized, Roy did not see the beautiful woman that was stepping into the door right next to the one that he was stepping out of.

As she whispered, "If you only knew!" a brilliant silver ring sparkled upon her finger.

A short time later, Roy found himself in front of his own suite. Uncertain as to how he arrived there, Roy smiled at the reflective and intimate focus that Rebecca had taken within his thoughts. As he began preparations for the following day of celebration, his silent thoughts elapsed into the sparkling glow of a golden card upon the nightstand. It rested against a golden vase with a yellow rose inside of it. As Roy took the envelope, his senses became absorbed into the intimate scent of a familiar perfume. In silver letters of Old English, the note read:

Singers Always Travel Around The World.
It Is Time For You To Settle In.
You Have Been Invited To A Birthday Celebration In Suite #7.
Come And Find My Heart Waiting For You.
After All, That Is Where It Has Always Been."

As he held the note to his heart, Roy smiled – his eyes blinded with tears. Softly, he whispered, *"Lucky Seven,* this one is for you!" As he worked, Roy whispered a prayer in deep reflection. ***"Almighty Father God, I Thank You For The Cherished Blessing Of Rebecca Davidson's Presence In My Life. In My Heart, I Know That She Is The Ethereal Vision Of One True And Everlasting Love That I Have Always Dreamed Of. I Ask You, In The Blessed Name Of Jesus Christ Your Son, My Lord And Savior To Guide Me In The Matter Of Paramount Importance Ahead And Speak Your Spiritual Blessing Upon It As I Declare Love And Praise To Your Name. Amen."***

Chapter 4

Within a few hours, it was October 4, 1977. Slowly, Roy stepped into the suite – only activating the lights to a gentle glow. Rebecca remained in her comfortable state of soft slumber – or so he thought. He woke her with the gentle melody of a birthday wish all of his own.

Happy Birthday My Angel And Everlasting Love…
*Sent to me in **God's Love**…*
One great year deserves another…
Let us spend it together, forever, in love…

In her thoughts, Rebecca hoped that Roy did not notice that she was making a concentrated effort to keep herself covered – in the name of keeping her new outfit a surprise for him. As Roy pointed to a room service cart, Rebecca smiled. With a bottle of "Dream Dairy Milk" behind it, her luscious yellow birthday cake was decorated with a unique red frosting and inscribed with "Happy Birthday Rebecca" in yellow letters and two hearts of whipped cream with "22" inscribed in the middle of them. On each side of it, Roy had placed a hot butterscotch sundae with two candles in the formation of "22" burning in a sentimental gesture that Roy would seal with a tender kiss and a few amusing words. Pointing at them, Roy asserted "You know the routine! Make a wish and make it quick! As you can see, you have already melted my heart!"

As she grinned with a kiss, Rebecca caressed his face and closed her eyes in a tender moment of reflection. Holding Roy's hand in a gesture of recognition that this was not just for her – but for him as well – Rebecca whispered "I love you, Roy."

As he whispered "I love you too!" she blew the candles out. In voluntary denial of the superstition that if she told her wish, it would not come true, Rebecca smiled once more. "I will tell you my wish – but first, you have to try and get it out of me!" she challenged. Upon these words, she raised her eyebrows. As Roy grinned, he noticed that Rebecca was pushing the blanket off of her body – slowly. Suddenly, his grin elapsed into a nervous sweat. Roy could not believe his eyes.

Rebecca was dressed in a bustier and long pants of sparkling gold satin and silver boots. Her beautiful breasts nestled beneath the comfort of thick white fur across them. The same beautiful fur was draped across her waist – stitched in tender accentuation of her navel Gulping a nervous lump that had risen in his throat, Roy began to formulate an amusing plan. A clever smile came across his face. In execution of his usual humorous distraction, Roy snickered, "Well, my vocal chords are warmed up, how about yours?"

Sensing that he was up to something, Rebecca decided to play along through her amused reply "Ah, yes! After all, if you have to work on my birthday, so should I." As she kissed him, Rebecca arose and stepped toward the door. Opening it, she raised her eyebrows and concluded with, "However, you are just going to have to work a little bit harder!"

As he pushed the cart with a mesmerized smile and nervous perception, Roy sighed, "Ah! The sweet sound of music to my ears!"

Within seven seconds, Rebecca was way ahead of him. In her intimate stride, she was blowing kisses with every few steps. Soon, Roy noticed that Rebecca was stepping into the elevator. In a sudden rush, Roy chuckled and shouted "Hey! Come back here!"

Even so, it was too late – the door was closing.

As Rebecca blew one more kiss and waved, she giggled "See you soon!"

In a final instant, Roy smiled and shouted "Come back here! You stole my heart!"

As the door closed, Rebecca grinned and whispered "I stole more than that!"

Their destination would be the place where *LUCK.7* once recorded and played many timeless songs. Now, the melodious magic of two of its greatest talents would be more than just one of a kind and legendary. Now, Roy Dawson and Rebecca Davidson would declare their *Everlasting Love* for one another united as one for all of Eternity through the tender intimacy of love songs that would relate the story of the cherished love behind their melodious union as *Lucky Seven*.

Upon entering the studio, Roy and Rebecca joined hands and spoke from their hearts in cherished blessing upon this special point of return for both of them.

"Father God In Heaven, In These Next Few Moments, We Seek To Lift Our Voices To You In Praises Of Love And Gratitude For The Journey That We Have Traveled Onto The Blessing Of One True And Everlasting Love Between Us And Declare In The Cherished Name Of Your Son Jesus Christ, Our Lord And Savior That Everything That Has Brought Us Here Was Not Only According To Your Will, But A Means To Make Us Aware Of Your Eternal Presence That Will Always Carry Us Through And Strengthen Our Dedication As Your Children To Serve You In Mind, Body, Heart, And Soul For All Of Eternity. Amen."

Upon Roy's activation of the *LUCK.7* monogram on the console, recording began. Roy had dreamed of this moment throughout many lonely days of a dream only to be realized through his powerful voice – until now. The moment of truth was upon him. Roy and Rebecca walked toward each other – slowly – with a mesmerized gaze into *The Eyes Of Everlasting Love*. Softly, Roy began to sing.

For so long...
I have been waiting to find you for so long...
And, the love that I have for you is genuine...
This love is true...
As I look into your eyes, I know that it is true – you were sent from ***Heaven****...*
Love that is mine, I cherish your love and its warm, tender shine...

Build my future upon this hope…
That you will be mine, Love – Eternally…
Will you unite in an everlasting bond of intimacy with me?
In The Name Of God's Love That United Us…
I am asking you to marry me…
In a life of love and happiness…
I will do my very best to make you very happy…
As My Everlasting Love And Dream Come True…
I pledge to love, protect, and take care of you…

Slowly, Roy produced a sparkling box of silver and gold velvet. In tender conclusion, Roy proposed "Rebecca Davidson, *My Beloved Angel And Everlasting Love*, will you marry me?"

As Roy opened the box, Rebecca could not believe her eyes. Inside, was a sparkling diamond ring with two hearts united amongst the glamour of diamond musical notes across the band of gold.

Through silent tears, Rebecca caressed Roy's face and inquired "Are you sure that we are recording?"

Amidst silent laughter, Roy replied "I am as sure about that as I am in declaring here and now that you are the most beautiful woman in the entire universe!"

Touched, Rebecca replied, "I am glad that you said that because now the entire world can hear this." As she wiped her eyes, Rebecca took Roy's hand and asserted "As I stand witness to a world anxious to hear the melodious echo of our love, I accept – on one condition. I now ask Roy Dawson, My Marvelous Minstrel and *Everlasting Love* to unite his voice with me – the future Mrs. Rebecca Dawson - in the song that was stolen from me in tragedy, but has always lived on within my heart with the strength to carry on – which I found through the tenderness of this special feeling of love that I will cherish for the rest of my life."

Upon these words, Roy placed the ring upon Rebecca's finger and caressed her face in a gesture of assurance that this love would last for all of Eternity. As they began to sing the soft melody of a familiar love song, Roy and Rebecca united as one for all of Eternity through the powerful declaration of Rebecca's first song, *"The Tie That Binds Us…"*

Upon completion of the song, Roy became lost in the moment. Blinded with tears, he looked into *The Eyes Of Everlasting Love.* The light of ethereal melody sparkled about Rebecca's entire body. Gently, he caressed her face once more. Sliding his finger across her lips in a heart formation, Roy placed Rebecca's hand upon his heart and whispered, "When I look into your gorgeous eyes, I see the intimate reflection of *My Beautiful And Loving Angel* before me." Upon these words, he kissed her. "When I hold you in my arms, I feel the warmth of your tender and *Everlasting Love* – guiding, protecting, and strengthening me for all of Eternity." Caressing the gentle beauty of her hair, he kissed her once more. Relieving himself of a deep sob, Roy concluded with "When I hear you sing, I hear the tender melody of *My Beloved Angel* singing her love song of *My Dream Come True.*

Softly, Rebecca whispered "Before me, I see that my birthday wish came true!"

Upon these words, Roy and Rebecca sealed one another into a tender embrace. In her thoughts, Rebecca was finding the cherished sentiment of Roy's touching words extremely difficult to resist amidst her own need to keep her deepest thoughts hidden – for now. ***"God's Love*** brought us together!" she sighed.

Holding her closer, Roy replied "Let us part – never!" Upon these words, Roy stopped the recording.

With a sweet kiss, Roy suggested "I propose that we allow ourselves some…" he paused – stepping toward the cart – "practice!" he concluded. Stepping behind him, Rebecca watched Roy cutting the cake. Holding his shoulders, she kissed him and declared "How appropriate!"

Turning around, Roy replied "Birthday responsibilities for *The Birthday Angel!*"

"On my birthday?" Rebecca inquired with interest.

"Ah, yes! You not only get the first slice, but you get the first taste! You see, I made this cake myself!" Roy asserted.

With a grin, Rebecca replied, "Do I dare?" As she paused – appearing to be thinking – she did not notice Roy's amusing maneuver behind her. Suddenly, Roy pinched her tummy. Before she could laugh, Roy placed a fork to her lips. With a confused grin, Rebecca gulped.

Never before had she tasted a cake that was so rich and sweet. Closing her eyes – savoring the flavor – she replied "Genius! Pure Confectionary Genius!"

Touched, Roy replied "Thank you!"

"I only speak the truth!" Rebecca replied. "Please, allow me to reward your baking expertise!" Upon these words, she took the plate. As Roy smiled in silent gratitude, Rebecca helped herself to a bigger bite and kissed Roy. Slowly, Roy consumed the sweet sentiment from her smooth lips. Grinning, Rebecca asserted, "You are going to pay for that instant of charming torture!"

Amused, Roy smacked his head in embarrassment. "Yes, of course!" he replied.

Removing a silver dollar from his pocket, he began to thrust it into the air and catch it with his thumb. "So, do you want cash?" He paused and raised the plate to his face. Absorbing the sweet scent, he raised his eyebrows and concluded "Or, would you rather have some more cake?"

In a gesture of distraction, Rebecca caressed his face. As Roy blushed, he forgot about the coin still in flight. As she kissed him, Rebecca caught it and slipped it into her pocket. Looking at Roy once more with a mesmerized gaze, Rebecca sighed "Why settle for one when I could have both?" – consuming another mouthful of cake.

Lost in the moment, Roy kissed her. "I love you!" he sighed.

"I love you too!" Rebecca replied with a final kiss. In the ideal moment of return to their new melodious journey, Roy activated the system once more.

Instinctively, Rebecca elapsed into her melodious focus once more. As he gazed at her with a warm smile, Roy was mesmerized by the love and passion within her beautiful eyes. His voice was prepared for anything. Softly, they whispered, "I love you!" in tender unison. Roy began singing a special song about the beginning of this *One True And Everlasting Love.*

When I am with you...
Nothing else matters in the world...
Being together, in a love that is sweet and tender...
Time passes slow and sweetly...
Lost in your beautiful glance...
In my heart, I memorize you...
And everything that you do...
Reflecting silent...
When I kiss you...
My deepest reflections overtake me...
I know that it is right...
Through the love in your eyes...
And with your loving touch...
I quickly resolve myself to the sweet truth...
That I love you so much...
By The Power Of God's Love...
This is only the beginning...
Of our True Love to last forever...
With just one look, you are into my heart...
As you stand beside me...
This Is Only The Beginning...

As the song ended, Rebecca caressed Roy's face and sighed "I began to reflect upon this song in the few moments that I had before we were reunited after the concert – hoping that we would be *"Together Forever."*

I think of me and you – it is true...
I reflect on love day and night – feels so right...
*To dream about My One True Love – sent in **God's Love...***
Together Forever...
My life is better than I ever knew...

In my heart, I know it is because of you...
Just please accept my Everlasting Love for you...
Together Forever...
If you see me wearing a smile...
It comes straight from my heart...
Take my hand and think of our future – we two...
Let us never part...

With a tender kiss, Roy began to sing about the sparkling light of *Everlasting Love* – with the sentimental title *"Light Of Love."*

You blessed me with happiness – In **God's Love**...
Shining upon me, with your Light Of Love...
From early day – into night...
I see in your eyes – gorgeous and bright...
You keeping me warm...
With your tender Light Of Love...
Precious Love, I hope you know...
My love grows – though time does go...
Love is more powerful with each new day...
The warmth that I feel as I see...
Your sweet, tender love as you look at me...
I see the sparkle of your Light Of Love...
I cannot resist your tender charm...
My Dream Come True, I love you so much...
The Blessing Of God's Love...
Brought us together as one...
Loving by day, afternoon, and night...
Beautiful and special, this feels so right...
This is only the beginning...
Of Our True Love as one...
How much I love you...
With all I say and do...
I will spend my life pledging my love...
Take my hand right now...
Our two hearts will allow the world...
To shine in our Light Of Love...

Upon resting, Roy and Rebecca stepped aside to eat a few luscious spoonfuls of their sundaes. As he ate, Roy could not relinquish the grin on his face in sentimental reflection upon a few sweet words not long ago. As Rebecca closed her eyes, she stretched. Roy gulped a nervous lump that has risen in his throat. As Rebecca ran her fingers through her beautiful blonde hair, she released her navel from the constraint of her pants. Upon opening her eyes, Rebecca giggled as she noticed Roy's amusing look.

As she ate, Rebecca grinned as well. "What is that look of mischief for?" she asked.

Smiling, Roy replied, "Look at these sundaes! They continue to melt – just like my heart does for you!" He paused for another spoonful. Dipping his finger into the center of the whipped cream hearts on the cake, he raised his finger to Rebecca's lips and concluded "Then again, it is all for you anyway!"

As Rebecca licked the sentiment from his tender touch, she replied "If you keep talking like that, I am going to melt even more than I already have!" She reclined into his arms – slowly – kissing him with tender passion. "Just like the first time I saw you on stage."

Blushing, Roy replied, "We cannot have that now, can we?"

Caressing his face, Rebecca kissed him once more. "Sure we can! But not now! Duty calls!" she asserted.

As Roy chuckled to himself, he was embarrassed – gulping a nervous lump that had risen in his throat. Wiping the sweat from his forehead, he gained composure and began recording once more. Holding Rebecca's hand in a gesture of encouragement, the love in Roy's eyes gave her the strength to begin her song of overcoming her deepest fears – strengthened by the guiding light of *Everlasting Love*.

No, not these feelings again...
No, not the same deep fears again...

To face them alone is hard...
But now I see that it's not my fault...
The way she served her own ends...
By stealing my greatest gift...
Before I knew it, I felt my life come to a halt...
I felt so lost and alone...
But now with you Love, I know through **Faith In God**...
Everything happens for a reason...
Whatever does not kill us will make us stronger...
You have given me the strength to rise up and carry on...
Now that I have seen all of my fears right before my very eyes...
I will never fear again...
With your tender love by my side, pain and fear are gone...
Because of a love so strong...
My Love, I thank you...
I will love you forever...

Despite her smile, Rebecca fell into Roy's arms in a moment of deep reflection. As she relieved herself of a deep sob within her throat, he slipped Rebecca's glass of milk into her right hand. As she proceeded with a drink to gain composure again, he caressed her face.

Gently, he took her left hand. In a tender whisper, Roy declared "Everything is going to be fine, My Love!" Softly, he raised Rebecca's head so that she could witness the brilliant light of *Everlasting Love* – sparkling upon her finger. "Look at this and remember what you said. You will never have to fear again."

As she wiped her eyes, Rebecca turned to him. Looking into *The Eyes Of Everlasting Love,* Rebecca held Roy close to her and whispered "No, never again! Neither one of us! I love you so much, Roy!"

"I love you too!" Roy replied. "Now and forever!" he concluded. With a loving gaze into *The Eyes Of Everlasting Love,* recording began once more.

In a sentimental declaration of encouragement, Rebecca whispered "I love you!"

84

As Rebecca took Roy's hand into hers in the same unified gesture of encouragement from moments ago, Roy repeated her touching words on his own behalf. Prepared to face this moment of resolution at last, he spoke. "This song is dedicated to the memory of a very special friend of mine who supported me during my earlier days in the music industry. He died of a broken heart. May ***Almighty God*** grant him eternal peace. Andrew Manchester, with the same melodious inspiration and love that you spoke of in your last words, this one is for you."

My heart cried…
When my friend died…
How hard he tried…
But still, she turned away…
Blinded by love and bewitched by her spell…
His heart was tied…
With his heart above his head, he died – leaving these words…
'See The Light Of Love - so bright…
Put up a fight…
Believing in yourself, you will find The Power Of Love…
It will be warm and kind…
Speak to hearts through your melodious voice and remember…
I will be with you…'
And now, as I sing from my heart about this painful tragedy…
I understand what he meant at long last…
Thank you, My Friend…
Inside, I know he did not die in vain…
Yes, he was right…
The Power Of Love is great…
And in my sight, I see True Love…
Thank you, My Friend…
May God Bless You…
I will not forget you…

As the last word echoed the song's soft ending, Roy and Rebecca joined hands once more. As Roy wiped tears that were felt from deep within his heart from his eyes, Rebecca said, "Fear not, My Love. In my heart, I know that he is watching down on us right now – leading the **Angels In Heaven** in a fanfare of blessings of love upon us."

"And, our love for one another!" Roy concluded – kissing her soft hand. With a unified expression of love, Roy declared "Two distant silver stars searching in the night – with only *The Light Of Love* within to find one another. The soft whisper of those ethereal words – resounding in the melodious echo of tender love songs from the heart – united us in our song of *Everlasting Love* for all of Eternity."

As their eyes closed in sentimental reflection, their hands drifted apart. Sparkling in *The Light Of Love* upon their fingers, Roy and Rebecca proceeded to communicate another chapter in their love story. Rebecca began to sing once more.

Singing to me, I can hear you calling...
Though distant, how close you seem...
In sweet melody, I reach for you, My Love...
Until now, you were a dream...
Endless searching – so close and yet so far...
Wishing you will hear my cries...
You rescue me with your tender kisses...
You heal me with your touch...
Singer, touch my heart with your voice...
Your tender words will ease my mind...
I hear a sweet melody...
I never dreamed that I would find an Everlasting Love, so true...
Love you always...
By The Power Of God's Love That United Us...
Throughout all of my days...
Softly resting in your arms...
Close my eyes and dream of us together...
Mesmerized by your tender charms...
Now until the end of time...
I will be yours and you will be mine...

Upon these words, they made a silent toast to the future. With a refreshing gulp of milk, Roy began his next song about being in the right place at the right time – in discovery of the unified absolute of this *One True And Everlasting Love.*

> *The passage of time is a difficult thing...*
> *Never knowing, of what it can bring...*
> *If you believe and be patient...*
> **Through God's Blessing Of Love...**
> *Words cannot explain the tender love you will get...*
> *Is it luck?*
> *Is it chance?*
> *It is meant to be...*
> *This Beautiful Romance...*
> *And now as I look to you – tender love that is mine...*
> *I see True Love in your gorgeous eyes...*
> *Our love will stand the passage of time...*

As they joined hands, Roy and Rebecca gazed into *The Eyes Of Everlasting Love.* As their tender touch drifted apart, Rebecca began to sing once more.

> *When you came into my life...*
> *You eased my restless mind...*
> *At that point, I did not know...*
> *Of The True Love that I would find...*
> *With you, I belong...*
> *In the arms of your love I will be...*
> *Forever in love, you and me...*
> *Thinking of what used to be...*
> *Life was so painful to live...*
> *Now it seems beautiful to me...*
> *Tender love – to you, I will give...*
> *This is True Love...*
> *And from now, until the end of time...*
> *I will cherish the love that is mine...*
> *Your tender love is all I need...*
> *In your eyes, I see tender beauty...*

My Tender Love And Dream Come True…
Within my heart, I know…
I will always love you so…
God's Blessing Of Love United Us…
As time goes by…
Just you and I…
You complete me, True Love…

With a tender smile, Roy began to sing a reflection upon their dreams together – past, present, and future - known as *"Golden Dreams."*

She is Dream Come True…
With just one look, I knew…
Now, my love grows stronger each and every day…
With one tender look, I knew it…
The pieces of my life fit…
Together in that sweet moment of True Love…
As I take this path…
Guided by **God's Love…**
These are Golden Dreams…
How great life seems…
These dreams are all I could ever hope for…
Now, I see her standing there…
Her eyes show how much she does care…
Lost in Everlasting Love, I will be…
She is my One True Love…
The one that I have dreamed of…
Her tender touch will guide me…
I see the silver lining of special Golden Dreams…
I know what this means…
My silver star and shining pure beauty…
These Golden Dreams give me the means by which to live through Eternity…
With My True Love And Golden Dream…

Rebecca stood before him – his *Golden Dream.* Mesmerized by her beauty, another glow was in his eyes – the glow of silent tears of *Everlasting Love.* Stopping the recording,

Roy repeated *"My Golden Dream"* until Rebecca silenced his beautiful sentiment with a kiss. Both of them were crying. As they held each other close, the last tear fell from their eyes. Rebecca activated the recording herself and declared, "I may be your *Golden Dream,* but you made that same dream come true – for me." As she blew a kiss, the vision of this *One True And Everlasting Love* flashed in the brilliant sparkles of silver and gold upon their fingers. In an instant, the intimate glow elapsed into Rebecca's sweet voice once more.

I am yours and you are mine…
Together, everything is fine…
Each new day into night…
Tenderly, I adore you…
As time goes by…
This Vision Of Love cannot deny…
It was In **God's Plan** *for us…*
Love, how My Eyes Adore You…
Silent tears, I cry when you are near…
Blessed with the magic of your love…
You are here by my side…
I will never again need to hide…
Because I see True Love in view…
Look and see My Eyes Adore You…

As Rebecca stopped the recording, she ran her fingers through her gorgeous blonde hair once more. She did not notice Roy's rapid maneuver around her.

Quickly, he held her waist in a tender embrace and whispered "Day in and day out, morning, noon and night, throughout all days for the rest of my life, every hour is made up of you – and all that the future holds with you, My Love!"

Upon activating the recording once more, Roy began to sing a song that was inspired by his intimate declaration just now.

Everyday, I dream of a future with you…
By your side, I will be – Eternally…
Every hour with you is so great…

My Love, it was well worth the wait…
Every minute keeps you in my heart…
Every second, I cherish the reality that you are a part of everything I do…
In His Love, God Watches Over Us…
This is how I know our love will grow…

Upon completion of the song, Rebecca turned the recording off and began to laugh. In amused recollection of Roy's sweet suggestion a few moments ago, Rebecca looked at him and raised her eyebrows. "I think that we need some more "practice!"" she suggested.

Grinning, Roy accepted "Ah, yes! Right you are!" As he took another slice of cake, he stepped toward her and placed the fork to her lips. "Although, I think that we know exactly what we are doing!" he added.

Touched, Rebecca replied, "I must admit, I knew what was going to happen from the start."

Overcome by the idealistic meeting of their minds, Roy swallowed a gulp of milk with sudden surprise. "Really? I thought that I was the only one! What exactly did you know?" he asked.

"Well, from the very first moment that I saw you, I knew that you were meant to find melodious stardom, *By The Power Of Almighty God!*" Rebecca began.

Confused, Roy asked, "Are you saying that you have seen me before?"

Blushing suddenly, Rebecca remained cautious against saying too much. "Yes, of course! Aside from your concerts here, I have seen you many times on television! Of course, you became a rapid success and I have always been very proud to call myself a fan." Touched, Roy kissed her – caressing her face.

Embarrassed and mesmerized by the love in his eyes, she continued. "The truth is that I felt a true personal connection to you from the very beginning. In my heart, I knew that one day – if *The Lord's Plan* would have it that I would meet you – I would do everything above and beyond the farthest limitations of my power to make you see…" She paused – relieving herself of a deep sob. "How much I love you!" she concluded.

Amidst the sentiment of the moment, they fell into *The Arms Of Everlasting Love*. Roy could not speak. In a soft voice, he declared, "Thank you so much, Rebecca. You have no idea how much that means to me." As he kissed her once more, Roy caressed her face and activated the recording. Rebecca was relieved that her deepest thoughts remained unspoken – for now. She began to sing once more.

> *With our tender love, we can give our all…*
> *In the name of Everlasting Love…*
> *And in all that we will confront each day…*
> *Our True Love will show us the way…*
> *There is no end to the dreams we will share together… forever…*
> *By your side, I will stay, be safe, and leave you – never…*
> *Can you feel it?*
> *Yes, I feel it…*
> *This love is true…*
> *From my heart to yours, I will cherish you…*
> *I will give you everything I can…*
> *With a tender touch in the arms of love…*
> *We can create sweet and true passion…*
> **Guided By The Love Of Almighty God…**
> *You are My One True Love And My Dream Come True…*
> *Your love is so special to me…*
> *Thank you for the love…*
> *It is soft and warm…*
> *Our two hearts will be full forever…*
> *I love you…*
> *Yes, I love you, True Love…*

As Roy placed his glass of milk to Rebecca's lips and she placed her glass to his, they indulged in a refreshing gulp. Roy began a song about the trials of endless search in love – only to be found at the most unexpected moment.

I thought love was just a distant fantasy...
Brilliant light that I would never see...
Love was within my reach...
It was there all along...
Now, it echoes in this tender song...
When I saw her face...
I knew it was **God's Will...**
All of my dreams came true...
She brought hope and peace to my mind...
This is love – lasting forever, one that I was glad to find...
I thought love was full of pain and endless search...
Seems the more I searched, the more lost I was...
Love will last forever...
One look... One kiss... One touch...
Everlasting Love, I love you so much...

As they joined hands, Rebecca expressed her gratitude by saying "I have been on a journey too. Allow me to tell you about it, My Marvelous Minstrel." As Roy blushed, Rebecca began.

Lucky Seven shined upon me when you sang to me against all distance...
Lucky Seven brought your song of love...
The powerful light in my existence...
My Love, I have lived in endless search of a life of love and happiness...
I would have never believed that I would find the man behind the melody...
It was **The Love Of God...**
Singer of sweet True Love...
We are meant to be together...
Soft love songs, this one is for you...
In all I say and do...
I pledge love forever...
You will never have to wonder...
I will keep you safe from harm...
As you sing to me with tender charm...

As you kiss my lips – so softly...
Their sweetness touches me deeply...
Tenderly, you caress my body...
The Power Of Love is in your touch...
Lucky Seven brought our hearts together...
You are all that I will ever need...
Our united bond will break – never...
Lucky Seven this one is for you...
Touch me once again...
United in this True Love...
Our voices pledge in sweet song, Everlasting Love...
Together, Forever is where we belong...

Smiling, Roy proposed a toast. "Here's to the end of our journey and the beginning of our lives – together as one!" As they drank, he concluded with "But, as they say in the music industry, the beat goes on!" Upon these words, he began singing.

Dream Come True...
With just one tender look, I knew it...
Everlasting...
Before I knew it, you were in my heart...
You are my one and only...
You stole my heart in that first moment...
All I ever needed...
From this moment on, I hope you see...
You are The Angel that I have dreamed of...
Dreamed of all of my life...
I will never forget it...
I know this is it...
In God's Blessing...
I will cherish and nurture you...
And, I will take care of you...
Never forget it...
How good it will get...
My love will never end – never, ever...
Take my hand – come, and I will show you...

We will find our way – together as one…
I am the one who will always love you…
Open up my heart to you…
Through the good and bad…
Cherish what we have…
There will never be another…
And, in time discover…
That in every way, love grows with each new day…
With each look, kiss, and touch – I love you very much…
You are My One True Love…
Now take me – I am yours…
One And One Makes Two…
Two Of A Kind…

As Roy wiped the tears of cherished love and sentiment from his eyes, he made a declaration in sentimental reflection upon a few words that he spoke from his heart in gratitude for Rebecca's ethereal presence in his life. Softly, he sang:

Rebecca, My Beloved Angel And Dream Come True
I Sing From My Heart.
Your Ethereal Beauty And Tender Love Sparkled In Intimate
Glow Upon Me In A Truly One Of A Kind Way.
*Blessed By **Almighty God's Love** That United Us,*
With Eternal Gratitude, I Seek One Goal -
Only To Spend The Rest Of My Life
Doing Everything Above And Beyond The Farthest Limitations
Of My Power To Shine The Same Reflection Of Everlasting
Love Upon Your Heart That You Have Onto My Own.
With Silver Wishes And Golden Dreams,
I Love You Always And Forever.

Blinded with tears, Rebecca sighed "OK! My Marvelous Minstrel and *One And Only Love*, this one is for you! This comes from the heart of a once and forever blushing fan. Now, it comes from the heart of your future wife!" Softly, she began to sing once more.

Every time I hear him singing from his heart to me…
I hear True Love, and dream that one day we will be…
Together in tender love…
I wish on the stars above…
Because I love him so much and I hope he will see…
The true happiness he has shown me…
Dreaming that one day he will love me…
One day he will be mine – all mine…
Then, it happened, By **God's Sweet Love…**
In that first sweet moment, our eyes met for the first time…
I began to reflect on this tender rhyme…
Now our hearts will become one…
We always have so much fun…
Though this song is done, Our Love Has Just Begun…

As the song ended, Roy smiled. Mesmerized by the intimacy of his love, Rebecca kissed him and began to eat another slice of cake. The light of melodious inspiration reflected around her – shining in the glow of ethereal beauty. She looked so beautiful standing there – enjoying the sentiment of his love. In his thoughts, he could not wait to wake up every morning with her – with the light of her love shining upon him. He thought about sharing every daily meal with her – as they indulge in the simple pleasures of **The Daily Blessings From Almighty God** to live the love within their hearts. As the sparkling light of each new day fades into the tender intimacy of night, he thought about holding her close to him with their hearts together as one – singing slumber tunes of simple words in reflection upon his *Everlasting Love*. As she kissed him and caressed his face, his reflection elapsed. With a mesmerized gaze into *The Eyes Of Everlasting Love*, Roy declared, "This is the story of *"The First Vision Of Love."*

Two distant hearts…
Committed to one dream…
When **God** *stepped in…*
A beautiful sight was seen…
They became one…

Finding all they dreamed of…
It was begun…
"The First Vision Of Love…"
They knew from the start…
They would never part…
Loving more and more…
Each and every day…
Together as one…
In a life of fun…
Joined in blessed union…
Love showed them the way…
Love, here now we stand…
Gently, take my hand…
Let us pledge our love…
From our hearts, we say…
I pledge love to you…
In all that I do…
For better or worse…
Sickness and health…
You are My True Love…
If we are rich or poor…
I will live life for…
The one that I adore…
You are My True Love…
Until death do us part…
The last beat of my heart…
Will declare infinite…
Everlasting Love…

As the song ended, Roy smiled at Rebecca. Amidst the tender warmth of his love for her, she sat in mesmerized gaze. As he caressed her face, she closed her eyes – cherishing his tender touch. "Hey there, our public awaits you!" Roy chuckled.

Embarrassed, her eyes remained focused upon this instant of the cherished love between them. "Ah, yes!" she replied. With a mesmerized gaze into *The Eyes Of Everlasting*

Love, Rebecca concluded "However, there is always time for a singing partner to reflect upon the most beautiful voice that she has ever heard! Remember Roy, I will always be your Number One Fan!" Before Roy could respond, Rebecca began to sing once more. Lost in her tender beauty, Roy could not take his eyes off of her.

> *Come to me, Precious Love…*
> *Reach out, let me take your hand…*
> *It has been so long, I have waited for you…*
> *Now, my dream came true…*
> *Stay close to me, My Love…*
> *I will cherish and take care of you…*
> *I have traveled around this lonely world – to find you at long last…*
> **In The Lord's Plan…**
> *Singer Of Love, my love for you grows stronger with each new day…*
> *Your love has given me the strength to find my way…*
> *Singer Of True Love, you charm me with all that you say…*
> *Look at all you have done – singing from your heart around the world…*
> *I still can hear you singing – just like it was the first time…*
> *Now, look at where we are – so far from the past left behind…*
> *Lost in love, we will never forget how we found True Love…*
> *My Singer Of Love, always remember how much I do love you…*
> *Take my love with you in all that you say and do…*
> *Romantic Of Song, I pledge Eternal Love to you…*

In his thoughts, Roy was reflecting upon the restless frame of mind that he felt prior to his cherished marriage proposal only moments ago. With a mesmerized smile, he sighed "Let me tell you about how the rest of our life together is going to be – beginning with our wedding night." Upon these words, he began singing once more.

> *Eternal Serenade…*
> *Led by **Almighty God**…*
> *The focus of plans I made…*

For you are an Angel and I am a dreamer…
With only looks to trade…
In my heart, I have dreamed of a night like this…
Lost in your tender kiss…
And where would I be without you near me?
Come, and be by my side…
Let me make your dreams come true…
Belong, with you I belong…
Let me love and cherish you…
Come and join me warm in our love tonight…
In your arms, I am safe and feel so right…
With the sweetness of the love we have made…
From in my heart, I sing this…
Eternal Serenade…

Amused and touched by his sentiment, Rebecca had an
intimate reply of her own. "Allow me to relate my ideas about
the night that will be here sooner than we both realize as well!"
she asserted. Amidst Roy's confused smile, she began singing.

Through Now And Forever…
For the rest of my life…
I will stand by you and love you…
As your sweet, loving wife…
By The Blessing Of God…
You gave me hope…
Sheltered me from pain and fear…
Your tender love lives on…
Even when you are not near…
In my heart, I love you with all that I know…
You are charming and sweet…
Wherever you go, I go with you – forever by your side…
You are my handsome husband…
I am your loving bride…
*And on the day that we become parents through **The Blessing***
Of God's Love…
Our True Love will live on again…
We will teach right from wrong…

With the love in our hearts...
There will be new life of love, so strong...

Softly, the song elapsed into a passionate kiss. In *The Arms Of Everlasting Love,* Roy and Rebecca placed their hands upon the loving hearts of their union. Blinded with tears, *The Light Of Love* sparkled upon their fingers. Softly, Roy whispered, "**The Plan Of Almighty God** brought us to this moment. We have become one through the melodious sentiment of our voices and united for all of Eternity through the *Everlasting Love* within our hearts. Together as one, there is nothing that we cannot accomplish and no trial that we cannot turn into triumph. Are you ready, Rebecca – *My Beautiful Angel And Everlasting Love?*"

With a smile, Rebecca replied, "Yes!" With a mesmerized gaze into *The Eyes Of Everlasting Love,* Roy Dawson and the future Mrs. Rebecca Dawson sang a few simple words in tender unison. *"Because All I Really Need Is You!"* Upon these words, they cherished the reality of their infinite love and elapsed into song. Roy and Rebecca sang their final duet with the melodious strength of this *One True And Everlasting Love* – united as one for all of Eternity.

Despite lonely years...
Of endless searching for love...
I did not know I would find...
Everlasting Love in you...
Take it all away...
All that I have in this world...
This I know is true...
All I Really Need Is You...
I will spend the rest of my life...
Hoping in some way to return...
The blessing of your tender love...
That I will cherish all my days...
With every beat of my heart...
Guided By **The Love Of God...**
Love from me to you...

All I Really Need Is You...
God's Love *brought us here...*
To become one now...
I will never forget...
The first sweet moment when...
You made all my dreams come true...
Whispering sweet words of love...
That will last forever...
My Love, this is true...
All I Really Need Is You...
Through all the pain and sadness...
All is well that ends well, with you...
I will always know...
That I will never let you go...
My Dream Come True, I will always love you so...
All I Really Need Is You...

Upon these words, Roy and Rebecca gazed into *The Eyes Of Everlasting Love* and whispered a few final words of tender sentiment in recognition of their melodious and sentimental journey – together as one. *"Lucky Seven*, this one is for you!"

"I love you, Rebecca!" Roy whispered.

"I love you too, Roy!" Rebecca whispered.

"Thank You, Almighty Father God!" they declared in blessed unison.

With a tender kiss, Roy switched the recording off. Roy and Rebecca stared into *The Eyes Of Everlasting Love* – mesmerized by the melodious magic behind these moments of true inspirational expression and intimate unity. Blinded with tears of sentimental happiness, they embraced. With a soft kiss, Roy caressed Rebecca's face. Softly, he whispered "Come, *My Beautiful And Melodious Angel.* Shall we go?" Upon these words, Roy took Rebecca into his arms.

Amidst peaceful reflection, Rebecca rested her head upon his heart and whispered, "Your love has given me the strength to carry on in the name of returning to my career.

100

Now, I look forward to our days as *Lucky Seven,* the ideal combination."

With a warm smile, Roy replied, "I have never had inspiration as strong and as sentimental as I have right now. In case you did not notice, I did not write a single word of any song that I just recorded. As I gazed into your eyes, the melodious sentiment simply flowed from the very essence of my entire being. All of this happened because of you and **The Powerful Blessing Of Almighty God!**' With a passionate kiss, Roy whispered "Thank you, *My Beautiful Angel*."

Mesmerized by the love between them, Rebecca whispered "No, thank you My Marvelous Minstrel!"

Upon these words, Roy felt that this was the ideal moment to capture the truly intimate and candid nature of their love. However, he reflected upon its purpose in his thoughts. As he carried her in their stride, Roy declared "Well, if that is how you truly feel, look at that flashing yellow light over there and smile." Confused, Rebecca looked. In a dark corner, she saw a solitary flashing light with no indication of its source.

Before she realized what was happening, Rebecca noticed Steve Fitzsimmons stepping from the shadows – with a camera. As Roy and Rebecca smiled amidst the sentiment of this *One True And Everlasting Love,* the flash bulb popped – crystallizing this moment within *The Eternal Capsule Of Time.* "Nice, My Friend! Very Nice!" Steve asserted - grinning. As he stepped toward them, Steve caressed Rebecca's hair. Upon kissing her, he smiled and said, "Roy is a very lucky man!"

Touched, Rebecca replied "Thank you!"

"I apologize for leaving in a flash like this, but literary inspiration has a very unpredictable impact on me! When it calls, I must answer! Congratulations and Best Wishes! **God Bless You Both!**' Upon these words, Steve departed.

"I felt that we needed a little more "practice!"" Roy chuckled – in subtle connection to their sharing of wedding cake and ceremonial photographs.

"I understand!" Rebecca acknowledged – raising her eyebrows. "Sweet! Very Sweet!"

As they left the studio, Roy replied "However, all is right – just as we are right for each other."

Upon these words, Roy and Rebecca turned to **Almighty God** and spoke blessings upon the past few tender moments, and those that lie ahead:

"Father God In Heaven, In The Beloved Name Of Jesus Christ Your Son, Our Lord And Savior, We Thank You For Your Spiritual Blessing Upon The Melodious Moments In Which We Spoke Glory And Honor To Your Name, And Declare Here And Now Upon Our Union Into The Sacred Institution Of Marriage In The Days Ahead To Live Our Lives Together As One In The Manner That You Alone Intended To Love One Another As You Love Us In Mind, Body, Heart, And Soul For All Of Eternity. Amen."

Amidst a passage of tender kisses, Roy carried Rebecca back to her hotel suite. Closing her eyes, Rebecca rested her head upon his shoulder. Placing her hand upon his heart, she sighed in comfort "I have never had so much fun recording!" Caressing his face, she concluded with "It is so much better with two!"

Upon these words, Roy stepped from the elevator and made an unexpected suggestion. "Rebecca, My Love, I have been thinking. This hotel is certainly one of the greatest places in *The City Of Lights*. As you know, I have always wanted to stay here ever since I was young. How would you feel about us buying your suite? That way, we can always have a place to escape to for some "R and R" when we need it."

Roy was unable to retrieve his key – which was a personal reflection of his unwillingness to release Rebecca from his intimate hold. Rebecca noticed this and reached into her pocket to retrieve hers. Unexpectedly, Rebecca replied "Wait right here! I shall return!" Upon these words, she jumped from his arms and opened the door. Amidst a confused smile, Roy complied. As Rebecca closed the door – slowly – Roy noticed that she was raising her eyebrows.

"Please, do not be long! I do not know how much waiting my heart can take!" Roy called.

From behind it, Rebecca smacked the door. Roy could hear her laughing. "More mushy talk! May we live a million years and never let it end!" she declared. Upon these words, she opened the door once more and blew a kiss.

Roy grinned. "That sounds good to me!" he asserted. With a smile, Rebecca motioned for him to turn around. As he complied, Roy noticed that Rebecca had a wooden stick in her hand. Confused, he heard six quiet taps on the door and one loud one.

"Welcome Home, Roy!" Rebecca declared. Upon these words, Roy turned around. In an instant, he was both shocked and confused. The wooden stick was a hammer. Rebecca had used it to place a golden plaque on the door. Amidst confusion, Roy read "Home Sweet Home" in silver letters of Old English formation. As Rebecca embraced him, Roy remained in a mesmerized state of confusion.

Noticing this, Rebecca giggled. "Let me explain." As she gazed into his eyes and kissed him once more, Rebecca's voice began to soften as she asked "Do you remember when I told you that Reese died by falling off of this very roof?"

"Yes, of course," Roy answered – holding her hand to his heart in assurance that she would feel safe and at peace at the mention of that painful name.

Noticing this, Rebecca caressed his heart and sighed "Thank you! I am fine! Being in your arms does that to me!" Touched once more, Roy was glad that she was very calm as she continued. "Well, the truth of the matter is that I have lived here ever since I was born. I practically grew up in the recording studio downstairs. So you see, this can be our "Home Sweet Home" away from home!"

Amidst silent laughter, Roy held Rebecca close to him. "You are truly sneaky!" he laughed.

"If you believe that now, you have not seen anything yet!" Rebecca replied.

"Why is that, *My Ever Beautiful Angel?*" Roy inquired.

"You will find that out in time, My Marvelous Minstrel. However, I am most grateful to you because you enjoyed that dinner that I made for you after the concert!" As they looked into *The Eyes Of Everlasting Love*, Roy and Rebecca burst into laughter.

Upon gaining composure, Roy added "In my heart, I knew that food did not come from any hotel kitchen. It only came from one place – the heart of the most caring, charming, and beautiful woman that I would ever come to know – your heart! I will make you a deal. If you keep making great good like that, I will make a cake anytime that you want when we are home between tours. After all, the public awaits the first tour of *Lucky Seven…*" He paused in amused formality as he made the concluding declaration "Coming soon to a venue near you!"

Caressing his face, Rebecca kissed him. "You have yourself a deal!" she accepted. "Something has just occurred to me. I have yet to show you the rest of our humble suite!" Rebecca snickered – reaching out to him.

Upon taking her hand, Roy sighed "Take me, I am yours."

"You know the routine! Close your eyes!!" Rebecca asserted.

Upon his compliance, she led him onto the rest of the suite. Caressing his face, Rebecca declared "Check this out!" – snapping her fingers. In an instant, Roy was mesmerized by the emergence of idealistic intimacy from the cool darkness. Amidst a procession of yellow neon lights, Roy noticed a table with two thick robes upon it – one silver for

104

Rebecca, and the other gold for him. Each was stitched with the letter "R" – Roy's in silver and Rebecca's in gold. A distant sound indicated their purpose.

As Rebecca led him further into the room, Roy could not believe his eyes. Heating lamps of yellow neon presented a beautiful swimming pool beneath the peaceful flow of a waterfall. Also, the room featured an antique fountain of red marble structure with aquatic sprays courtesy of seven frosted globes – each inscribed with black musical notes.

Mesmerized by the sentimental reflection of one of his cherished love songs, Roy turned to find Rebecca.

From behind him, she giggled and declared "I told you that you always have been a truly special source of inspiration for me!" Roy noticed that she was preparing two fruit juice cocktails.

"Is that our recommended daily allowance of Vitamin C?" he inquired.

"You know me too well!" Rebecca replied - stepping toward him. Roy and Rebecca drank with a tender kiss. Slowly, they slipped into the pool. In the peaceful calm of the water, Roy took Rebecca into his arms. As their bodies drifted upon the surface, they relaxed in a comfortable duration of passionate kisses. Suddenly, they were swept through an unusual aquatic blast.

Once underwater, they joined hands and arose in laughter. Inadvertently, they had drifted through the path of the waterfall. With a final kiss, Roy and Rebecca swam to the opposite end of the pool and exited.

Upon slipping into their robes, Roy carried Rebecca to the bed. Reclining her delicate body – softly – he kissed her once more. "I have everything that I have ever wanted or needed right here!" Roy whispered.

"So do I!" Rebecca replied. "So do I!" Upon these words, Roy noticed that Rebecca appeared tired. As he held her close to him, Roy began to sing a song about *The Ethereal Power Of Love*.

Loving You is what I was meant to do…
Loving You made all of my dreams come true…
God's Love *did bring us together*
Just you and I as one…
This True Love is ours, we have just begun…
Because of you, the future is so bright…
Always by your side – day into night…
In your eyes, I realize…
In all you say and do…
All I need is you…
This I found – Loving You…

Upon these words, Rebecca whispered "Once a beautiful and intimate singer, always a beautiful and intimate singer."

Touched, Roy chuckled "That may be true! However, I am dedicated to the intimate focus of my melodious magic now more than ever. A certain *Beautiful And Loving Angel* seems to have had something to do with that. Would you happen to know who it is?"

Lost in the cherished declaration of his love, Rebecca rested her head upon Roy's heart and whispered, "If you only knew!"

Softly kissing her, Roy did not hear her last words. "What did you say?" he asked.

Quick to keep her deepest thoughts hidden for a while longer with some humor of distraction, Rebecca replied, "If I must repeat myself!" In an instant, she elapsed into a cherished love song about the warmth and comfort of their *One True And Everlasting Love.*

He holds me close…
Caresses my face…
He places my hand…
Upon his heart…
It is meant to be…
Everlasting…
He kisses me and begins to sing…

106

It feels so good to be here…
Relaxing, with My True Love near…
By The Power Of God's Blessing…
Until the end of time…
I will cherish the love that is mine…
I am yours and you are mine…
I hear in his melodious voice…
The truth that we have made the right choice…
From now and throughout the rest of my days…
The warmth of this True Love will shine upon my face…
These tender words elapsed into a sweet kiss. Softly, Roy whispered "Sweet Dreams, *My Beautiful And Melodious Angel.*" Drifting onto the peaceful comfort of Dreamland, Rebecca whispered, "After my life took that devastating turn, I was afraid to go to sleep at night for so long. Now, I will never have to be afraid ever again. You have strengthened me with the love and peace of mind that I only dreamed about through the tender melodies that only you can create. Now, we can create everything that has never been created before and more – with loving hearts and powerful voices united as one for all of Eternity. I cannot wait for our first appearance together! I love you so much, Roy!"

As he soothed Rebecca to rest, Roy arose – caressing her gorgeous hair. Kissing her once more, Roy whispered, "I love you too, Rebecca! I love you always and forever." Stepping toward the door, Roy was reflecting upon the matter of paramount importance that was at hand. Turning around for one final intimate gaze at his sleeping *Angel*, Roy whispered "It will be here sooner than you think!"

Roy's destination was the promotion room for *The Solid Gold Hotel And Casino*. Upon stopping to retrieve the intimate photograph from a short time ago, Roy activated the *LUCK.7* inscription once more and sighed, "*Lucky Seven,* this one is for you!" Upon entering the promotion room, Roy began to design a sentimental declaration of his love for Rebecca – one that would last from that moment onward and into Eternity.

By the force of habit, Roy checked his watch. It was the morning of October 5, 1977. Surprised, Roy's mind began to wander. He knew that *The City Of Lights* was a "24: 7: 365" place. Even so, he was reflecting upon the sentimentality of the fact that he and Rebecca had spent an entire day discovering the melodious intimacy of their love. Smiling with a sigh of resolve, he looked at the sparkling declaration of her love upon his finger and said, "One special day deserves another. Two days from now, the reality of our *Everlasting Love* will reflect upon the painful days of endless search in the past as their darkest shadows elapse into ***The Guiding Light Of Blessings From Almighty God*** in the present, and onto *The Silver Wishes And Golden Dreams* of our loving future ahead – forever you and me!"

Chapter 5

Impressed with his creation, Roy placed it into the mass distribution box. Quick to return to Rebecca, she remained in her state of peaceful slumber. As he woke her with a tender kiss, a unique idea caused them to turn to each other and declare in amused unison "I have a plan!"

A short time later, Roy held Rebecca's waist in a tender embrace. His senses became absorbed in the unison of three of the truly greatest smells – the intimate scent of her perfume and the luscious scents of barbecue chicken and sugar cookies. Rebecca placed an exotic fruit salad into the cooler. With a rapid maneuver, she reached into the cabinet and retrieved a jar of "Sticky Banana." Glancing at Roy behind her as he sealed the cooler, Rebecca raised her eyebrows – rapidly closing the picnic basket. As Roy stepped aside to retrieve their keys, Rebecca slipped a bottle of "Smooth And Sweet Whipped Cream" into the cooler as well.

As they prepared to leave, Roy and Rebecca spoke blessings upon their journey ahead. *"Heavenly Father, We Declare Gratitude In Mind, Body, Heart, And Soul As You Continue To Watch Over Us And We Seek To Do Your Will Every Step Of The Way. We Ask For Peace And Safety In Our Travels At This Time, In The Precious Name Of Jesus Christ Your Son, Our Lord And Savior. Amen!"*

With a tender smile, they kissed and declared, *"Melodious Mountain* is about to sing with the loving and melodious intimacy of *Lucky Seven."* Amidst a passage of sweet kisses, Roy and Rebecca proceeded onto the parking garage. Once on their motorcycles, their hearts traveled at the speed of *Everlasting Love.*

Their destination would be the scenic intimacy of the place where two distant hearts would unite in an everlasting bond of love as the warm sunlight and cool breezes carry their songs upon *The Wings Of Love* onto the ethereal chorus of the place from which **The Power Of Almighty God** had united them – **The Ethereal Essence Of Heaven.** As they approached the crossroads of *Melodious Mountain*, Roy and Rebecca's hands separated. "See you in the center of the heart!" they shouted.

Once they reached the highest point, Roy and Rebecca stepped from their motorcycles. Slowly, they moved toward each other. Amidst the gentle winds, Rebecca ran her fingers through the sparkling beauty of her blonde hair. Lost in the tender intimacy of *His Charming Angel* before him, Roy was blinded by *The Light Of Love* in her gorgeous eyes. "I love you, *Angel.*" Roy whispered.

"I love you too, My Marvelous Minstrel!" Rebecca replied. With a tender kiss, they began to prepare their meal and spoke a few words of gratitude and praise. *"Heavenly Father, We Thank You In Mind, Body, Heart, And Soul In The Blessed Name Of Your Son, Our Lord And Savior Jesus Christ For This Food And The Cherished Gift Of One True And Everlasting Love Between Us. We Declare Glory To Your Name For Your Endless Blessings Upon Us For All Of Eternity. Amen."*

Mesmerized by her beauty once more, Roy tried to remain cautious against saturating his fingers in barbecue sauce. As she poured two fruit juice cocktails, Rebecca began to laugh. "Hey, Sticky Fingers! How is it that you always manage to get us into these sticky situations?" she inquired. Dipping her finger into the sauce, she licked it and sighed "Very tasty!" Presenting Roy with a drink, Rebecca snickered "You cannot drink this with fingers like those!" As he took a drink from the tenderness of her helping hand, Roy placed some chicken to her lips. Upon tasting it, Rebecca sighed "Compliments to the chef!" As Rebecca raised her eyebrows in recognition of his culinary genius, Roy grinned – swallowing some chicken and replied "Thank you very much."

Upon finishing the first course of their meal amidst the comfort of *Everlasting Love,* Roy held Rebecca in his

110

arms – caressing her sparkling hair. As they continued to drink, Rebecca smiled and declared, "I said it before and I will say it again…" She paused – caressing his face. "Good food is best when eaten in *The Arms Of Everlasting Love!* Agreed?" she concluded.

Touched by her intimate twist to the same words in a special moment from a short time ago, Roy sighed "Agreed!"

Reaching for the cooler once more, Rebecca retrieved the fruit salad. In a gesture of assurance that Roy would not see her inclination, Rebecca raised her eyebrows and shielded his eyes. Retrieving the whipped cream, she poured a splash upon both portions of fruit – making sure that they were heart formations. Spreading some of it across her lips as well, Rebecca uncovered Roy's eyes and accentuated his appetite with a kiss. They continued to eat.

Reaching for the picnic basket, Rebecca retrieved the cookies. She opened the "Sticky Banana" and licked a scoop from her finger. As she offered some to Roy, he placed a cookie to Rebecca's lips. Upon her first taste, Rebecca asked, "Do you realize that you have a truly great sweet talent?" Before he could answer, she concluded with "Then again, it is not difficult to understand with the sweetest guy that I have ever known sitting right before my very eyes."

Upon kissing her, Roy sighed, "That may be true. But, you are sweeter!"

As she took another drink, Rebecca began to laugh – reclining her body. Lost in the moment, she felt the sweetness of Roy's tender caress upon her tummy. Softly, she whispered "Sticky Fingers, I am stuck on you!"

As he gazed into her eyes, Roy sighed, "Sexy Sweet One, I am happy to be stuck with you!" Amidst the tenderness of soft kisses, Roy and Rebecca rested in *The Arms Of Everlasting Love.*

As the evening hours drifted across the sparkling intimacy of *Melodious Mountain,* Roy and Rebecca returned to *The City Of Lights.* They spoke unified praise in their travels.

"Father God, We Ask In The Cherished Name Of Your Son Jesus Christ, Our Lord And Savior For Your Blessing Of Continued Guidance In Safety Onto Our Return Home As We Speak Gratitude Upon This Time Together And Cherished Blessings In The Days Ahead. Amen."

Rebecca was very tired. Gently, Roy took her into his arms and carried her to the comfort and intimacy of Suite #7. As he reclined her delicate body onto the bed – with every intention of going to sleep – Roy could not resist the sudden impulse of his intimate desire. Gently, he began to caress Rebecca's tummy once more. Although her eyes remained closed, Rebecca began a silent giggle - amidst the sentimental charm of Roy's endless love for her. These thoughts were united with Roy's silent reflection upon the dawn of each new day fading into night of listening to her heart beating next to his own, kissing and caressing her, and above all, living out their dreams together and loving her with the warmth of this *One True And Everlasting Love* until the end of time.

"I can see that some things will never change! Then again, it is not as if I would ever want them to!" Rebecca chuckled.

Blushing, Roy grinned, "My only defense is that I simply cannot resist your ethereal beauty or tender charm!" he reasoned.

Amused, Rebecca replied "Very interesting!" Lost in the moment, she sighed "I can assure you right here and now that you will never hear any complaints out of me! However, let me ask you one question..." She paused – raising her eyebrows. Grinning as Roy looked at her – soothing her tummy – Rebecca asked "Are you still going to kiss, caress, look at me, and love me this way before, during, and after there is a baby in there?"

"I could never get enough of you!" Roy repeated through rapid breaths. "In response to your question..." He paused as she giggled at his discovery of another sensitive area.

"Just as long as you promise that Angel Starr will look as beautiful as you!" he concluded in intimate reply.

Amidst silent laughter, Rebecca replied "Angel Starr! I like that! I really do! Where did you..." She paused – lost in the moment once more.

Knowing of her question, Roy breathed, "You see the reason for that name every time that you look in the mirror. I see it every time I think about you, am near you, and kiss, caress, and love you more with the passage of each tender moment between us. The years ahead of us will only strengthen my intense passion and *Everlasting Love* for you. Even so, every special and cherished moment always has been and always will be just like the first. Our beautiful daughter will live as a sparkling reflection of that very same love – with a beautiful, healthy, and loving mind, body, heart, and soul. Just as we two have these very special aspects of our being, our two hearts truly do make the ideal combination. Through it all, the fact remains that Angel Starr deserves to be born with your truly one of a kind beauty, tender charm, and melodious singing voice."

As she caressed Roy's face, Rebecca proceeded onto his neck and chest – stopping on his heart with the sentimental conclusion "That is fine with me! However, that will only happen if she is born with the special melodious, and one of a kind love that can only be found right here!" Upon these words, she raised her body and kissed Roy's heart – encircling it with a heart formation.

In intimate unison, Roy and Rebecca declared **"Thank You, Almighty Father God!"** Upon these words, their two loving hearts united in the absolute of *One True And Everlasting Love* spent the remainder of the evening in the warm comfort and pleasure of their infinite love – amidst the melodious sentiment of their debut album.

Chapter 6

The next morning, Rebecca arose to the sound of Roy bouncing a basketball in the corridor. Rubbing the sleep from her eyes, she arose. Opening the door, she looked at him – giggling. Roy was dressed in a shirt, shorts, and shoes of sparkling yellow. Spinning the ball upon his finger, Roy inquired, "Do you still love the competitive edge?"

"Yes!" Rebecca replied – blowing a kiss. Looking closer, she giggled as she noticed the monogram on his shirt – in sparkling silver letters. Rebecca read *"Lucky."*

Noticing this, Roy blushed and declared "Well, now it is my turn to express myself with this truly idealistic word because we both know that I am the lucky one!"

"I am going to have to challenge that one!" Rebecca asserted – reclining into a familiar chair with an amused grin.

"Anytime, *Angel!* Downstairs, the basketball court is dark and smells strange. Just think! You can brighten it up with your ethereal charm and absorb it into the intimate scent of your perfume!" Roy suggested.

"Game on!" Rebecca declared.

Upon these words, Roy and Rebecca spoke blessings of gratitude. ***"Heavenly Father, We Thank You For This New Day And Declare Blessings To Your Name For The Challenges That Lie Ahead. With Love And Praise In Mind, Body, Heart, And Soul In The Beloved Name Of Jesus Christ Your Son, Our Lord And Savior. Amen."***

As Roy arose and ran to the door, he paused and snickered "Do not trouble yourself by searching for something to wear!" Upon these words, he tossed a package wrapped in golden tissue paper toward Rebecca and raised his eyebrows.

As Rebecca opened it in amused confusion, she asked "What do you…" Rebecca paused. Surprised once more, she grinned and chuckled the conclusion, "I see what you mean!" Rebecca could not believe her eyes. In her hands, was a similar outfit. Suddenly, Rebecca marveled – *"Seven"* was inscribed on her sports bra. Touched, she blew a kiss in recognition of his unique creativity and stepped toward the bedroom to change her clothes. Amidst laughter, they ran out of the suite and shouted, "We are *Lucky Seven!*" Turning to each other, they exchanged a high-five and concluded with "This one is for you!"

Suddenly, Roy and Rebecca stopped – Rebecca had noticed something on the wall. Quick to make sure that she did not see it, Roy pinched her tummy. "What was that?" Rebecca wondered.

"I am a firm believer in grabbing hold of *One True And Everlasting Love.* You are now mine and I will never let you go!" Roy replied with amusingly sinister laughter.

Unable to resist her laughter, Rebecca asserted, "Although that was sweet and you know that you are going to pay for that, that is not what I meant and you know it! What was that poster on the wall?"

To extinguish her curiosity, Roy did the only thing that he could. Gazing into her eyes, he took her into his arms and declared, "You are incredibly beautiful!" As Rebecca blushed, Roy proceeded with a tender kiss upon her unsuspecting lips. Slowly, the elevator door closed.

Once inside the basketball court, Rebecca threw the ball onto the court and jumped from Roy's arms – running to the center of the court. "There is only one way to settle this!" she resolved.

As Roy followed, he declared, "Now, the real game begins!" In the center of the court, Roy suggested "How about a kiss for good luck?"

"That is fine with me, but who starts the game?" Looking at each other, Roy and Rebecca grinned and shouted *"Rock, Scissors, Paper!"* and proceeded with a tender kiss. Placing the ball on the floor, they executed their decisive exchange. Suddenly, Rebecca had another idea. Sliding her foot beneath the ball, she kicked it into the air. As she raised her arms, Rebecca's navel slipped from the constraint of her shorts. Blushing, Roy was distracted. Quickly, Rebecca smacked the ball behind his head. As Roy dodged – caressing her hair – Rebecca flipped into the air and landed behind him.

"Paper!" I win!" she shouted. Mesmerized, Roy chuckled but began to run after her by pure instinct. Turning three cartwheels with the ball in continuous bounce, Rebecca shouted "Three points! Here they come!"

Impressed with her speed and agility, nothing could have prepared Roy for what she was about to do. Flipping once, Rebecca shouted "One!" With another, she declared "Two!" On the third maneuver, Rebecca grasped the ball between her ankles and flipped once more – landing on her hands with a rapid release of the ball. Mesmerized, Roy watched as it flew into the air and landed in the basket. As Rebecca landed upon her feet once more, she declared "Three!" in victory.

Amidst shock, Roy jogged toward the ball. "How did you do that?" he asked.

As she ran toward him, Rebecca answered, "Let me put it this way. Anyone who believes that someone cannot learn a great deal by watching the unique aerial tactics of professional wrestling is very mistaken!"

"That was great! In fact, such unique entertainment has taught me a trick of my own!" Roy admitted. "Observe!" With a high bounce of the ball, Roy jumped into the air and kicked it toward the basket with a maneuver that resembled a dropkick. Sinking the basket, Roy landed on his feet.

"I suppose we have revealed our signature moves!" Rebecca resolved.

"You are correct!" Roy asserted. Upon these words, the game began. As Roy and Rebecca ran amidst the amusing spirit of competition, Roy inquired, "There is something that I would like very much to ask you. You know where my **Walk With The Lord** has led me to attend church services. He paused – thrusting the ball toward the basket. With a successful score, he concluded with, "However, you never did tell me where you attend."

As Rebecca cheered with a successful shot of her own, she said, "You know, I find it very interesting that you attend *Heaven's Paradise Christian Union*. I think that it is time for me to let you in on a little secret!"

Raising his right hand, Roy pledged, "If I have any intention of telling anyone, may this next shot not find its mark!" He began to spin the ball upon his finger. Quickly, he released the ball upward. As it rotated in flight, he gained more points and declared, "OK! You can tell me now!"

"Well, the truth of the matter is that after Reese died, I felt lost personally and spiritually for awhile. I was convinced that **Almighty God** was angry with me for what happened."

"Well, nothing could be further from the truth!" Roy asserted – kissing her.

"Well, yes, of course! I know that now!" Rebecca replied. "Anyway, nothing happened to me to make me believe it. It was my own personal struggle. Until…" Upon these words, Rebecca paused – in intense excitement toward the revelation that was about to occur.

"Until???" Roy inquired – grinning in confusion.

You are going to be very surprised by this, but I have been attending there ever since you left to go on tour!"

Shocked, Roy inquired "Ever since I left?"

"Yes!" Rebecca replied. "As you know, I had been trying to find a way to meet you for some time before the concert. Anyway, **The Lord** led me there on the Sunday prior to your departure. I could hear you singing inside – as I sat outside, praying for **Almighty God** to bless you in your good fortune and keep you safe in your time away. However, I was far too nervous to go in."

"Another missed opportunity for us to meet!" Roy regretted.

"Very true! Even so, after you left, a truly one of a kind experience occurred!"

"What happened?" Roy asked

"I walked in and Pastor Mulholland could sense the intense burden upon my heart. I proceeded to the altar and fell to my knees. Pastor Mulholland laid hands on me and I felt a strong sense of peace that I never knew before and declared ***"Almighty Father God, You Have Always Been There For Me. Since The Beginning Of Time, You Declared The Universal Truth That No One Should Be Alone. I Ask In The Cherished Name Of Jesus Christ Your Son, My Lord And Savior That You Shine The Powerful Glow Of One True And Everlasting Love Upon Me."***

Upon these words, Roy's eyes blinded with tears. ***"The Lord Reveals Himself In Mysterious Ways***, My Love!" he declared. "Now more than ever, I know that we are meant to be together because…" He paused – caressing her face. "I said the exact same thing right before the concert!" Upon these words, Roy and Rebecca declared in spiritual union ***"To Almighty God Be The Glory Now And Forever! Amen!"*** Upon sealing this sentiment with a loving embrace, they began to play once more.

As the game progressed, Rebecca asked "What colors are we going to dress our adorable Angel Starr in when we bring her home from the hospital?"

Confused, Roy inquired "Who said anything about a hospital? I believe that there is nothing more safe, intimate, and special than a family developing amidst the tenderness of natural childbirth in the very place where it is going to live out its life of love and happiness together. All of this begins at home! But, to answer your question, we will have nothing but the best silver and gold for our sparkling reflection of Immortality. Then again, she will look beautiful in any color – just like her mother!"

Touched, Rebecca could not resist the humorous reality of her next thought. "I can just see you running around the house like the charmingly nervous guy that you are! Not that I would be complaining by any means. The only complaints that I would have..." she paused – rubbing her tummy - "would be painful ones!" she concluded. "In my heart, I know that any amount of pain can easily be alleviated by a song from My Marvelous Minstrel!" Rebecca sighed in comfort.

"Although your pain is my deepest fear, I will do everything above and beyond the farthest limitations of my power to ensure your comfort, health, and safety. Although, I do have one simple request!" Roy mentioned.

"What might that be?" Rebecca asked.

"Well, after she is born, I would love to kiss the very beautiful and intimate place where she came from!" Roy admitted – blushing in a subtly intimate reference to her tummy.

"But of course you do and of course you will! After all, we have already established that some things will never change!" Rebecca recalled - rubbing her tummy once more.

"Thank you so much! That means just as much to me as the cherished thought of you becoming the mother of my child!" Roy expressed – in cherished hope for the future ahead.

Blowing a kiss, Rebecca replied, "Since she is going to be born with your heart, how do you think I feel?"

"I have no idea!" Roy snickered.

Gently, Rebecca pushed the basketball toward his chest and kissed him. "The answer is right here!" she asserted – with a tender kiss. As they resumed the game, Rebecca executed her signature move once more and said "Now, I have a question for you! How old should she be when we begin to guide her onto the realization of her own melodious talent?"

"I have two feelings about that. First of all, with you as her mother, she is going to have a natural talent that is going to be realized with her very first breath. Therefore, we must give her the freedom to discover it on her own. Second of all, although the two of us always had dreams of our stardom through the early discovery of our *Gifts Of Song* **From Almighty God**, we did not live in the spotlight since birth.

For that reason, we should raise her in a manner that far too many other stars do not – by ourselves. That way, we can guide, protect, and nurture her in the loving family bond that many children of stars miss out on. All of the while, we will encourage her to live out her dreams with the everlasting inspiration, security, and love that only we can provide!" Roy explained – executing his own signature move.

"Just like us, your true words represent the ideal combination!" Rebecca declared with a sentimental smile.

As Roy stood in the middle of the court, he scored again and asked "Are we in complete agreement as to what Angel Starr's first meal should be?"

"But of course!" he confirmed. Rebecca grinned with a successful shot. "French onion soup!" she began.

"Garden salad!" Roy continued with another score.

"With Thousand Island Dressing!" Rebecca added – shooting once more.

"Sourdough rolls!" Roy continued – talking and playing.

"With garlic butter!" Rebecca added – in play once more.

"Chicken Vesuvio!" Roy snickered with another shot.

"With onion potatoes!" Rebecca added with the ball in flight to its intended target.

Upon these words, Roy and Rebecca walked toward each other – passing the ball between them.

As Roy began with "And last but not least…" They paused – shooting the ball in amused unison and concluding with "Yellow pound cake with vanilla ice cream!"

Snickering at an amusing thought, Rebecca inquired, "Do you think that baby food is made in such delicious flavors?"

With an amused grin, Roy reflected upon the delicious sentiment of their first meal. "Baby food could never taste as good as…" He paused – raising his eyebrows – "Mom's home cooking!" he concluded. Blushing, Rebecca caressed Roy's

121

face and kissed him. With a rapid maneuver, they threw the ball into the air and executed their signature moves in unison one last time.

"What about toys?" Roy asked. "I speak from the experience of knowing that no aspiring singer can discover his or her true talent without toys." Suddenly, Roy and Rebecca looked at one another – each knowing what the other was thinking. However, neither of them would have ever thought that the words to follow would represent a very special projection into the future that they would experience in *The Arms Of Everlasting Love* very soon – with their hearts together as one.

Grinning, Rebecca said "OK, Genius! You started this thought, now finish it!"

Amidst laughter, Roy revealed his thought. "I see her picking up a toy microphone and using the beautiful voice that her mother gave her to sing her first rhyme – at a very early age," he began.

"So do I!" Rebecca replied. "Since great minds do think alike and we both know that anything can happen, I know in my heart that with my looks and voice and the love and talent from your heart, Angel Starr will shine like the beautiful vision within our hearts through her existence of ethereal innocence and adorable charm."

As they gazed into *The Eyes Of Everlasting Love*, Roy and Rebecca thought that they were going to make a final declaration in unison. Instead, an amusing difference of opinion was asserted. As Roy said "Just like you, Mom," at the same time, Rebecca said "Just like you, Dad." As they laughed, they did make the unified statement "Not even *"Rock, Scissors, Paper"* can solve this one!"

As the game ended, they threw the basketball into the air once more. As they proceeded to embrace, the ball fell right through the center of them and onto the floor. As he caressed Rebecca's sparkling hair, Roy said, "Well, just as **The Power Of Almighty God** brought us together..." As he paused, Rebecca concluded with *"The Good Lord* can handle this one too!"

As they moved their lips toward each other for a kiss, Roy and Rebecca whispered a final sentiment in unison "With the love of *Lucky Seven* – the ideal combination!" Amidst a procession of passionate kisses, they returned to the tender intimacy of their "Home Sweet Home" in Suite #7.

On the way, Roy felt his heart stop in anticipation of the matter of paramount importance that was at hand. In his nervous stride, he was intent on deliberately passing by the billboard that he had created. "Rebecca, I have something very important to tell you!" he admitted.

Confused by his nervous frame of mind, Rebecca wiped the sweat from his forehead and declared "Anything, My Love!"

Taking a deep breath, he began to explain. In deep hope that she would not notice the silent mystery of his thoughts, Roy reached into his pocket. "This is my new contract proposal for another year of promotion with *LUCK.7,*" he began.

Suddenly, Rebecca had to avoid revelation of a silent thought of her own. "Please, continue!" she insisted.

"The next step for me is to go on tour around the world and as you know, I still have another appearance to make in recognition of my homecoming celebration. Well, the radio station contacted me and told me that there was a schedule conflict with the tour and in order to accommodate it, I am going to have to make my second appearance tomorrow – and begin the tour the very next day," Roy explained.

Laughing at Roy's nervous frame of mind now, Rebecca said, "Well, I know that you will never disappoint your fans. So, what is the problem?"

Upon these words, they stopped. Roy covered her eyes. With a kiss, he whispered, "I do not want to tell you. Instead, I would rather show you!" Upon these words, he uncovered her eyes – revealing the billboard and his new silent mystery.

Mesmerized, Rebecca saw a familiar image of their love with the words:

"Lucky Seven"
Two Loving Hearts Unite In The Melodious Echo
Of Their Tender Intimacy And Cherished
Love Songs Of Everlasting Love
The First Appearance Of Roy Dawson And Rebecca Davidson
As They Become One
In The Institution Of Marriage
October 7, 1977

As Roy descended onto one knee, his eyes blinded with the tears of *Everlasting Love*. Taking Rebecca's hand, he placed it upon his heart. The wave of love swept over them. "So, I am asking you, Rebecca Davidson, as *My Beautiful Angel, My Dream Come True, And My Everlasting Love*, will you marry me tomorrow and begin the journey of our *Everlasting Love* for one another – united in our melodious bond for all of Eternity?"

As Rebecca's eyes blinded with tears, she accepted through her soft words "I am yours and you are mine – for all of Eternity. It does not matter if it is seven minutes from now or seven lifetimes from now – I would travel to the ends of the universe with you at anytime. Tomorrow sounds great to me! I only wish that we could have gotten married sooner!"

"So do I!" Roy replied. As he took her into his arms, he whispered "Thank you so much! I love you, Rebecca!"

"I love you too, Roy!" she replied. "By the way, it is a great picture!" Rebecca added. Upon these words, they kissed in intimate reflection upon their melodious partnership and *Everlasting Love* – in gentle stride back to Suite #7.

Upon reaching the door, Roy took Rebecca into his arms and raised his eyebrows. "I believe that we have proven that "practice" is a truly good thing!" he said.

Opening the door, Rebecca sighed in amused acceptance "Yes, we certainly have done just that!" Upon these words, Roy stepped over the threshold of *Everlasting Love*.

Once inside the cool darkness, Rebecca jumped from his arms and whispered "Do not concern yourself with the lights!" By the gentle glow of *The Solid Gold Hotel And Casino* sign in its brilliant declaration just outside the window, Roy followed the ethereal intimacy of her shadow – but he was not sure as to what she was doing. Amidst sudden confusion, he heard the sound of effervescence – followed by activation of the 8-track machine. As the first recording of *Lucky Seven* began playing once more, Rebecca snapped her fingers. Roy's face flooded with sweat. Rebecca sat in the spa – glistening in aquatic glamour. Slowly, Roy stepped toward the spa with nervous perception and slipped into it. Roy and Rebecca began to kiss. As Rebecca's gentle touch held him closer to her, Roy began to soothe her tummy – softly. Only love remained.

A short time later, they stood together in tender reflection upon everything that they had been through in the name of this *One True And Everlasting Love*. Roy declared "*My Beautiful Angel*, I must leave now, but after tomorrow, I will follow you to the ends of this world and back again through an infinite number of lifetimes – in the name of falling in love with you all over again throughout every minute of each new day – knowing that the warmth of your sweet voice, tender beauty, and *Everlasting Love* all represent *My Dream Come True*."

As they joined hands – blinded by *The Light Of Love* upon their fingers – Roy and Rebecca cried silent tears of *Everlasting Love* and spoke a final prayer in blessed gratitude toward their departure from this moment onto the cherished future ahead. ***"Father God, We Thank You, In The Precious Name Of Jesus Christ Your Son, Our Lord And Savior For Showing Us Once Again By The Power Of Your Infinite Love That As We Reunite In The New Day That You Alone Will Make, The Blessing Of One True***

125

And Everlasting Love Will Shine Within Our Minds,
Bodies, Hearts, And Souls And Through Your Spiritual
Blessing Become Our Source Of Strength And Guidance
Through All Days Ahead In Our Cherished Love For You
And One Another For All Of Eternity. Amen."
"I love you, Roy Dawson!" Rebecca sighed.
"I love you too, Rebecca Davidson!" Roy replied.
Upon these words, Roy and Rebecca sealed the moment with a
tender kiss. Roy departed. Only love remained. With their
hearts together as one, Roy and Rebecca drifted into a restful
sleep - onto an intimate vision into the future.

In their dream, the day was July 17, 1984. After being
on tour for another year, Roy and Rebecca returned to *The
Solid Gold Hotel And Casino* for a homecoming concert. Since
the very beginning, **The Power Of Almighty God**, *The One
True And Everlasting Love* between them, and the constant
promotional guidance of *LUCK.7 Radio* had been the ideal
elements in the name of *Lucky Seven* being recognized as the
greatest singing duo in history. After the success of their debut
album, Roy and Rebecca had been selected as *"The Best New
Recording Artist Of 1977,"* and had been awarded *"Album Of The
Year"* and *"Song Of The Year"* every year since then. In true
intimate and sentimental reflection, Roy and Rebecca renewed
their wedding vows every year on their anniversary during their
homecoming concert. This sentiment was of a particular
intimate nature because their first *"Song Of The Year"* was *"The
Tie That Binds Us…"* All of their dreams had come true at long
last.

Even so, this homecoming concert would stand out
amongst days of the past, present, and future in true idealistic
sentimental and personal fulfillment because five years ago on
this visionary day, Roy and Rebecca became the loving parents
of a beautiful daughter who was going to make her singing
debut with them on this very special night. Her name was
none other than the cherished words that they had spoken

during that special night of tender love and intimacy – October 5, 1977 – Angel Starr.

Before stepping out on stage, Roy and Rebecca gazed into *The Eyes Of Everlasting Love*. Roy marveled at Rebecca's ethereal beauty. She was dressed in a black shirt – tied in tender accentuation of her navel and inscribed with the same photographic image of their *Everlasting Love* that appeared on their latest best-selling album, *"As Time Goes By..."* – and pants of black satin. Her sparkling blonde hair flowed in ethereal union with her gorgeous blue eyes and beautiful smile of pure warmth. Roy and Rebecca spoke a few words in loving reflection upon this special point of return.

"Heavenly Father, We Thank You For This Special Moment In Time Where We Return With The Cherished Being Of Tender Innocence That You Alone Have Blessed Us In Mind, Body, Heart, And Soul With - Our Beloved Daughter Angel Starr – And Unite Our Voices In Declaration Of Our Everlasting Love For You And One Another, In The Blessed Name Of Jesus Christ Your Son, Our Lord And Savior In The Same Sweet Verse Through Which We Continue To Speak Melodious Words Of Honor And Praise To Your Name For All Of Eternity. Amen." With a mesmerized gaze into *The Eyes Of Everlasting Love*, they eased their restless minds by singing a song in sentimental reflection upon everything that they had been through to arrive at this cherished moment.

Giving of ourselves to one another, we became one...
As we opened up our hearts to each other...
We united our two hearts into one...
In God's Love, *we became a loving family...*
Built on dreams and tenderness...
I love the way it feels – forever loving one another...
In an Everlasting Love...
In our hearts, we will always be together...
As Time Goes By...

127

Amidst a unified expression of love, they whispered "*Lucky Seven,* this one is for you!" in sentimental declaration. With a tender kiss, they stepped out on stage.

In the same sentimental manner as Roy's homecoming seven years ago, a touching declaration was made from the box seats billboard. As the crowd cheered, Roy and Rebecca waved and read *"Lucky Seven! The Greatest Love Story Ever To Be Told!"*

"Thank you very much! *City Of Lights,* it is great to be home! ***May Almighty God Bless You Always And Forever!*** they began in unison.

"My Marvelous Minstrel and I wish to express our warmest gratitude for your cherished appreciation for our melodious success over the past seven truly great years!" Rebecca continued.

Upon these words, Roy turned to Rebecca and blushed – laughter had taken control of the audience.

"Thank you, Rebecca!" Roy sighed. "Friends, *My Beautiful Angel* is trying to tell you that we have a very special guest here with us this evening!"

As the crowd cheered in wonder, Rebecca continued. "We know this person better than anybody. In fact, we have the genuine privilege of letting you in on a secret that the three of us have kept hidden for the past five years."

"The fact of the matter is that we were the first people to hear this person sing her first note in declaration of the fact that she was born with a marvelous and melodious talent!" Roy added. Upon these words, Roy and Rebecca joined hands. Taking their microphones, they stepped backstage – all of the while, continuing to speak to the audience. "We must stress the word "born" because…" As Roy paused, they stepped out on stage with a beautiful child. As they each held one of her hands, the child was jumping as they were swinging her in between them. As the crowd cheered, Roy and Rebecca concluded with "This is our beautiful daughter, Angel Starr."

Angel Starr was dressed in the same shirt as Rebecca and denim jeans. Her blue eyes and long blonde hair sparkled with adorable innocence and charm. Every time Roy and Rebecca looked at her, they were truly blessed by how she was growing in the idealistic reflection of their dreams of a special and loving family bond. Smiling, their eyes blinded with the tears of *Everlasting Love*. She was wearing a hat that featured a picture of Roy and Rebecca's album that they recorded during Rebecca's pregnancy.

As the crowd cheered, Roy took her into his arms. Roy and Rebecca laughed at the fact that her shirt was bigger than she was. Even though they did have a tour shirt that was exactly her size that she was wearing underneath, she said that she wanted to wear a shirt that was just like her Mommy's. In their hearts Roy and Rebecca reflected upon the amusing and sentimental gratitude that she was not growing up too fast. As they kissed her, Roy whispered in sentimental reflection of his nickname for her "Your shirt is too big, My Heart!"

"That is because she is a big girl, Daddy!" Rebecca replied.

"Yes, I am a big girl, Daddy!" Angel Starr repeated – giggling. Waving, Angel Starr leaned toward the microphone and shouted "Hello Everybody! My name is Angel Starr and I am five years old today!" Upon these words, she extended five fingers to the audience.

Laughing, Roy and Rebecca kissed and turned to the audience. "*Our Little Dream Come True* here, wants to give you a present on her birthday!" Roy declared. Upon these words, Roy and Rebecca lowered her to the floor and pushed the microphone down to her height. "So, we are going to step back and let her take center stage!" Rebecca said.

"My Heart, the spotlight is yours!" Roy declared – caressing her hair. As they kissed once more, Roy and Rebecca declared in unison "Remember, Mommy and Daddy are right behind you – every step of the way." Upon these words, Roy and Rebecca stepped back – cheering for her as she stepped toward the microphone.

"My Mommy and Daddy said that all of you are our friends. So, I am going to sing a song for you about my Mommy and Daddy. I will sing the words and then you go after me. At the end, I am going to show you that I know my ABC's. When I stop, you clap, OK?" As the audience laughed and smiled, they said "OK!" in unison. With Roy and Rebecca standing in the background – proud of their beloved daughter - Angel Starr began to sing.

My Mommy and Daddy like to sing songs and they are Lucky Seven...
L-U-C-K-Y...
L-U-C-K-Y...
L-U-C-K-Y...
And they are Lucky Seven!

"Now, you go. But, they are not your Mommy and Daddy. So you just sing the ABC's." Upon these words, Roy and Rebecca united with the audience – following her through the entire song. Upon clapping the word "LUCKY" – in progression of one letter at a time – the song ended. As the audience cheered, Roy and Rebecca took her into their arms. Smiling and giggling, Angel Starr said "Thank you! Thank you! Thank you!"

As their eyes blinded with the tears of love and happiness, Roy and Rebecca said "That was beautiful!"

Tenderly, Roy explained, "My Heart, Mommy and Daddy have to sing some songs for our friends for a little while."

"But, when we are all done, Daddy baked a birthday cake for you!" Rebecca continued.

"Yellow cake?" she asked – excited.

"You got it! Mommy made your favorite meal for you too!" Roy added.

"Onion soup, lettuce, tomatoes, cucumbers, and celery with orange sauce, chicken, mashed potatoes, and yellow cake with vanilla ice cream!" Angel Starr declared - smiling.

"Right again! Is she not the most adorable cutie that you have ever seen?" Rebecca asked the audience. Upon these words, the audience laughed and cheered once more.

"She should be! After all, she looks just like you!" Roy replied.

Caressing his face, Rebecca sighed, "That may be true! But, she has a heart of gold – just like you!"

"But, before we start..." Roy began. As Rebecca stepped backstage once more, she returned with a yellow inflatable chair for their daughter. "You have to sit in your favorite seat because Mommy and Daddy want to sing a song for you!"

As she clapped, Angel Starr shouted "My song! My song!" and went to sit down.

Joining hands, Roy and Rebecca stepped forward – turning to the audience. "As you know, we wrote and recorded this song when we found out that **Almighty God** was going to bless our lives with her adorable presence five years ago," Rebecca explained.

"We have been singing it to her every day and every night since then. Tonight, we would like to sing it for you!" Roy declared.

As their eyes blinded with tears, Roy and Rebecca looked back at their beautiful daughter and sighed "Happy Birthday, Angel Starr!" Gazing into *The Eyes Of Everlasting Love*, they kissed and began to sing.

> *To you, we sing this sweet song...*
> *As our love for you grows strong...*
> *With the passage of each new day...*
> *In love, we wait...*
> *Each day, we celebrate...*
> *In the name of love, you were made...*
> *Sweet, innocent...*
> *From **God**, you are sent...*
> *To us, your loving parents...*
> *You are Our Dream Come True, Angel Starr...*

131

You have a Musical Father...
You are the light in his eyes...
He loves you with all that he has to give...
Melodious Mom, with her musical charm...
For your happiness, she will live...
Love and guidance...
Strength, through life's chance...
You will know we will not be far...
As you grow in love, Angel Starr...
Sweet and Precious Child, through the good and bad...
We will love you always and forever...
Far from now, please do not forget how...
We pledged love that will end – never...
Make your dreams come true...
Love, from us to you...
Catch and hold your star...
Love, Mom and Dad, Angel Starr...

As the crowd cheered, the wave of *Everlasting Love* swept over *"The Triangle Of True Love"* – Roy, Rebecca, and Angel Starr Dawson. Roy and Rebecca took Angel Starr into their arms and kissed her. Softly, Roy sighed *"My Two Beautiful Angels,* I love you always and forever!"

"My Marvelous Minstrel and adorable image of Immortality, I love you too!" Rebecca asserted.

"My Mommy and Daddy, I love you three!" Angel Starr concluded. Upon these words, the visualization elapsed.

Chapter 7

The next morning, Roy arose in cherished reflection upon the first magical moment that had brought him to this one. As his love would continue to strengthen, he would look back upon the moment of *Everlasting Love* when he looked into Rebecca's beautiful eyes and fell in love with her as not only an aide in the conquer of the inevitable trials of life and love but as an intimate monument to the times in an endless rebirth of this love throughout the passage of each new day until the end of time as well. As he proceeded onto his dressing room that he had used six days ago, the door was locked. Confused, Roy noticed a note written in golden letters of Old English formation. Smiling, he read:

My Beloved Roy,

> *Today, I Will Experience One Of The Greatest Moments In My Entire Life. After I Heard The Melodious Voice From Your Heart For The Very First Time, **The Blessing Of Almighty God** Showed Me The Cherished Magic Of Your Love. Now, I Am Going To Become One With You In A Bond Of Everlasting Love For All Of Eternity. The Warmth Of Your Love Has Solved The Complex Mystery Of Romance For Me. Now, It Is Time For Me To Do The Same For You. "The Tie That Binds Us Is Love From Me To You! Remember, Lucky Seven Is With You Always And Forever.*
>
> *With Silver Wishes And Golden Dreams,*
>
> *Rebecca*

The day was October 7, 1977. As Roy ventured onto the next dressing room, he noticed a note from Steve Fitzsimmons expressing his regret for not being able to attend due to an unexpected meeting with a publishing company that he had been waiting to hear from for quite some time. Amidst this resolve, Roy began to reflect upon the ethereal reality that had led him onto this – one of the greatest moments in his entire life. On this day, Roy would come to believe in the *One True And Everlasting Love* that he had only been able to communicate through his tender melodies from the heart – until now – once and for all time. On this day, the tender love song of his *Dream Come True* would be sung in two voices united as one for all to hear – forever until the end of time. On this day, October 7, 1977, Roy and Rebecca would declare their love for one another and unite their hearts together as one through their tender love song of *Everlasting Love* within the ethereal bond of marriage - in communication of *The Greatest Love Story Ever To Be Told.*

Roy wore a tuxedo of sparkling gold. With his hand upon his heart, the vision of this *One True And Everlasting Love* united with the gentle glow of sentimental declaration upon his finger. As he stepped toward the door, Roy would have never believed that he was about to solve the special mystery that had remained throughout the past year – as well as the one that materialized six days ago.

As Roy stepped onto the stage, the crowd cheered. As he waved, Roy turned to Pastor Clifford Mulholland. **"God Bless You,** Pastor!" Roy said.

"God Bless You, as well, **Brother In Christ,** Roy Dawson!" the minister replied.

Upon these words, Roy presented the minister with his latest financial offering in recognition of **The Spiritual Blessing** of his melodious success and declared "Blessings upon you and everyone at *Heaven's Paradise Christian Union* as I share blessings of my literary success bestowed upon me by **Almighty God!"**

Upon these words, they shook hands. In an instant, Roy read a message displayed upon the box seats platform. *"Roy, Your Dream Come True Is Right In Front Of You!"* Smiling, Roy witnessed **The Ethereal Power Of Almighty God** once more – right before his mesmerized eyes.

Rebecca appeared before him with the brilliance of *The Golden Dream* that came true for him six days ago. Amidst the sparkling *Light Of Love,* her ethereal beauty defined and personified the vision of love that he had only realized through the melodious echo of his tender melodies – until now. Her gorgeous blue eyes reflected the ideal light to shine the cherished reality of this one moment in time upon him. Beneath a halo of red and yellow roses, the gentle beauty of her gorgeous blonde hair flowed amidst the reflection of Roy's *Golden Dream*. The warmth of her smile provided Roy with the belief in the reality of *Everlasting Love* that they would share together from this moment onward – until the end of time.

She was dressed in a golden evening gown – sparkling in the intimate reflection of silver stars and vented in glamorous enhancement of her beautiful breasts and tender accentuation of her navel. Around her neck, she wore the sparkling locket of sentimental declaration of a love to last for all time. She was his *Beautiful And Melodious Angel* – defined and personified for all of Eternity. As the wave of love swept over them, Roy and Rebecca began to sing with the strength of their **Melodious Blessing From Almighty God** – united as one for all of Eternity.

> *It looks like we made it…*
> *This is our Dream Come True…*
> *We have come a long way…*
> *But, this is where we will stay…*
> *This is truly meant to be…*
> *Looking back, life was so hard…*
> *To our hearts, we were true…*
> *Dedicated to one dream…*
> *Some things are not what they seem…*
> *It was only a dream until I met you…*
> *It was Love At First Sight…*
> *Everlasting Love that seems so right…*
> *Everything I need is in your heart…*
> *Reach out now and take my hand…*
> *Stay with me until the end…*
> *It is meant to be…*
> *Forever you and me…*
> *Let us never part…*

God did truly step in…
Now, the best days begin…
Granting this One True Love…
I love you more each day…
In each and every way…
*You were sent in **God's Love**…*
Seemed so close and yet so far…
In that distant silver star…
My Love, "Some Dreams Really Do Come True…"

As they joined hands, Roy Dawson and Rebecca Davidson whispered, "I love you!" in unison.

Pastor Mulholland smiled. ***"God Bless You, Sister In Christ,*** Rebecca Davidson!"

"May God Bless You, Pastor!" Rebecca replied.

Upon blessing them, Pastor Mulholland spoke:

"In the beginning, ***To Almighty God Be The Glory,*** for *The Essence Of Creation* was *The Gift Of Song.* This special gift touched the heart of a man and woman through their unified creation of beautiful and melodious magic. Throughout the passage of time, *The Gift Of Song* brought much happiness to their lives. Even so, they both knew that something was missing. In their hearts, they were united in one dream – to find a kindred spirit with whom they could realize ***The True Power Of This Cherished Gift From Almighty God*** through the discovery of *One True And Everlasting Love.* On ***"The First Day,"*** *The Power Of Almighty God* shined the brilliant light of ***His Spiritual Blessing*** upon them. Mesmerized by the ethereal mystery of that moment, neither of them could sing one word. On ***"The Second Day,"*** they found the strength to communicate their deepest feelings within *The First Kiss Of One True And Everlasting Love.* On ***"The Third Day,"*** they traveled the endless path that they had both used in search of one another – with their hearts together as one. On ***"The Fourth Day,"*** they united their ***Melodious Gift From Almighty God*** through their creation of beautiful and melodious magic – together as one for the very

136

first time. On *"The Fifth Day,"* they created a beautiful child in the image of their ethereal bond and melodious union. On *"The Sixth Day,"* they united with the child in a loving and melodious family bond – shining in the gentle glow of *Everlasting Love.* On *"The Seventh Day," "The Triangle Of True Love"* began to travel throughout the entire world in communication of their melodious message – united in the ethereal absolute that they had found at long last with their hearts together as one, *One True And Everlasting Love.* The story that I have just related represents the past, present, and future of the two special beings of melodious talent and *Everlasting Love* that you see before you right now – Roy Dawson and Rebecca Davidson." As the crowd cheered, Rebecca gazed at Roy. Blinded with tears, she stepped forward – taking the microphone. As the wave of love swept over them, nothing could have ever prepared Roy for the words that would come to follow.

"Friends, before I met the man standing by my side at this moment, I was a fan of his just like you. This sentiment will live on within my heart always and forever. He was such a special inspiration for me, that I found the courage to pursue melodious aspirations of my very own. Unfortunately, an egotistical family member stole that chance away from me. My reason for telling you this now in his presence is that I had the genuine privilege of being the first person to ever hear his melodious voice." Wiping sentimental tears from her eyes, Rebecca smiled. "Roy, I have something for you!" she declared. Caressing his face, she stepped backstage – returning with a familiar box of sparkling silver.

Amidst amused confusion, Roy opened it. He could not believe his eyes. Inside, were the recordings that he had lost in a moment of great personal tragedy and triumph one year ago and a sparkling revelation of a mystery that remained for the past six days – the solid gold heart that had been waiting outside of his dressing room door was not divided anymore. Now, it was united in the absolute of this

137

One True And Everlasting Love – inscribed with Roy's name next to Rebecca's.

Amidst deep sentiment, Rebecca repeated the familiar words that Roy read in that cherished moment. *"From My Heart To Yours, Everlasting Love Is Sent To You From Me. Now That You Have It, Let Us Unite* **By The Power Of Almighty God** *– And Complete Our Romantic Journey."* As she paused to caress his face, Rebecca concluded with *"Lucky Seven Is With You Always And Forever."*

Slowly, Roy took his microphone and replied *"Everlasting And True, Now That I Have Found You!"* Upon these words, Roy solved another mystery. The tender sweetness of Rebecca's voice made him realize at long last that hers was the voice that he heard over the *LUCK.7* airwaves in recognition of his first melodious masterpiece on that special day one year ago. As they joined hands, Roy said, "Rebecca, you stole my recordings!"

"Yes, I know! After it happened to me, I wanted to right that wrong by doing something good for someone – you, and you alone." She paused – caressing his face. "Are you…" she paused once more.

Chuckling, Roy placed his finger to her lips – silencing her. "Anger is not even a thought. All that matters is that it was you all along! In my heart, I knew that it could be no one else in the entire world. However, you stole much more than that." As he took her into his arms, Roy concluded with "You stole my heart! Now, it belongs to you – forever, until the end of time. I love you always and forever!"

Amidst silent tears, Rebecca replied "I love you too!" Upon these words, Roy and Rebecca sealed one another into a loving embrace. As the crowd cheered, this intimate story of *Everlasting Love* was about to begin its next chapter.

Blessing them, Pastor Mulholland continued. "The reality of *One True And Everlasting Love* can only be realized between the unity of a man and a woman whom **The Good Lord** intends to be together for all of Eternity. Just as *"Every* *picture tells a story,"* every tender love song echoes its special melody into the heart of anyone and everyone who seeks it. *Everlasting Love* has united the hearts of Roy Dawson and Rebecca Davidson and brought them to this one moment in time to profess their love for one another amidst their tender intimacy and melodious bond."

In a final instant of cherished reflection, Roy placed Rebecca's hand upon his heart. Blinded with tears, he caressed her face. As they joined hands, Roy spoke. *"With This One Voice..."* I declare that I, Roy Dawson, take you, Rebecca Davidson, to be my wife. As my *Everlasting Love* for you grows with the passage of each new day for all of Eternity, I pledge to love, honor, cherish, and nurture you for better or for worse, for richer or for poorer, in good times and in bad, and in sickness and in health for as long as we both shall live. As the tender intimacy of our love story echoes its cherished melody – sung in my one voice of loving declaration – I pledge to live my life with you amidst the cherished reflection of **The Power Of Almighty God** that has united us."

As he gazed into *The Eyes Of Everlasting Love,* Roy reached into his pocket – all of the while, their eyes never left one another. He retrieved a golden box – sparkling in the melodious reflection of silver musical notes. As he opened it, Rebecca could not believe her eyes. A gorgeous diamond watch sparkled in brilliant union with a central band of gold around it. On one side, Rebecca noticed the inscription:

To My Beloved Wife, Rebecca
*On The Day That **Almighty God***
United Us In Everlasting Love
October 7, 1977
With Love, Roy

The other side reflected in the cherished sentiment *"Time Is On Our Side."* As he placed it upon her wrist, Roy opened the secret compartment in the center of the box. Rebecca cried silent tears. A glamorous diamond wedding band sparkled in the intimate glow of *"Lucky Seven"* - inscribed in golden letters. Placing the ring upon her finger, Roy spoke a final declaration of his love. *"With This One Voice..."* I pledge *Everlasting Love* from my heart to yours – always and forever until the end of time."

In cherished sentiment, Rebecca spoke. *""As The Tie That Binds Us Is Love From Me To You..."* I declare that I, Rebecca Davidson, take you, Roy Dawson, to be my husband. As my *Everlasting Love* for you grows with the passage of each new day for all of Eternity, I pledge to love, honor, cherish, and nurture you for better or for worse, for richer or for poorer, in good times and in bad, and in sickness and in health for as long as we both shall live. As the tender intimacy of our love story echoes its cherished melody – uniting *'The Tie That Binds Us..."* for all of Eternity – I pledge to live my life with you amidst the cherished reflection of **The Power Of Almighty God** that has united us."

As she gazed into *The Eyes Of Everlasting Love*, Rebecca reached into her pocket. Roy could not believe his eyes. In her hand, a solid gold watch sparkled in a tender inscription. On one side, Roy noticed

To My Beloved Husband, Roy
*On The Day That **Almighty God***
United Us In Everlasting Love
October 7, 1977
With Love, Rebecca

The other side reflected in the cherished sentiment *'Time Is On Our Side."* As she placed it upon his wrist, Rebecca reached into her pocket once more. In her hand was a solid gold wedding band. *"Lucky Seven"* sparkled in an intimate inscription of diamonds. Placing the ring upon his finger, Rebecca spoke a final declaration of her love. *""The Tie That Binds Us Is Love From Me To You"* – always and forever until the end of time."

As the crowd cheered, Pastor Mulholland smiled. As he blessed them once more, he said "In declaration of your *Everlasting Love* for one another and exchange of these rings, you have begun a new journey onto your lives together – with *The Love Of Almighty God* that has united you as one for all of Eternity."

Upon these words, Rebecca smiled and raised the microphone to her lips once more. "As we begin this special journey together, I have one final intimate mystery to reveal to My Beloved Husband. Roy, do you recall when I told you that I knew what was going to happen between us from the start?" she inquired.

Smiling, Roy declared, "Yes, of course!"

"Well, I knew of the journey that we were going to embark upon in a life of *Everlasting Love*. However, I also knew when and where it would begin!" Rebecca explained.

Grinning at the charming mystery of the previous tender moment between them – but cherished once again in Rebecca's bright smile – Roy inquired "What did you know?"

"Nothing much! All that I knew was that it was going to begin today with our loving declaration of *Everlasting Love* in marriage and that our first stop along the way would be the first city of our international tour. I spoke these words with my heart first…" She paused. Retrieving something else from her pocket, she concluded with "Then with this golden pen. You see My Marvelous Minstrel and Beloved Husband, I drafted your new promotional contract with *LUCK.7*!" She paused once more. Raising her eyebrows, Rebecca concluded with "Now, the real fun begins!"

"You are truly one of a kind!" Roy declared.

"So are you, My Marvelous Minstrel!" Rebecca replied. "So are you!"

Upon these words, Roy and Rebecca declared in tender unison "*Lucky Seven,* this one is for you!"

As they gazed into *The Eyes Of Everlasting Love,* Pastor Mulholland proceeded. "Thus, by the authority vested in me by *The City Of Lights* and **The Power Of Almighty God And His Son Jesus Christ** that has united you, I now declare that you have become one within the spiritual bond of marriage."

Upon these words, he shook their hands and declared *"City Of Lights,* it is an honor and privilege to present to you Mr. and Mrs. Roy and Rebecca Dawson – *Lucky Seven!* **May Almighty God Bless You Both!"** As the crowd began to cheer and throw confetti of sparkling gold, Pastor Mulholland stepped from the stage and joined the audience. The wave of love swept over them. Moving their lips toward each other in tender intimacy, Roy and Rebecca sealed their first intimate moment as husband and wife with a passionate kiss and declared their love in tender unison. With a unified expression of **Faith, Hope, And Love,** Roy and Rebecca declared **"Thank You, Almighty Father God!"** Joining hands, they stepped forward. In one final moment of surprise, Roy stepped backstage once more – all of the while, their eyes never left one another.

Roy returned with a sparkling silver object. "Friends, I have something very important to share with My Beautiful Wife – as well as every one of you. Six days ago, I realized the final dream that I had only sang about through my cherished *Gift Of Song.* Defined and personified in *The Beautiful Angel* that you see before you right now, I found my *One True And Everlasting Love.* Three days ago, Rebecca and I realized a new dimension to our cherished relationship. We became more than just two loving hearts united in the absolute of *Everlasting Love.* Uniting our voices in the melodious echo of our debut album, we became *Lucky Seven.* As we speak, *LUCK.7* – the radio station that has meant more to us in the name of making it possible for us to stand before you right now in communication of our melodious message than words could ever hope to express– is producing copies of our debut album for each and every one of you. Upon our departure tomorrow morning, this album will be released around the world."

As the crowd cheered, Rebecca concluded with "Before we leave, Roy and I wanted to make this final appearance for you in expression of our deepest gratitude for your kindness and support."

Upon these words, Roy and Rebecca declared, "Thank you very much! *City Of Lights*, this one is for you!"

As they gazed into *The Eyes Of Everlasting Love*, a sudden sense of intense confusion came over Rebecca. Roy said, "Before we proceed any further, I have two special gifts for My Beautiful Wife."

Grinning at Rebecca's sudden expression of confusion, Roy placed the sparkling silver mystery into her hands. Upon opening it, Rebecca could not believe her eyes. Inside, was a solid gold replica of the cover of their debut album – inscribed with the photographic image of their love that they had taken upon the conclusion of recording. Upon it, a sentimental inscription sparkled in silver letters of Old English. In spiritual union, Roy and Rebecca cried silent tears and whispered, ***"Thank You, Almighty Father God And Our Lord And Savior Jesus Christ!"***

"I love you, Roy Dawson!" Rebecca sighed.

"I love you too, Rebecca Dawson!" Roy replied. As they sealed the moment with a passionate kiss, Roy and Rebecca stepped forward and began the concert. Suddenly, Rebecca was very confused as Roy grinned and declared, "I have one more story to tell. *City Of Lights*, I am going to need your help with this one. I am going to tell you the story of how much I truly do love the woman that is standing beside me right now." As Roy began to sway to the cheers of the crowd, he sighed, "Mrs. Rebecca Dawson, will you dance with me?" Amidst silent tears, Rebecca smiled and blew a kiss in tender acceptance. As they began to sway together as one, Roy and Rebecca danced to the rhythm of reflection of this *One True And Everlasting Love* – through the melodious communication of his tender melody.

Sweet Rebecca I…
Love you very much…
Because of you, all I do…
Is touched by True Love…
My Rebecca…

Come now, take my hand...
Stay until the end...
In your arms, I am safe – lost in your sweet charms...
Dear Rebecca...
Look into these enchanted eyes...
Touch the warmth of my love...
By your side, everything seems so right...
As I look to the future with you...
I see beauty morning, noon, and night...
And My Dream Come True in your eyes...
Your sweet eyes...
Angel eyes...
Rebecca, I love you...
Tender, sweet, and true...
With our hearts as one, we look to tomorrow...
Sweet Rebecca...
Everlasting Love...
*Sent in **God's Love**...*
Rebecca, My Love...
Let us part – never...
This is forever...

As the song concluded, the new husband and wife kissed once more and declared, "*Lucky Seven*, I love you!" The wave of love swept over them. Roy knew that he was dreaming no longer. Amidst the tender intimacy of this *One True And Everlasting Love*, Roy and Rebecca Dawson spoke the words that would remain inscribed upon their debut album in sentimental declaration of their silver wishes for the future upon the solid gold foundation of their melodious bond and *Everlasting Love* for all of Eternity - ***"True Love Is Only Found In The Heart."***

"True
Love
Is
Only
Found
In
The
Heart"

Chapter One

Steve Fitzsimmons' dream came true on July 7, 1984. He had dedicated his entire life to the pursuit of this dream. This ethereal circumstance materialized at a truly ideal point in time for him. One year prior to this cherished day, he published his first literary masterpiece.

At a young age, Steve's **Walk With The Lord** led him onto *Faith, Hope, And Love Christian Haven* and the spiritual guidance of Pastor Samuel Kiplinger.

After graduating from Orange State University in 1977 with a Bachelor's Degree in Creative Writing, Steve was touched by a unique sense of literary vision – dedicated to solving the complex *Mystery Of Romance*. Unfortunately, a painful sense of uncertainty left him unable to take the first vital step in communication of his message and definition of the place that he truly believed was his own in a changing world of complex realities. Also, futile impulses over the past few years left him plagued by rejection.

Even so, Steve remained dedicated to his **Literary Gift From The Lord** – and inspired by a few powerful words that **The Lord** had given him. These words became a true source of strength for him throughout his literary pursuits: *"A Writer's Life Is His Work."* As the years progressed, these words were an idealistic declaration of the reality that Steve was able to use his **Creative Gift From The Lord** with a capability that was so natural, it reflected in absolutely every aspect of his life.

Still, one of the most difficult trials within his life became a true source of inspiration to believe in himself and never give up – guiding him onto the creation of his first literary masterpiece, *"True Love Is Only Found In The Heart."* *A True Romantic Idealist* at heart, all that he ever hoped for was to find *One True And Unconditional Love* in someone willing to accept him for everything that he was – as a visionary of his **Gift From Almighty God** and as a human being. Although he knew that as **A Child Of Almighty God**, he would always be accepted for all that he had been and would ever be, this fundamental desire of his heart was never truly fulfilled in his life. Even so, his strong sense of dedication to the realization of it made his dream of creative success come true at long last.

At a young age, Steve developed a strong belief that became an ideal source of strength and peace of mind in triumph over the harsh realities of the world around him. He believed that no being of life should experience the degradation of having superficial judgments passed upon him or her by any other.

Shortly after his birth, Steve developed an uncertain medical condition called Hydrocephalus. Over the years, Steve had learned not to live in fear of it – but with awareness of its potential dangers at all times. In a church sermon, he heard some very powerful words and took them to heart in the name of viewing his health in the proper perspective as a source of strength and determination to overcome any and all difficulties in life – *"Whatever does not kill us, will make us stronger."*

Due to the fact that he was now at the age of 29, he found himself lost in the harsh reality of being at a difficult age to find women who were motivated by the notion of a serious relationship. Around him, he noticed that all of the most sensitive and beautiful women were married or deeply resentful. No one seemed to believe in the existence of someone with his truly sensitive and caring focus in life. To make matters even worse, he came to realize that no one seemed to believe that someone of his idealistic nature existed. Furthermore, his past relationships reflected the reprehensible truth that understanding and acceptance by others of the reality of conflicts with his health that he had no control over was very difficult.

Despite all that was happening around him, Steve remained devoted to his **Faith In Almighty God** and the fulfillment of his idealistic dream. Throughout his painful years of endless searching, he resolved never to engage in a relationship with any expectations or take anything for granted – with complete disregard for the strength of his initial feelings. These beliefs were the direct result of his own defenses against needless pain and loss.

In visionary reflection upon this dream, Steve made this special wish known through powerful communication in a very special place. Every night before *The Ethereal Essence Of Almighty God* that would eventually grant it, he would gaze onto the spiritual haven. Amidst deep reflection, he would reach out into the cool darkness and whisper *"Almighty Father God, You Have Always Been There For Me. In The Blessed Name Of Jesus Christ Your Son, My Lord And Savior, I Ask You To Shine The Powerful Glow Of One True And Unconditional Love Upon Me. Distant Spirit, Wherever You May Be, It Is Meant To Be One Day – Forever You And Me."*

As time passed on, the strong passion within Steve's heart began to provide a feeling of determination that had a power all of its own. With the acquisition of this new confidence, he grew to interpret it as the source of strength that he had lacked for so long. Thus, having felt this *Supreme Power From Almighty God,* Steve knew that his dream was within his grasp and that it had been there all of the time. However, no amount of desire or dedication could have ever been strong enough to prepare him for the moment when *Almighty God* would shine the brilliant light of ethereal blessing upon him once more when his dream would materialize at long last – July 7, 1984.

This day began in a manner that Steve had never known. Ironically, it occurred at the stroke of midnight. He sat in his hotel room and gazed at the stars – unable to focus on the personal fulfillment of the final installment of his first book promotion tour that would occur in a few short hours. Amidst deep reflection, he repeated his wish once more. However, nothing could have ever prepared him for the events that would come to follow.

As he gazed at the moon, Steve could not believe his eyes. In the center of it, a light of sparkling green flickered in a gentle glow. Suddenly, it flashed – blinding him. As his visual senses restored, Steve was confused. As the visualization elapsed, he heard a beautiful voice call to him in a tender whisper. *"Steve, I Am Here For You – And Will Always Be. Reach For The Light – And You Shall Find Me!"* With a smile, he reached out as he had so many times in the past. Mesmerized by the sparkling green light, his restless frame of mind drifted into a restful sleep.

Chapter Two

The next morning, Steve arose in a declaration of praise upon the special moment from the night before and spoke blessings upon his idealistic journey. *"Almighty Father God, I Thank You For All Days Of The Past, Present, And Future Through Which The Spiritual Blessing Of Idealistic Literary Vision That You Alone Have Given Me Will Continue To Bring Glory And Honor To Your Holy Name. I Ask You, In The Cherished Name Of My Lord And Savior Jesus Christ Your Son To Solve The Mystery Of Romance Within My Own Life In Your Time And Shine The Ethereal Light Of One True And Unconditional Love Upon Me. Amen."*

In a few short hours, he arrived at the signing. Reflecting upon the ethereal mystery of the night before, Steve was led to alter his usual frame of mind in the direction of an intense sense of anticipation toward an event of monumental proportions that seemed close at hand and inevitable. Ironically, this complex enigma provided Steve with a unique spirit that he felt would be useful in even the most impossible of feats. In a sudden and unexpected manner, the dream that he had dedicated his entire existence to the realization of materialized right before his eyes. Steve saw *A Beautiful Angel*.

Selena Ferriday shined with the charming elegance of his *Dream Come True* that had been lost in a distant silver star – so close and yet so far - for so long. Her blue eyes illuminated with the light of ethereal reflection. Her delicate skin sparkled in the glow of one of a kind beauty – defined and personified right before his mesmerized eyes. Her gorgeous hair flowed with a long, soft, and gentle mirage of the most beautiful shade of sparkling pink carnation that Steve had ever seen. Her fingers and toes reflected in the glow of red gloss. Her smile exuded warmth and happiness. She was dressed in a yellow sports bra, green denim shorts, and yellow sandals. She was a true monument to her time. Never before had Steve seen a being of such ethereal beauty. He knew at once that she was the most beautiful woman that he had ever seen in his entire life.

"Hello! My name is Selena Ferriday. It is a genuine pleasure to meet you at long last. You have a truly special way with words!" she declared – as they shook hands.

"Thank you very much! The pleasure is mine! Thank you for your support. I would have never made it to this special point of return without you!" Steve replied.

With a nervous smile, Selena sighed "No! Thank you!"

Signing her copy of his novel with a warm smile – in silent gratitude to **Almighty God** for this special moment, Steve could not speak another word. Amidst mesmerized nerves, he could not take his eyes off of her. Fortunately, the one aspect of his being that he had always used in communication of his deepest feelings did not abandon him in this one moment in time – one that would come to change the course of his life as he knew it – forever.

He wrote:
To Selena Ferriday,
Thank You For Your Kindness, Warmth, And Support.
You Are A Beautiful Angel.
With Love And Best Wishes From My Heart To Yours,
God Bless,
Steve Fitzsimmons

As he returned it to her with another smile and handshake of gratitude and appreciation, there were no words left to speak. As Selena walked away, Steve watched her in her gentle stride. As Selena looked back once more and blew a kiss, Steve was mesmerized by her ethereal beauty once again. Due to the fact that she stepped out of his life with the same rapid and unexpected means by which she stepped into it, he hoped that there would be some chance of their paths crossing again.   However, neither of them would have ever believed how soon it would occur. The rest was in *The Loving Hands Of Almighty God.*

Chapter Three

Upon returning to his hotel room, Steve could not stop reflecting upon the beautiful glimpse of intimate mystery that had passed through his field of vision a short time ago. Resolving to take advantage of the secured beverage cabinet, he mixed a favorite combination of "Sweet Springs Ginger Ale and Tropical Blast Fruit Punch." Guided by his heart, he gazed at the beautiful sunshine outside of his window. In one glance, nothing could have ever prepared him for what was about to occur.

Selena was sitting on the veranda of a hotel room right next door – relaxing with a beverage of her own. They smiled at one another in shocked surprise. "Hello! It is great to see you again!" Steve said – raising his glass in a warm greeting.

"You are so charming - just like your words in my book! Thank you again!" Selena replied with a drink.

With a smile of touched and sentimental reflection, Steve replied "No! Thank you!" – proceeding with a drink. "Might I have the pleasure of knowing what you are drinking?" he inquired.

"Sweet Springs Ginger Ale and Tropical Blast Fruit Punch!" Selena responded – drinking once more. "How long are you going to be in town?" she asked.

"Well, I have to leave tomorrow. I have to get home to see a concert that I have been waiting for. If you do not mind my saying this, I would like to take this opportunity to thank you very much again!" Steve answered.

"For what?" Selena asked.

"For showing me that true kindness and beauty exists in this world and is not only present in my books!" Steve sighed.

"Thank you very much. Please forgive me if this seems too direct, but I was wondering if you might be interested in coming over so that we can get to know one another before you leave. You see, I love your book. Aside from being far too nervous to contact you through your fan club, I knew that you were on tour and did not think that you would receive my mail!" Selena admitted.

Upon these words, Steve smiled and replied, "If you do not mind, I wish to take this opportunity to accept your invitation. That way, we can continue this conversation…"

Before he could finish, she concluded with "Over some Turkey Melts?" Amused by his sudden look of confusion, she added "I do not mean to brag, but I happen to be a champion Turkey Melt chef!"

Grinning, Steve suggested "Would ten minutes be too soon?"

"Only if you promise to try and get here faster!" Selena accepted.

Upon their unified conclusion "See you in a few minutes!" Steve and Selena stepped into their rooms and closed the doors – slowly.

Nervous as he headed out of the hotel, Steve noticed some beautiful pink carnations at the service desk. Amidst the excitement of the moment and cherishing the intimate rainbow of Selena's beautiful hair, Steve grinned. Taking one, he thrust a silver dollar in payment – raising his eyebrows. As it landed on the counter, he stopped in front of the hotel fountain of a brilliant crystal structure that featured a beautiful angel in the center. In the same manner of deep focus with which he made his wish from the heart every night, Steve closed his eyes – in a gesture of hope that his nerves would hold together just as they had when he met Selena only hours ago and a silent prayer to **Almighty God** – thrusting a copper coin into the fountain.

Stepping outside, he gulped a nervous lump that had risen in his throat and stepped toward the next hotel – unaware of the beautiful vision that was about to materialize before his unsuspecting eyes. In an instant, he saw Selena sitting in the hotel lobby. As she looked up and smiled, Steve noticed that she was reading his book. "I know what you are thinking. First of all, I realized that I did not tell you my room number.

156

Also, this book means so much to me that everywhere I go, it goes along with me!" she asserted – raising her eyebrows.

Amused but still nervous, Steve sighed "Thank you very much!" As she arose, Selena closed her eyes and reclined her head – running her fingers through her beautiful hair of intimate rainbow. Smiling, Steve presented the rose to her – amidst this sentiment "Visions come and go with each passing glance, but the vision of your beauty will live on forever in my eyes."

Gently, Selena caressed his face. As Steve's senses absorbed into the warmth and tenderness of her touch, Selena blushed – mesmerized by the charming intimacy of his words. Smiling once more, she sighed "My heart said it a short time ago and my voice speaks it now…" As she paused for an instant of reflection upon the intimate revelation of her own senses, Selena sighed in tender conclusion "A face much cuter in person!"

Upon these words, Steve blushed. Noticing this, Selena smiled once more and said "Follow me, Ever Romantic One." In their stride, they joined hands – slowly. With one glance, Steve and Selena cherished the warmth of this tender feeling. Upon reaching Selena's room, Steve noticed that the table was already prepared – complete with Turkey Melts, turkey bacon, French fries, onion rings, and Bleu Cheese Dressing. "Please, make yourself at home!" Selena offered – placing the carnation into a vase and onto the table. Grinning at the unique meeting of their minds only moments ago, she concluded with "I should take my own advice because I have to go home tomorrow as well."

Upon these words, Steve and Selena sat in declaration of a blessing before their meal.

"Father God, We Thank You In Mind, Body, Heart, And Soul In The Beloved Name Of Your Son Jesus Christ, Our Lord And Savior For Your Spiritual Blessing Through This Food And Bringing Us Together. We Declare Praise To Your Name And Look To You With

Gratitude And Love As We Continue To Do Your Will Throughout The Ages. Amen."

As they began to eat, Selena inquired "Now, what were you saying before?"

Although his nervous frame of mind remained as he savored the flavor of his Turkey Melt, Steve was able to resume the conversation at the exact point where it had ended – after a simple expression of gratitude. "Before I say anything, I wish to express my gratitude for your kind invitation and compliments to the chef. This is the most delicious Turkey Melt I have ever tasted."

"Thank you very much! Now, I have shared something very special of my own with you!" Selena replied – blushing. "So tell me, was there any chance that you would have seen my mail before we met?" she asked.

Upon these words, Steve explained, "I find it very interesting that you should ask me that. Believe it or not, I am the only one who sees and responds to my mail. The fan club is set up through some very special people in my life. As a matter of fact, they are the people that I am going to see in concert tomorrow. Have you ever heard of *Lucky Seven?"*

As she gulped her beverage with sudden surprise, Selena responded "Yes, you might say that! The truth of the matter is that I know them quite well and am going to see them very soon as well."

Through his own surprised frame of mind, Steve asked "Did I understand you correctly when you said that you have to go home tomorrow?"

"Yes, of course! Unless there is an echo in here!" Selena acknowledged – grinning.

Amused, they declared in shocking unison "Home Sweet Home in *The State Of Orange."*

"Only two questions remain!" Steve asserted.

Raising her eyebrows in interest, Selena inquired "One?"

"Can I tell you something that just might surprise you?" Steve asked.

"Only if you promise to try and shock me as well!" Selena replied.

"Believe it or not, Roy and I went to college together!" Steve declared.

"Are you serious?" Selena asked with true surprise.

"I am as serious about that as I am in declaring right here and now that my life has been touched by *A Beautiful Angel!*" Steve asserted.

Blushing once more, Selena whispered "Thank you." Placing her hand upon her copy of his book in a gesture of sentimental reflection upon his touching inscription, she proceeded with a futile gulp to relax her restless frame of mind. "Two?" she inquired in conclusion.

"How long have you known Roy and Rebecca?" Steve asked.

"You have shocked me. Now, I am going to shock you as well. First, tell me - do you remember Rebecca's sister, Reese?" Selena asked.

"Yes, of course! Roy and I were always thankful that we never met her when she was dating our friend Andrew Manchester!" Steve reasoned.

Upon these words, Selena wiped a tear from her eye.

Concerned that he had said something wrong, Steve apologized. "Please forgive my brash audacity if I have upset you in some way."

"Absolutely not!" Selena replied - slamming her fist onto the table. Upon gaining composure, she asserted "Please forgive me but I only wish that I could have been that fortunate because she was far more trouble to all of us than she was worth!" In her thoughts, she did not realize that Steve was reaching for her hand.

As he took it, Steve asked "What are you trying to tell me?"

159

As he proceeded to touch her face with a gentle caress, a sudden warmth and comfort mesmerized Selena. Smiling, she held his hand to her face and caressed it - amidst the same sentiment. Softly, she sighed "I am glad that Roy and Rebecca found each other! I was with Rebecca throughout all of that and more. You see, she and I went to college together as well!" "We truly do live in a small world!" Steve replied.

Laughing, Selena took another drink to calm her nerves in revelation of her deepest thoughts. "One more question remains…"

As she paused, he answered "Ask away!"

"Do you really believe in *Love At First Sight?*" Selena asked.

Surprised once more, Steve took a drink and asserted "I believe that *Love At First Sight* is something that remains unrealized for a very long time. I speak from that experience. Although we search for it, **The Power Of Almighty God** shall shine it upon us at the most unexpected moment – right before our unsuspecting eyes. How about you?"

Touched, Selena took Steve's hand. "Yes!" Mesmerized, she paused for an instant of reflection. "Yes, of course I do! Thank you! This was far better than any letter I could have ever sent to you – or received from you!" she concluded.

As they arose, Steve said "This was the most genuine pleasure that I have ever experienced. Thank you very much for inviting me. Perhaps, the four of us could get together sometime."

"I would like that very much. It might be easier now that Roy and Rebecca have decided to take some time off after their homecoming concert next week. Thank you very much for coming. I will see you tomorrow at the concert. Thank you for showing me the man behind *The Mystery Of Romance* that you solved in your book," Selena sighed.

As they shook hands and their hands drifted apart – slowly – Steve and Selena could not take their eyes off of one another. "No! Thank you!" Steve whispered. With a warm smile, he departed.

Lost in the moment, Steve returned to his hotel – slowly. Before returning to his room, his destination would be the brilliant crystal fountain. Standing before it, he gulped a nervous lump that had risen in his throat. Amidst a deep sense of gratitude and hope, he retrieved another copper coin. With a rapid thrust of his thumb, he declared *"Almighty Father God, You Have Always Been There For Me. If This Is According To Your Will, Guide Me In The Discovery Of One True And Unconditional Love And Reveal The Power Of Your Infinite Love In The Days Before Me."* Upon these words, he returned to his room.

Throughout the many painful years within his past, Steve had always been a staunch believer in the words that he had spoken only moments ago about *Love At First Sight.* Unfortunately, no tangible evidence in support of this view had ever touched his life at any point within the past. However, *The Blessings Of Almighty God* and the ethereal presence of Selena had turned these words into a cherished reality.

Mesmerized, he had to make a very important telephone call. However, he would have never believed that Selena was doing the very same thing – right next door. They were calling the people that had eased their restless minds for many years as they searched for a moment as special as this one – through their eternal bonds of friendship with Steve and Selena that were formed in their younger days and most recently through their success in the music industry for the past seven years.

As Steve began with "Hello, Roy," Selena began with "Hello, Rebecca." As their conversations progressed, Steve and Selena stared at one another through the window - with a warm smile.

161

Chapter Four

The next morning, Steve sat on the airplane – reading a message that Rebecca had left him before he left the hotel.

Hello Steve! Congratulations once again on your successful book promotion tour. Roy told me about the conversation that you had last night. I am very glad that you met Selena at last. You know, you left so quickly before Roy and I got married that I never had the chance to tell you about her. She is a truly special person. She is very warm, sensitive, caring, and loving. The only advice that I can give you is the same thing that Roy and I did when we met – listen to your heart and always remember: **"True Love Is Only Found In The Heart."** *I wanted you to know this right here and now because a great guy like you has nothing to fear. I cannot wait to see you tomorrow. By the way, there will be a very special surprise waiting for you on the airplane.*

Take Care, Best Wishes, And **God Bless**!

Love,
Rebecca

Touched, Steve did not notice the beautiful woman that was sitting next to him – doing exactly the same thing. Selena was reading a message from Roy.

Hello Selena! Rebecca told me about the conversation that you had last night. I am very glad that you met Steve at last. You know, Rebecca and I always said that you two should meet. He is a very special person with a great deal of love to give. I know that you are the one and only person that can make a true difference in his life. The only advice that I can give you is the same thing that Rebecca and I did when we met - listen to your heart and always remember: **"True Love Is Only Found In The Heart."** *I wanted you to know this right here and now because a Sweetheart like you has nothing to fear. I cannot wait to see you tomorrow. By the way, there will be a very special surprise waiting for you on the airplane.*

Take Care, Best Wishes, And **God Bless**!

Love,
Roy

As they smiled at the special sentiments in touched unison, Steve and Selena noticed each other – shocked. Once again, Steve was mesmerized by her ethereal beauty. Selena was dressed in a yellow sunflower hat, green bustier – envisioned by a yellow cardigan – and denim shorts. The cardigan was stitched in a charming pattern of hearts. Her fingers and toes reflected in the glow of yellow and green gloss. Around her neck, was the pink carnation that he had given her – sealed in a sparkling green crystal heart. As she lowered her sunglasses, Selena asked "Did Rebecca mention something to you about a very special surprise? Roy was kind enough to mention something about that to me!"

"Well, she could not have been any more correct!" Steve replied.

"Neither could he!" Selena asserted – raising her eyebrows. Noticing that Steve was aware of the heart, she sighed "Since this came from your heart, I will keep it close to mine for the rest of my life!"

"It touches my heart to know that something so simple means so much to you!" Steve replied.

As their travels began, Steve and Selena joined hands in prayer for their safe return home. *"Heavenly Father, We Thank You For The Peace And Protection That You Have Always Provided Throughout Our Daily Lives As We Seek To Do Your Will In All That We Do. We Ask For Your Blessed Guidance In Our Travels At This Time, In The Precious Name Of Jesus Christ Your Son, Our Lord And Savior. Amen!"*

Upon these words, they became lost in conversation which brought forth the realization of powerful growth within their past lives that had brought them to this very special moment in time. From the very first moment, they felt as if they had known each other throughout their entire lives.

"Can I tell you something that might surprise you?" Selena asked.

"Please forgive my brash audacity, but I must tell you right here and now that since I am still recovering from the shock of being mesmerized by your ethereal beauty, nothing else could ever have that impact upon me!" Steve replied.

Blushing, Selena said "Well, now I know that what I have to say will have even more meaning because of your cherished way with words. You see, since I read your book, I have been inspired to pursue a dream to write poetry that I have never truly thought was possible – until now."

Slowly, Steve took her hand and sighed "It is a genuine pleasure to know that I have been a source of inspiration to someone as warm and kind as you. Now, I have something to tell you."

Touched, Selena replied "I am ready when you are!"

"The fact of the matter is that although my writing comes from the heart, it is a reflection of my dream to find someone who will fulfill my two fundamental desires of the heart and know that I would do the same for her. With our mutual belief in this connection, I have always believed that everything else will fall place – as we live out our dreams together in a love that began with **The Blessings Of Almighty God,**" Steve began.

"Amen!" Selena declared. "We do indeed serve an **Awesome God!"**

"Amen!" Steve repeated in spiritual sentiment.

"What would these two desires of the heart be?" Selena inquired – holding his hand tighter.

"*The Unconditional Love* and acceptance of all that I am of another. I know that **Almighty God** will always accept me in all ways as **His Child**. However, I have loved and lost many times over the years. Even so, no one has ever even tried to fulfill these basic human needs because every time I start to open up, they leave without giving me so much as a reason. I admit that I am not perfect by any means. However, I stand firm in my resolve that I have a great deal of love to give.

165

Even so, there must be something wrong with me because no one has ever given me so much as a chance!" Steve explained.

Upon these words, Selena asserted, "If I may be direct for a moment, I knew from the very first words of your book that any woman would be the most fortunate person to ever have anyone to love – if she had you. Also, I find it impossible to believe that there could be anything difficult to accept about you."

"If you only knew!" Steve sighed.

"Knew what?" Selena asked.

Upon these words, the plane descended. As they arose, Steve and Selena continued to hold hands. "That is a story for another time. Thank you for listening!" Steve declared.

"No! Thank you! Hopefully, we will be able to talk more about this at a later time!" Selena suggested.

"I would like that very much. Furthermore, if I may say so, it would be a genuine pleasure and privilege to hear some of your poetry some time!" Steve replied.

"From one writer to another, there is nothing that I could ever want more!" Selena sighed – as they stepped off of the plane. Joining hands once more, Steve and Selena declared *"Thank You, Lord!"* upon their safe return. After claiming their luggage, Steve and Selena stepped onto the escalator transport. From all around, they were impressed by the first visual signs of their arrival – although they were very familiar to both of them.

Amidst a passage of brilliant lights of orange neon, they noticed a scenic mural that projected a remarkable view of the ocean. However, they knew that nothing could compare to the visionary spectacle that was about to materialize before their eyes. As they stepped out of the terminal, they united with Nature in this beautiful setting that had always been very special to them. The first breath of air produced a peaceful freshness that gave a new meaning to life. This life could be seen from far and near, heard from close at hand or at a distance, and sensed by the smells of rest and relaxation.

The sun produced the ideal light in reflection of the scenic orange groves that grew in secluded beauty. Above, countless birds communicated their song of life in the floating world of the clear blue. From all around, various water dwelling creatures splashed in their aquatic procession of welcome.

Turning to Selena, Steve declared "There is a first time for everything. I must say that it is much nicer and warmer to witness the beauty of *The State Of Orange* now more than ever because I now realize that pure beauty has existed here all along – for as long as I have lived! Thank you!"

"No! Thank you!" Selena replied.

Lost in the moment, Steve and Selena were interrupted by the cheerful declaration "Hey there!"

Amidst laughter, Steve looked and shouted "Can it be? It is! *"The Triangle Of True Love!"* Steve and Selena stepped forward to greet their friends, Roy and Rebecca Dawson and their daughter, Angel Starr.

Roy was 29 years of age with dark brown hair and eyes. He and Steve had spent their entire lives writing about their idealistic visions of love. In fact, their inspiration had carried them though successful college careers as they stuck together through Roy's major in Music and Steve's – of course – in Creative Writing.

Rebecca was 29 years of age as well with sparkling blonde hair and gorgeous blue eyes. In her younger days, she was an aspiring singer – inspired by Roy's melodious singing voice. However, her sister Reese – who died in a fatal accident – had tried to steal Rebecca's chance at stardom away from her. With Roy's help, and **The Guidance Of Almighty God**, she found the courage to try again.

They met and fell in love at Roy's homecoming concert in their hometown of *The City Of Lights* back in 1977. With the help of Rebecca – that he did not know about until after they met - and the radio station that she worked for, *LUCK.7 Radio*, Roy became a legendary singer. Amidst the intimacy of the love that had united them, Roy and Rebecca joined forces and became *Lucky Seven* – the greatest singing duo in history.

Angel Starr was almost five years old and she sparkled in the vision of her parents' love. She was about to make her singing debut at Roy and Rebecca's next homecoming concert the following week. As she ran up to Steve and Selena, she shouted "Hey! Uncle Steve and Aunt Selena!" As they picked her up into their arms, Steve and Selena kissed her.

"Have you been taking care of Mommy and Daddy?" Selena asked.

"Are you excited about going home and singing with Mommy and Daddy?" Steve asked.

"Yes! Yes! Double Yes!" Angel Starr giggled.

As they all laughed, Roy and Steve exchanged a high-five. Roy declared "See? I told you that a true literary vision is a terrible thing to waste!"

"When you are right, you are right!" Steve chuckled. Upon these words, they embraced.

Rebecca and Selena embraced. In amused reflection upon the words in her message to Steve – knowing full well that Roy had written the same thing to Selena - Rebecca whispered "There certainly are surprises around every corner!"

"You two are so sneaky!" Selena giggled.

As Rebecca embraced Steve, she whispered in amused inquiry "So, what do you think?"

"My life has been touched by an *Angel!*" he sighed in reply.

Upon these words, Roy embraced Selena and asked "Great guy, is he not?"

Blushing, she raised her eyebrows and asserted "Awesome! Truly Awesome!"

The five of them joined hands and closed their eyes in blessing upon their reunion. ***"Heavenly Father, We Thank You For The Love, Peace, And Safety That You Have Spoken Onto Our Blessed Reunion At This Time. We Look To You With Gratitude And Love, In The Blessed***

Name Of Our Lord And Savior, Your Son Jesus Christ For The Everlasting Bond Of Friendship That Has Continued To Bring Comfort, Strength, And Happiness To All Of Us In Mind, Body, Heart, And Soul And We Declare Praise To Your Name As We Continue To Do Your Will Throughout The Ages. Amen."

Upon these words, they traveled back to Steve's beachside suite. Suddenly, they looked up to see a hot air balloon in flight with a special advertisement upon it:

One Night Only
The Orange Grove Theatre Welcomes
Roy And Rebecca Dawson
"Lucky Seven"
July 8, 1984

This would be a night to remember. In the distance, Steve noticed a beautiful island. As he looked at Selena, she was smiling at him – she had noticed as well. However, neither of them would have ever believed how special the scenic beauty of that island would become for them – very soon.

As they proceeded onto Suite #10, Roy and Rebecca shielded Selena's eyes. Since she was carrying Angel Starr, Selena could hear her laughing. "OK! What are you up to?" Selena snickered.

"It is time for us to reveal our special surprise for you!" Rebecca said.

Upon these words, she and Roy looked at Steve as well. "Just to let you know as well, the three of us have kept this hidden since your book was released!" Roy concluded.

Amidst confusion, Steve opened the door. As they stepped inside, Roy, Rebecca, and Steve snapped their fingers. As they uncovered Selena's eyes, she was surprised at the uniquely cozy and creative quality of their environment.

The room sparkled in the brilliant glow of track lighting and was furnished with Forest Green carpet – illuminating in the colorful contrast of Sunlit Glade green paint upon the walls. The walls were further decorated with framed replicas of

169

Roy and Rebecca's multi-platinum albums, photographs taken after Roy and Rebecca's wedding and during subsequent tours, and photographs of Angel Starr – arranged by her age progression. In the center of all of the photographs, was a poster of Steve's literary masterpiece. Beneath it, was a computer with an animated graphic depiction of his book cover on the screen as well. Above the bed, was a large video library – with a green lava lamp on one side and a yellow one on the other.

Amidst amused confusion, Selena asked "OK! Where are we?"

As Roy rested his arm upon Steve's shoulder, Rebecca did the same to Selena. "OK! Tell her, My Friend!" Roy said - smiling.

Still confused as Rebecca looked at Selena and raised her eyebrows, Steve smiled at Selena and said "This is where I live!"

Upon these words, Selena set Angel Starr down and looked at Roy and Rebecca amidst shock. "Wow! This is a great surprise! The three of you sure do know how to keep a secret!" she laughed.

Upon these words, Steve was confused. "OK! What is the big mystery here?" he asked.

"You tell him, My Heart!" Roy said to Angel Starr – in sentimental declaration of his nickname for her.

"Aunt Selena lives right next door to you!" Angel Starr giggled. Mesmerized, Steve and Selena stared at one another – they were unable to speak.

"Well, this certainly is most cozy!" Rebecca chuckled.

"Ah, yes!" Roy replied. As he looked at Steve and Selena, he inquired "Too close for comfort?"

Comfortable at last, Steve and Selena replied in amused unison "Not a chance!"

"That sounds good to me! Well, now that we have established that, it is time to get ready for our melodious afternoon!" Roy said. Upon these words, Roy, Rebecca, and Angel Starr departed.

Steve smiled at Selena. "I think that this is the ideal moment for a new beginning!" he suggested.

"What did you have in mind?" Selena inquired.

With a warm smile, Steve said "I have wanted to do this ever since I met you." Extending his hand to her, he said "Thank you for coming into my life *Beautiful Angel*"

As Selena took it, she sighed in reply "Thank you very much, Ever Romantic One! I have waited for this moment for a very long time!" Upon these words, Steve and Selena sealed one another into a warm embrace and spoke a blessing upon this special moment. ***"Almighty Father God, In Our Walk With You Through This Life, You Have Blessed Us In Great Abundance. We Declare Love And Gratitude In The Cherished Name Of Our Lord And Savior, Jesus Christ Your Son For The Spiritual Blessing Within The Warmth And Tenderness Of This Truly Special Moment. Amen."***

Chapter Five

A short time later, Steve was preparing for the special afternoon. As he poured a splash of "Leather Essence Cologne" upon his face and slipped into his orange tropical shirt, black denim shorts, and white shoes, Selena appeared at his suite in all of her splendor.

She was dressed in a bright bikini of orange shade. Her sparkling pink hair remained wet from her shower and droplets dripped in aquatic glow across her entire body. The beauty of her gorgeous blue eyes sparkled through the unique shade of her orange sunglasses.

As he wiped the sweat from his forehead, Steve raised his eyebrows and put his own sunglasses on – they were very dark. "It heightens my sense of security. Earlier in the year, this hotel hosted a book signing for me," he explained.

Upon these words, Selena grinned and sighed "Yes, of course! The one that I was far too nervous to take part in and meet you sooner. Well, as I said yesterday, this is much better!"

Blushing, Steve sighed "Trust me, these fans give new definition to the term "adoring public!""

"Well, in your case, it is impossible to think anything different!" Selena replied. As she paused, Selena blushed and grinned at the amusing reality of her sudden thought. "If I had only known that you live here…" she began.

As he blushed, Steve snickered and concluded her thoughts with "Trust me! I know exactly what you mean!" Reaching out to her, he sighed "The best days now begin!"

"Truer words have never been spoken!" Selena replied. Joining hands, they stepped toward the door. With a final gaze into each other's eyes, Steve and Selena proceeded onto the concert.

Opening the door, they could hear the excitement from inside. *The Orange Grove Theatre* was an aquatic auditorium of sparkling magnificence. Heating lamps reflected their orange glow across the stage that featured palm trees and an effervescent window with *"Lucky Seven"* inscribed upon it in sparkling red and yellow neon. Holding hands at a comfortable stride, they proceeded onto the comfort of two floating chairs. Suddenly, Angel Starr drifted toward them upon another floating chair.

Steve and Selena laughed. She was dressed in a green shirt – inscribed with her name on the front in yellow letters and an amusing monogram upon it: *"Angel Of Today... Starr Of Tomorrow..."* – sunglasses, denim shorts, and green rubber sandals. On her wrists, were rubber bracelets in a rainbow of colors. She was wearing a hat inscribed with the *"As Time Goes By..."* tour monogram.

"Hello Sweetheart!" they chuckled in unison.

"Where did you get that shirt?" Steve asked. Suddenly, he and Selena looked at one another in amused and sarcastic recognition of the common sense behind the answer. "Daddy!" they declared in unison.

As she lowered her sunglasses, Angel Starr giggled. "Thank you! Please, no autographs! I am practicing for my singing debut on my birthday in a few days!" she said.

As he lowered his sunglasses, Steve asked "Will you make an exception for your Aunt and Uncle?"

Giggling once more, she said "OK! But, just for you!"

Upon these words, Steve and Selena placed their fists upon her chair. Angel Starr reached into her pocket. Upon retrieving a green ink stamper – inscribed with her name, stars, and hearts – she stamped their hands. In amused unison, Steve and Selena declared "Thank you! We will never wash these hands again!"

"Yuck!" Angel Starr replied in confusion.

As Steve and Selena kissed her in amused gratitude, all three of them laughed. "Excuse me, Beautiful Ladies! I will be right back!" Steve said. He proceeded onto the juice bar and mixed a familiar combination of "Sweet Springs Ginger Ale and Tropical Blast Fruit Punch" into three green glasses. In accentuation of their design and flavor, he placed an orange slice and tropical umbrella of a unique mixture of red, yellow, orange, and green shades into each one.

Upon returning to them, Steve noticed that Selena and Angel Starr were playing *"Rock, Scissors, Paper."* "Ha! Ha! *"Paper"* beats *"Scissors!""* Selena chuckled.

"No way!" Angel Starr shouted.

Upon these words, Selena took Angel Starr into her arms – snuggling and kissing her. "I know! I know!" Selena laughed.

As Steve joined in their laughter, he said "Try this! I call it "Sweet Paradise!""

Looking at Angel Starr in amused wonder, Selena whispered "What do you think? Do we dare?" Thinking for a minute, they looked at Steve and said "OK! We trust you!"

Presenting their drinks with a smile, Steve proposed a toast. "Here's to *The Two Most Beautiful Angels* that I have ever seen!"

Amused, Angel Starr pointed at Selena and then at herself and counted "One… Two… Hey! You forgot about my Mommy!" she said.

"I know! I was only kidding. Make that three!" he concluded. Raising his glass toward the stage in recognition of Rebecca's beauty, Steve began kissing and cuddling Angel Starr in his arms. As the three of them drank, the crowd began to cheer. As the lights went out, the three of them began to cheer as well. "Here we go!" Steve declared. Roy and Rebecca began to sing the tender melody of *"As Time Goes By…"* As the monogram on the stage began to sparkle, the window arose. In an instant, the spotlights presented the greatest singing duo in history, Roy and Rebecca Dawson - *Lucky Seven.*

Roy and Rebecca were dressed in identical red and yellow tropical shirts, black denim jeans, and white shoes. They were wearing dark sunglasses. In their hands, plastic red machine guns were inscribed with *"Have A Blast!!!"* in large yellow letters. As the crowd continued to cheer, Roy and

Rebecca stepped forward. Steve, Selena, and Angel Starr began to laugh – they knew exactly what was going to happen.

In an instant, Roy and Rebecca began to fire large red and yellow projectiles into the audience. As individual fans caught them, they were delighted to find an autographed hat, shirt, photograph, or audiotape in each one.

As they looked at one another and nodded, Roy and Rebecca removed their sunglasses and shouted *"State Of Orange,* thank you very much! By the way, there is plenty more where that came from – like always! We are truly touched **By The Blessing Of Almighty God** to see all of you here today!" Roy declared. Upon these words, the crowd proceeded with warm applause.

Amidst deep gratitude, Roy and Rebecca smiled and waved to the crowd once more. "Thank you very much for joining us here in the beautiful *Orange Grove Theatre* for one of the greatest moments of the *"As Time Goes By…"* tour of 1984 in dedication to the tender melodies from our hearts that could never have become the cherished source of our happiness and personal fulfillment that it is today without your special and touching support over the past seven years. We will be recording a live album and video here tonight! Thank you very much and **May God Bless All Of You!"** Roy began.

"However, before we begin, we wish to take this opportunity to welcome our three very special guests. First, you know him as a best-selling Romance novelist and author of *"True Love Is Only Found In The Heart."* Second, you know her as the successful poet of *"Forever We Will Be…"* Finally, we have someone who is going to make her professional singing debut at our homecoming concert next week," Rebecca added.

"Friends of *The State Of Orange,* we present to you our very special friends, Steve Fitzsimmons and Selena Ferriday and our beautiful daughter, Angel Starr!" they concluded in loving unison.

As the crowd cheered, Steve and Selena looked at one another – shocked. "Well, I certainly did not expect that!" Selena asserted in confusion.

With a smile, Steve raised his eyebrows and asked "Do you remember what I said to you about an "adoring public?"" As Selena nodded in confused acceptance, Steve concluded with "Come, *My Poetic Angel!* Our public awaits us!" Upon these words, they took Angel Starr into their arms and arose from the pool.

As Roy and Rebecca took Angel Starr into their arms, Roy said "Thank you for joining us."

Looking at the audience, Angel Starr giggled "No! Thank you for being such a nice Mommy and Daddy!"

As Steve and Selena stepped forward, they embraced Roy and Rebecca. As Steve said "Thank you for inviting us," Selena concluded with "It is a genuine pleasure to be here."

"Let me assure you that the pleasure belongs to us," Roy replied. Turning to the audience, he added "Friends, would you join us in recognition of their literary accomplishments and the truly special feeling of *One True And Unconditional Love* within them?"

As Roy and Rebecca proceeded with warm applause, the entire audience joined in. As Steve and Selena joined hands and waved in nervous acceptance, nothing could have ever prepared them for the touching request that Rebecca was about to make of them.

"Please forgive our brash audacity, but we were wondering if you might grant us the pleasure of joining us for our autograph session after the show!" Shocked, Steve and Selena gulped the sudden nervous lumps that had risen in their throats and said in unison "I do not think we should..." Before they could finish, Angel Starr leaned toward the microphone and shouted to the audience "What do you think?"

The crowd began cheering and shouting "Go-'fer it!"

As Roy, Rebecca, and Angel Starr began to laugh, Steve and Selena looked at one another and smiled in sentimental reflection upon the moment. All of the while, their eyes never left one another. They accepted in unison "How could we ever think about disappointing our fans?"

Upon these words, Roy and Rebecca replied "Thank you very much. We hope that you enjoy the show." As Rebecca reached for Angel Starr's chair, Roy kissed their beloved daughter. He and Rebecca embraced Steve and Selena once more and suggested "How about some more applause for our three special guests?" As the crowd responded with more warm cheers, Steve and Selena waved once more and returned to their seats. Roy and Rebecca kissed Angel Starr and reclined her into the chair. Amidst laughter from the audience, they stepped forward and declared "A special seat for our special girl!" In an instant, Roy and Rebecca gazed into *The Eyes Of Everlasting Love* and whispered "I love you!" in tender unison. With a passionate kiss, the concert began. Softly, Steve asserted "Now, I know that I have some intense literary competition!"

Blushing, Selena inquired "What do you mean by that?"

"Are you kidding me? I never knew that the most beautiful woman that I have ever seen wrote the most beautiful poem that I have ever read. You said that I have a way with words..." As he paused and took her hand, Steve concluded with "I am not the only one, *My Beautiful And Poetic Angel!*"

Upon completion of the concert, the five of them sat together in sentimental communication with their fans. Mesmerized by her ethereal beauty, Steve could not take his eyes off of Selena. In sentimental reflection upon the special familiarity of a moment from a short time ago, Selena grinned – knowing of Steve's deepest thoughts because hers were exactly the same. As they reached for their favorite drinks – now known as "Sweet Paradise" - Steve and Selena toasted the moment in unison with the special words ***To Almighty God Be The Glory!*** I will never forget the day that we met!"

Chapter Six

As the evening hours drifted upon the horizon, Roy, Rebecca, and Angel Starr appeared at Steve's hotel suite. They were dressed in similar orange bathing suits of a unique tropical design. Roy was wearing shorts. Rebecca was wearing a bikini. Angel Starr was wearing a mermaid costume.

"Would you care for some cool and refreshing swimming by the soft glow of the moonlight?" Rebecca asked.

As Steve and Selena looked at one another – grinning – they declared "Let's Go-'fer it!"

As they descended the spiral staircase that led to the beach, they noticed that a recent tide had made its presence felt. All that remained were the gentle pacific waves. In his thoughts, Steve knew that this scenic beauty would be the ideal setting for the matter of paramount importance that was at hand.

"I think that we should have a parting of ways right now!" Roy suggested.

"Yes, we should! After all…" Rebecca paused – glancing at Steve and Selena as they held hands in their comfortable stride – "You two seem to be in good hands!" she concluded. Upon these words, Roy and Rebecca snickered and raised their eyebrows.

Amused, Selena replied "You three should have some fun."

In the same manner, Steve concluded with "After all, "Home Sweet Home" in a few days!"

As Roy, Rebecca, and Angel Starr ran down the beach, Roy shouted "Do not do anything that we would not do!"

Giggling, Rebecca played along and declared "If you do, be careful!"

As Steve and Selena laughed, they began to walk once more. "Those two are absolutely crazy!" Steve sighed.

"Crazy in love with one another!" Selena replied.

In his nervous frame of mind, Steve knew that the moment of truth was upon him. "I was thinking, the future has many great possibilities just waiting to be..." he paused, "discovered!" he began. Blushing, he continued "Of course, it is always nicer and well, warmer..." he paused again "to share in these discoveries with someone."

Confused, Selena giggled "What are you... searching for, Ever Romantic One?"

Suddenly, Steve's attention made a rapid shift. In the distance, the moon reflected upon a minute glow. At once, he felt as if he knew what it was. With hope that Selena had not seen it, he requested that she close her eyes. Confused, she did so. Steve headed toward his visionary assumption. Once near it, he marveled the sight. At his feet, sat a remarkable coral shell with a brilliant pearl inside of it. Picking it up, Steve knew that Selena would love to own this masterpiece of the aquatic world. Looking back, he noticed that she remained in her waiting state. With no desire to keep her in further suspense, Steve rushed back to her.

Amidst the laughter of excitement, he located a large stick that had washed up on the shore. He had an artistic impulse and intended to act upon it. In further confusion and impatience, Selena declared, "Hey Slowpoke, I am going blind!"

With hope to eliminate her intolerance, Steve ran to her. As he caressed her face, Steve replied "Patience, *My Beautiful Angel*." With that, he finished and brought her to her feet. Above, the moon emerged from behind a passing cloud. This would be the ideal light that Steve's surprise would need. Upon his word, Selena opened her eyes in anticipation. Astonished, she rubbed them – blinking.

At her feet, Selena saw a heart that Steve had constructed with his footprints. Inside, he had inscribed a powerful declaration. In the center, the beautiful coral shell sparkled in aquatic beauty. Steve could see the reflection of the pearl within her beautiful eyes. They glowed with cherished sentiment and happiness as Selena read *"Steve Loves Selena."*

"I could not tell you at first. I had to show you." Steve sighed. Stepping toward her, Steve placed his arms around Selena and gazed into her eyes. Amidst the warm tenderness of this one moment in time, Steve spoke.

"I love you! I have been in love with you from the first magical moment that I saw you. I have spent my entire life writing about my dream of the discovery of *One True And Unconditional Love.* Throughout many years of endless searching, the ethereal vision of your charming beauty that flashed before my unsuspecting eyes in that first sweet moment made me realize at long last that the trials of pain and sadness that I had lived through and had given me the inspiration to write about *The Idealistic Vision Of One True And Unconditional Love* that I had always dreamed about - but did not know if I would ever find – had brought me onto my blessed union with you yesterday. I knew then that the love that I have written about for so many years truly does exist. Selena, when you came into my life **By The Blessing Of Almighty God,** all of my dreams came true at long last. I love you so much!"

At a loss for words, Selena sighed "I love you too! I always have and I always will!" Amidst the tender love between them, Steve and Selena cried silent tears, but the smiles of love and happiness remained. There were no words left to speak.

They embraced. Upon looking into *The Eyes Of One True And Unconditional Love,"* each whispered a unified expression of love once more. As each of them caressed the other's face, the last tear fell from their eyes. Suddenly, Steve noticed a wondrous sight from behind Selena. In a rapid maneuver to turn her around, Steve pointed. Across the horizon, a familiar green glow sparkled in the center of the moon.

"What do you think about that?" Steve asked – kissing Selena.

"That is one of the most beautiful sights that I have ever seen. But, where did it come from?" Selena asked – in deep hope that her thoughts would remain hidden for now.

"By The Power Of Almighty God, All Things Are Possible!" Steve declared.

"Amen!" Selena asserted.

"Believe it or not, I saw that very same awesome spectacle on the night before I met you!" Steve explained.

Upon these words, Selena rested her head upon Steve's shoulder. Smiling, she closed her eyes in silent reflection upon the moment of truth that was about to occur. "Steve, My Ever Romantic One, I have something to tell you. I have cherished this sentiment within my heart ever since I read the first touching words of your book. I have dreamed by *The Blessing Of Almighty God* of a complete change in my life by which the only sight that I can see is the vision of you beside me, the only smell is the scent of your cologne, the only taste is the soft tenderness of your kiss, the only sound is the soothing expression of your love for me, and the only sensation that I can feel is you holding me in your arms until the end of time. In my heart, I cherish a sentimental connection to your last name. It is a name that I wish to share with you in a life of *One True And Unconditional Love* and tender intimacy and pass onto my children as their mother..." she paused – caressing his face - "and your wife."

"As have I, *Sweet Angel*!" Steve agreed. "You have no idea how glad I am that you said that because in my heart, I cherish the day upon which *A Charming And Beautiful Angel* named Selena Ferriday blessed the life of *A Romantic Idealist* named Steve Fitzsimmons amidst the gentle glow of her sparkling elegance that became the light of *His Dream Come True*.

Descending onto one knee, he reached into his pocket. As he took Selena's hand, Steve retrieved a box of sparkling yellow, orange, and green velvet and opened it. Inside, was a brilliant diamond ring of heart formation that nestled amongst the glamour of red, yellow, and green hearts and diamond stars across the band of gold. Nervous, Steve relieved himself of a deep sob within his throat. Tears flooded his eyes. In a final instant, he took notice of the charming intimacy of Selena's ethereal beauty once more. As the wave of love swept over them, Steve spoke. "Selena My Love, since the first sweet moment that you came into my life, I knew that **The Power Of Almighty God** did bring us together. So, I am asking you, Selena Ferriday, *My Beautiful And Poetic Angel* - as the ethereal vision of beauty, charm, and tenderness, warm and sensitive kindness, and *One True And Unconditional Love* that I have always dreamed of, will you marry me?"

With a warm smile, Selena placed her hand upon Steve's heart and whispered "Yes," in tender acceptance. By now, both of them were crying. As they stared into *The Eyes Of One True And Unconditional Love*, Steve witnessed a visionary spectacle that would unite him with the very haven from which **Almighty God** had sent his *One True And Unconditional Love* to touch his life upon *The Wings Of An Angel*. In his heart, he knew that she was a spiritual blessing from **The Ethereal Essence Of Heaven.** From behind Selena, multiple stars began to fall. The wind began to flow through the gentle beauty of her sparkling pink hair.

As the moon emerged from a passing cloud, its warm glow focused upon her and cast its ethereal presence across her entire body. As Selena blew a kiss, the sparkling visualization elapsed. All at once, Steve knew that he was dreaming no longer. All that remained were Steve's soft and simple words of love. "For all of Eternity – shining in the glow of my *One True And Unconditional Love* for you alone. I love you, Selena"

Gently, Selena took Steve's hand and placed it upon her heart amidst this tender pledge. "For all of Eternity – shining in the glow of my *One True And Unconditional Love* for you alone. I love you, Steve."

Steve and Selena united in a prayer of spiritual blessing upon their cherished union. **"Father God In Heaven, We**

Thank You In Mind, Body, Heart, And Soul For Uniting Us In The Blessing Of One True And Unconditional Love That You Know We Have Searched For Throughout Our Entire Lives And Pledge In The Beloved Name Of Jesus Christ Your Son, Our Lord And Savior To Love One Another As You Love Us. Thank You, Almighty Father God!" Upon these words, Steve placed the ring upon Selena's finger. Only love remained. The moon produced a cool and sparkling sight in unison with the remarkable freshness of the warm summer air of the night. All at once, it was clear that both elements were conducive to the formation of an ideal setting for the impeccable new beginning that was about to occur. However, the moon was dimmed by the gorgeous glow of Selena's beautiful eyes, and the air became absorbed into the intimate scent of her perfume.

As Steve and Selena reached for each other, the silent tears of intimate realization of the discovery of this vision of *One True And Unconditional Love* elapsed into a tender kiss. Steve began to caress Selena's beautiful body with a soft and gentle touch. He ran his fingers through her hair of sparkling pink carnation – onto the smooth tenderness of her face. The wave of love swept over them. As they kissed, Steve and Selena sealed one another into a loving embrace. Amidst their gentle caress, the warm glow of the moon and the cool breezes of night were the ideal witnesses to this – *The First Kiss Of One True And Unconditional Love.* With a unified expression of love, Steve and Selena united together as one in their ethereal bond of love for all of Eternity.

Softly, Steve whispered "I love you, *My Poetic Angel And Dream Come True!*"

Upon Selena's tender reply "I love you too, My Ever Romantic One!" Steve knew that he was dreaming no longer.

Gently, they reclined their bodies and rested in *The Arms Of One True And Unconditional Love.* A barrage of fireworks began to explode above them. Unexpectedly, the heat of the moment was interrupted by an arctic blast from the world of water. As the tide rushed through the horizon, Steve and Selena became submerged in the sea breeze.

Amidst laughter, they began to kiss once more. Steve was caressing Selena's tummy. As they gazed into *The Eyes Of One True And Unconditional Love*, Steve opened his mouth to speak. Selena placed a finger to his lips – silencing him – and whispered "Kiss me!" Upon these words, Steve and Selena elapsed into a passionate kiss. Amidst his gentle caress, she began to sigh and speak his name. In an instant, the current grew stronger. This was of no concern to them. As they continued to kiss, the heat of the moment provided a warmth that presented an intimate contrast to the liquid flow around them. Steve and Selena cherished one another as the powerful love between them united them together as one - amidst the tender rhythm of the beating of their hearts. With each tender kiss and gentle caress, they became one in this vision of *One True And Unconditional Love*. Upon resting for a brief moment, they discovered that the tide had relinquished. As they reclined into *The Arms Of One True And Unconditional Love*, Steve began caressing Selena's tummy once more.

Selena's tummy accentuated its tender beauty with pure intimacy. Slowly Steve raised his body and began to cover her tummy with soft kisses. Amused and excited, Selena's silent giggle mesmerized her into Steve's charming sentiment as she gently caressed his back. Softly, she spoke his name. Only love remained. Tenderly, they rested in *The Arms Of One True And Unconditional Love*. Amidst the tender gaze of this *One True And Unconditional Love*, Steve and Selena could not take their eyes off of one another. Only love remained.

As their visual senses became exhausted, a unified expression of love drifted them into the secret safety haven of sleep. In his dream, Steve saw himself and Selena sleeping together in the peaceful calm of their tender love. From somewhere within **The Ethereal Essence Of Heaven**, a yellow, orange, and green cloud of heart formation emerged

185

upon them.   Settling around them, the cloud lifted their sleeping bodies and carried them to the comfort of their hotel suites. With that, his visualization elapsed.

Chapter Seven

Despite the mesmerizing confusion that remained throughout the night, Steve arose to the sound of seven taps on his bedroom wall. He laughed as he heard a familiar voice calling to him from the other side. "Wake up, My Beloved Future Husband! You have exactly seven seconds to get over here!" Selena shouted – giggling. Without saying anything, he rushed to her door and responded with seven taps of his own. As she opened the door, he inquired with amused sarcasm "Wow! Are you sure that we are not already married?"

In spite of being too shocked to laugh, Selena simply responded with a rapid embrace and dragged Steve across the threshold. As she sighed "I love you, My Ever Romantic One," he replied "I love you too, *My Beautiful And Poetic Angel.*" Upon their first kiss, Selena concluded with "I truly hope that you know what you are getting yourself into, because you are going to pay for that charming bit of amusement for the rest of your life!"

Steve sighed "That is a mission that I accept from this day forward because…" He paused for a soft kiss and concluded, "My life truly has been touched by *A Beautiful Angel!*"

Mesmerized, Selena whispered "If you only knew!"

Upon these words, Steve and Selena spoke blessings of gratitude upon another day together. ***"Heavenly Father, We Thank You For This New Day And Declare Gratitude And Love In Mind, Body, Heart, And Soul For The Ability To Continue To Serve Your Blessed Name In The Challenges That Lie Ahead With Love And Praise In The Precious Name Of Our Lord And Savior Jesus Christ, Your Son. Amen."*** As she took his hand, Selena sighed "Come, My Ever Romantic One! Let me show you how much of an inspiration that you have been to me."

As they walked a few steps in the cool darkness of the suite, Steve could not see very much – with the exception of a poster of his literary masterpiece and photographs that were similar to his of Roy, Rebecca, and Angel Starr upon the walls. As she shielded his vision, Selena pressed a button. As yellow, orange, and green lights flashed through his field of vision, Steve could hear the sound of effervescence. Selena smiled. As she pointed, she raised her eyebrows. Steve could not believe his eyes.

Before him, sat an exquisite spa of red marble structure and heart formation. Around it, steam and water flowed from hearts at alternating intervals. All at once, the relaxation of the night before did not matter any longer – his entire body was drenched in sweat. He gulped a nervous lump that had risen in his throat.

"It sure is getting hot in here!" Steve sighed. As he wiped a flood of sweat from his face, she brought his face to hers. Kissing him, she sighed "If you believe that now, you have not seen anything yet!" With a mesmerized look into his eyes, Selena kissed him once more.

As they kissed, Steve and Selena lowered themselves onto their knees. Reclining to the floor, Steve kissed Selena once more. Smiling in amusement, she whispered "Hold onto me as tight as you can." Confused, he complied. With that, she proceeded with a slight push motion. In an instant, they were submerged in a warm blaze of bubbles.

They floated to the surface. As Steve's mind began to wander, he laughed at the sentiment of an intimate chapter in his book that was similar to this moment. He recalled the sentimental unity of excitement and nerves that he felt as he wrote it. He would have never believed that he would ever experience it – let alone in the unique idealism of this special moment in time. By now, Selena was resting in his arms. As the aquatic comfort swept over them, she inquired "What are you snickering about?"

His answer was a kiss. "Another one of my literary inspirations comes to life at long last! Thank you very much!" Steve sighed in amused excitement.

"You are very welcome!" Selena replied with a kiss. "However, you must understand that the pleasure is all my own!"

Snickering, Steve asserted "I am going to have to challenge you on that one!"

"Anytime! Any place!" Selena accepted – caressing his face. Upon these words, they relaxed in a peaceful duration of soft kisses.

A short time later, Selena was escorting Steve through a tour of the rest of her suite. As they held hands, they walked in tender stride with Roy and Rebecca's latest album that was playing throughout the suite. Suddenly, Steve noticed a nostalgic pastime before his unsuspecting eyes – Selena owned an air hockey table. "Ah! The games that people play!" he laughed.

"Is that a challenge?" she asked.

"You know me all too well, *My Poetic Angel!*" Steve answered.

Upon these words, they launched into the competitive spirit of fun. With a draw declared, Steve heard Roy call to him in his suite from the two-way radios that they had used to keep in contact with one another on campus during their college days.

"*"Super Singer"* to *"Romantic Avenger!"* Come in, *"Romantic Avenger!"*"

As he laughed at the codenames that they used in the old days, Steve responded. "*"Romantic Avenger"* to *"Super Singer!"* I read you loud and clear. What is our battle plan for today?"

"This just in from the investigative report of *"The Beautiful Angels."* There is a dance competition today and the presence of our entire operation has been requested for evaluation and award presentation. Confirm…" Roy continued.

Upon these words, Selena looked at Steve with amused charm. "*"Romantic Avenger?"*" She paused – chuckling. "*"Super

189

Singer And The Beautiful Angels?'" she inquired. "I must say that this is an interesting twist upon the games that people play!" she asserted – giggling. Rebecca and Angel Starr must be impressed!" With a tender kiss, she gazed into his eyes and concluded with "You are so adorable!"

Gulping a nervous lump that had risen in his throat, Steve continued to play along and asked "Do you wish to take part in this mirthful excursion?"

Selena responded by raising her eyebrows. Kissing him once more, she began to run back toward her own suite. In her travels, she declared "A super heroine needs a proper uniform!"

Amidst laughter, Steve responded to the waiting invitation. "*"Romantic Avenger"* to *"Super Singer."* *"The Legion Of Love"* has a new member!"

"*"Super Singer"* to *"Romantic Avenger!"* We did not copy that transmission. Requesting elaboration!" Roy inquired.

Upon these words, Steve could hear Rebecca and Angel Starr laughing in the background. Suddenly, Selena appeared once more. Mesmerized, Steve's face flooded with sweat. In this tender glance, he knew that Selena's sparkling beauty was the key to a special victory at the dance competition.

She was dressed in a costume of yellow spandex – vented in glamorous enhancement of her beautiful breasts. Her navel remained invisible by the constraint of her green utility belt. The gorgeous reflection of her blue eyes sparkled in brilliant unison with the green mask upon them. Boots of sparkling green extended up to her knees upon her long and beautiful legs. A green cape rested upon her shoulders. A green inscription reflected upon a golden shield around her neck – *S XO S*.

"Greetings! I am *"The Romantic Visionary."* I have lived by the powerful reflection of my vision of *One True And Unconditional Love* for many years. Unable to realize my own dreams, I have sought to encourage others to believe in *The*

Power Of Love and to never give up in their search for it through the poetic words of my crime files. However, one individual is responsible for the fulfillment of my own dream at long last. From the very first words of his own literary vision, I felt a true personal and sentimental connection from my heart to his. Now, I look forward to joining forces with him in a life of *One True And Unconditional Love* as we fight against the inevitable trials of life and love **By The Power Of Almighty God** – together as one for all of Eternity. Perhaps, you know him. His name is *"The Romantic Avenger."*" Selena said with the triumphant passion of a true super heroine.

Nervously, Steve replied "Well, the fact of the matter is that I am a very special friend of his and he informed me that he should be here any minute now! If you will indulge me for a moment, I am sure that he would love to meet you."

Suddenly, Steve heard Roy's amused declaration. "We copy that Steve. Tell *"The Romantic Avenger"* that we will meet him faster than he can say *"Legion Of Love!"*"

Looking at his communicator, Steve laughed to himself – he had his finger on the transmission button the entire time. "Over and out, Roy!" he chuckled. Stepping toward the bedroom, Steve looked at *"The Romantic Visionary"* and declared "If you see him, please inform him that I will be back before he can say *"Legion Of Love!"*" Raising his eyebrows with a nervous grin, Steve stopped to cherish the heroic beauty of *"The Romantic Visionary"* once more. Blushing, he sighed "Please forgive my brash audacity, but I would never forgive myself if I let this opportunity slip by without telling you that *"The Romantic Avenger"* is a very lucky man!"

Touched, *"The Romantic Visionary"* replied "A superhero must always be in the right place at the right time." Selena paused. Smiling, she concluded with "I certainly was!"

As Selena blew a kiss, Steve declared "I shall return."

A short time later, *"The Romantic Avenger"* appeared at *"The Romantic Visionary's"* door. He was dressed in a costume of green spandex. The vision of love within his eyes reflected through a yellow mask as a yellow cape rested upon his shoulders. *"The Romantic Visionary"* was mesmerized by the intimate power within the moment as *"The Romantic Avenger"* stepped toward her amidst the sparkling stride of yellow boots and spoke. "Greetings! I am *"The Romantic Avenger."* I live by *The Power Of Love* that beats within my heart. It has strengthened me in my search for *One True And Unconditional Love* that has come to an end at long last – all because of one beautiful and special individual. From the first moment that I was touched by her ethereal beauty, I pledged my love to her amidst the cherished realization of *One True And Unconditional Love.* In my heart, I know that together, our love is strong enough to overcome absolutely anything. I see the reality of her beauty, charm, and tenderness before me right now. I love you, *"Romantic Visionary"* – **My Blessing From Almighty God.**"

"I love you too, *"My Ever Romantic Avenger* - **My Blessing From Almighty God!**" *"The Romantic Visionary"* replied. "By the way, is it ethical for superheroes to accept gifts?" she asked.

Rapidly, *"The Romantic Avenger"* examined every direction of the room. Focusing his mesmerized gaze upon her once more, he replied "Only if the gift comes from the heart of a super heroine." Upon these words, *"The Romantic Visionary"* stepped toward the dresser. They could not take their eyes off of one another. As she retrieved a green box, he retrieved a yellow box from his cape. These gifts would come to serve as monumental representations of their cherished love and commitment to one another.

Selena's gift to Steve was a photographic diary that featured an image of her sweet beauty and the words that would remain inscribed upon his loving heart until the end of time – *"Steve, Forever Yours, Selena."* Inside, she had placed a photographic representation of herself as a beautiful and delicate child. Also, she produced a medallion – identical to the one that she had around her neck.

192

Steve's representation of his love for Selena was a musical box that featured a minute photographic image of his book cover. Around it, he had inscribed the same words that he had written from his heart during their cherished first meeting. As she caressed his face in gratitude, Selena noticed that she did not recognize the song.

Noticing this, Steve declared "Fear not! That song will become very familiar to you – soon!" Taking her into his arms amidst the enchantment of her tender beauty, Steve sighed "Through the dreams of my heart that long for your touch, My Beloved Selena, I love you very much!" Softly, he caressed her face – ending his words with a sweet kiss and warm embrace. Amidst their unified declaration "Come, My Beloved! Our fair city awaits us!" they ran out of the room and proceeded onto the dance competition.

Once near the room, Steve stopped. Reaching for Selena, he held her waist in a tender embrace. Slightly reclining her body, he kissed her lips - looking into her eyes once more. They joined hands. This would be a truly special afternoon. At a comfortable stride, they looked into *The Eyes Of One True And Unconditional Love* and kissed – turning all heads in the procession. Exchanging a glance and smile, they confirmed attendance by presenting superhero identification – heads turned once again. Paying them no mind, Steve and Selena entered the dance competition. Outside, the arrival of the cherished love story would become the main event of the evening and many to follow.

Inside and unsuspecting of anything, they surveyed the scenery. From all around, statues of fictional superheroes and super heroines from the world of comic books and television and their famous vehicles stood in vigilance around the room. Upon the walls, famous weapons and promotional toys were presented in display cases. Impressed, Steve sighed "This is a superhero's paradise!" Upon these words, Steve and Selena stepped forward. Suddenly, the room stood in instant darkness. The words *"ZAP! POW! BAM!"* began to flash upon the large projection screens around the room. As neon lights began to flash from the ceiling at alternating intervals of red, yellow, orange, and green, a large cloud of steam covered the entire stage in front of them. As the crowd cheered, the festivities began. In an instant, Roy, Rebecca, and Angel Starr – now known as *"Super Singer And The Beautiful Angels"* – slid downward and onto the stage on large cables. Angel Starr giggled with excitement from a carrier on Roy's back. They were dressed in identical costumes of sparkling gold spandex as well as red masks, capes, utility belts, and boots. Their names were inscribed in large red letters upon their chests.

"Greetings! I am *"Super Singer!"*" Roy began.

"And we are *"The Beautiful Angels!"* Rebecca and Angel Starr declared in unison.

"Together, we are *"The Triangle Of True Love!"* the three of them asserted in unison.

"We are thankful that you have joined us here this afternoon to assist us in our special mission!" Roy continued.

"We are in search of new members for our justice league – known as *"The Legion Of Love"* - and knew that a competition such as this one would be a suitable means by which we could determine who has all of the right moves – essential to a superhero!" Rebecca explained.

"Let's Go-'fer it!" Angel Starr shouted.

Upon these words, Steve and Selena stepped forward. Leaning into a soft kiss, Steve said "Come, *My Poetic Angel!*"

As he paused, she concluded with "Let us dance and disappoint the competition, My Ever Romantic One!" Upon these words, the competition began – amidst a timeless selection of melodious classics and the greatest hits of *Lucky Seven*.

As they danced to the rhythm of reflection of the unified absolute of *One True And Unconditional Love*, Steve and Selena stepped in complete unity with their every move. Soon, a visionary spectacle materialized right before their unsuspecting eyes. From all around them, fellow superheroes and super heroines were cheering and surrounding them. Above, the neon lights began their sparkling reflection once more - in illumination of their brilliant light within the shadows. Steve and Selena had taken center stage.

As *"The Triangle Of True Love"* cheered from the stage, *"Super Singer"* declared "Our superhero senses have recognized victory. Fellow crime fighters, the new members of *"The Legion Of Love"* are *"The Romantic Avenger And The Romantic Visionary!"* In shocked amusement, Steve and Selena stood back-to-back in a victorious pose and raised their fists in acceptance of their spectators.

Steve was presented with a ceramic heart of sparkling green. A solid gold shield reflected upon it. Amidst surprise, Steve grinned as he read the inscription upon the heart - *S XO S*. A gold letter *"S"* sparkled at each side of it as he noticed the gold inscription at the bottom as well – *Legion Of Love, July 9, 1980*. Also, Selena was presented with one dozen pink carnations.

Finally, both of them received jackets with *"Legion Of Love"* inscribed upon the front and back, and the year '84 representation on each shoulder – a gesture that Steve would come to reflect upon as *"The Year Of His Heart."* Upon shaking hands with Roy and Rebecca, Steve and Selena sealed their special victory with a tender kiss. As Roy and Rebecca began to sing the sweet melody of their first duet *"The Tie That Binds Us…"* Steve and Selena danced amidst the tenderness of this *One True And Unconditional Love*.

Upon the conclusion of the song, Steve kissed Selena and took her by the hand. As the crowd of spectators began cheering and spreading itself in their path, Steve and Selena ventured onto the area of ceremonial photography. After slipping into his jacket, Steve helped Selena with hers. As Steve held the ceramic heart close to his own, Selena cradled her flowers.

She appeared in all of her splendor. As they stood amongst the vision of this *One True And Unconditional Love*, the flash bulb popped – crystallizing this moment into *The Eternal Capsule Of Time*. Steve knew that he was dreaming no longer.

Chapter Eight

As the evening hours drifted upon the horizon, Steve and Selena found themselves cruising across the aquatic world of *The State Of Orange* in its nocturnal splendor – riding Steve's new boat. Although the darkness seemed to alter his navigation, the glow of Selena's beautiful eyes served as his guiding light. Amusingly, he was confronted by another obstacle – Selena's feet. In intimate distraction, she ran her toes down his back. As the moon reflected the gloss of orange shade upon them, Steve turned to marvel her fluorescent beauty.

Selena was dressed in a sports bra of orange shade – envisioned by a transparent shirt of white shade that was tied in tender accentuation of her navel – and white denim shorts. Her ethereal beauty guided the intense passion within Steve's heart onto the matter of paramount importance that was at hand. The moment of truth was upon him. As he blinked his eyes, Steve's personal reflection elapsed into the reality of their destination – a familiar scenic island that was located in ideal observatory glance of the genuine Orange sunrise. Steve pointed. The moon reflected the aquatic glow that splashed upon the sandbar in a pathway of welcome. Beautiful palm trees and cactus plants stood in visionary wonder around the island. Above, countless birds soared in search of their safety haven for the evening. In melodious echo, crickets sang their slumber tune. Steve docked near the sandbar.

As he held Selena's hand in exit, Steve declared "Come, *My Poetic Angel!* Let us search and discover the meaning of this island paradise!" Upon these words, Steve and Selena began their trek across the island. Upon locating a comfortable circle in the sand, they reclined their bodies and Steve began to massage Selena's feet. With her strength renewed, she reached for him and held him until he was rested at her side.

Selena closed her eyes and breathed the fresh air. Placing her hand upon his face, she noticed the silent tears in his eyes. She knew at once that Steve appeared to be very troubled. As his nervous frame of mind surged through his entire body in fearful anticipation of this moment, Steve relieved himself of a deep sob within his throat. "I need to feel your arms around me! I am so scared!" Before Selena realized what was happening, Steve was crying in terrified pain.

Concerned, Selena declared "Fear not, My Precious Love! Please, try to calm yourself. *I Am Here For You And Will Always Be.*" Holding Steve closer to her, Selena placed his hand upon her heart - in a gesture of reflection upon one of the most powerful pledges that she had made up to this moment in time. This made him even more upset. Gently taking his other hand into hers, she said "Please, tell me what has frightened you so much."

Upon these words, Steve found the strength to calm himself long enough to firmly grip her hand and whisper "I love you so much!" As another deep sob took control of his senses, Steve declared in a soft whisper "But, there is something that I must tell you before we get married. I fear that your feelings will change after this," he regretted. In his troubled frame of mind, Steve did not notice the unique familiarity of Selena's previous declaration.

In loving reply, Selena asked "What is it? There is nothing in this entire universe that you could ever tell me that would cause me to stop loving you or leave you! I have dreamed of the vision of this *One True And Unconditional Love* with you throughout my entire existence. Your love for me has been one of the most cherished feelings that I have ever known. Tomorrow, I will marry you and love you forever in the name of *My Dream Come True.* However, open communication is essential – no matter how painful or difficult. Please, tell me and this painful burden will be gone once and for all time!" Selena promised.

"Just hold me while I tell you!" Steve requested.

"I am right here, My Love - ready, willing, and loving!"
Selena asserted – taking him into her arms and holding his
hand to her heart. "Since shortly after I was born, I have lived
with an uncertain medical condition," Steve began.

"Please continue! I am right here!" Selena asserted – in
firm grip of his hand upon her heart.

"It is known as Hydrocephalus. It involves the
build-up of fluid in the brain – which normally circulates
through the body by way of the spinal chord and circulatory
system. You see, I was born a premature infant and bleeding
in my brain caused blockage to my spinal column. When I was
about a month old, a neurosurgeon inserted a rubber tube in
me – known as a shunt. It collects the fluid in my head and
circulates downward and drains and absorbs into my stomach."
Pausing, Steve took Selena's hand and guided it in location of
where the device was and continued. "This serves as the
drainage pathway. The only problem is that it is an imperfect
device that can malfunction at any time due to a number of
factors such as a severe injury or – as in my case over the
years – excessive growth of scar tissue around it. Just to set
you at ease, I have had six of them installed in my lifetime,"
Steve explained.

"How do you know if there is a problem with it?"
Selena asked.

"Symptoms range from dizziness, nausea, blurred
vision, and swelling to the worst case scenario in my
position – pressure headaches," Steve continued.

"Is there any way to determine when and if a
malfunction might occur?" Selena asked.

"Unfortunately, no! One shunt lasted ten years for me.
Another only lasted for four years. If I sense that something is
wrong, I have to get a CT scan taken of my brain and a shunt
revision if a fluid build-up is seen. Fortunately, I have not had
any problems for twelve years. In fact, I am one of the most
successful Hydrocephalus cases ever to be known," Steve
replied.

"I am very glad to hear that!" Selena sighed with a sensitive smile. She was suddenly curious about the scars on his left arm. Caressing them, she said "Might I ask where these came from?"

"Those represent a development as a result of Hydrocephalus. I developed Cerebral Palsy on the left side of my body. If you look closely, you will see that I do not have full extension in my left arm and leg. Also, I do not have the best coordination in my left hand." Upon these words, Selena took Steve's left hand and placed it upon her face. Steve felt the tears of sensitivity drifting from her loving eyes.

"Please, continue!" Selena sighed.

"When I was five years old, I had a corrective tendon-separation surgery performed on my arm. The same surgery was done on my leg when I was nine. As you can see, I am fully functional. The only restriction that was ever placed on me was that I can never engage in contact sports. In spite of all that I have ever been through, I always knew that *"The Power Of Almighty God Carried Me Through."* Now that I have found you, I now realize something for the first time in my life. Everything that I have ever been through has been worthwhile. I love you so much, Selena!" Steve concluded – in the silent comfort of gratitude to be in her arms. Softly, he cried silent tears in deep reflection of everything that he had been through and the vision of this one moment in time. Unfortunately, his pain and fears did not allow him to see that nothing had changed – or would ever change.

Softly, Selena took Steve's left hand and placed it upon her heart once more. She was thankful that her deepest thoughts had not been revealed as of yet. Gently, she kissed him and said "OK, My Sweet And Precious Love! Do you feel better now that you told me?"

"Yes and no. I am so scared!" Steve whispered.

A smile of love and peace came upon Selena's face. Softly, she whispered "Everything is going to be fine! Please, tell me what you are so frightened about!" she said.

200

"Almighty God Has Always Blessed Me With Unconditional Love And Acceptance, but…" Steve began.

Smiling, Selena finished his thought. "Did you really think that I would stop loving you because of that – much less leave you?" she inquired.

"Selena, ever since I met you, I have been strengthened and fulfilled because…" He paused – relieving himself of a deep sob within his throat – "Not everyone comes face to face with their *Angel*. But, even *Angels* get scared!" he concluded. "Selena, *My Poetic Angel And One True And Unconditional Love*, I declare here and now that **My Faith In Almighty God** and your blessed presence in my life have both given me the strength and courage to realize two very important truths about myself and us. First, although the complex realities about my health are beyond my control, you alone have shown me that *One True And Unconditional Love* truly does exist. Second, although in my previous relationships I never had anyone to truly love or understand me, you alone are **The Blessing From Almighty God** that I have always dreamed of. I love you always and forever!" Steve concluded.

"I love you too, Steve! Please, listen to me for a moment. After you hear me out, I promise you here and now that you will never have to be afraid ever again! Close your eyes!" Selena replied.

"But…" Steve stammered.

"But, nothing! Close them!" Selena repeated with a soft kiss. Gently, she pressed his hand to her heart. Although he was still shaking, she spoke. "This heart fell in love with you for all of Eternity – without reservation or purpose for evasion."

"Promise?" Steve breathed.

"Definitely! I promise! But, I am not finished!" Selena declared. "From the first words of your book, I fell in love with you and dreamed of a day when I would have you all to myself. I am not about to let the reality of your health prevent my love for you in any way – and I certainly never would to

201

begin with. My only fears are seeing you in pain if anything were to ever happen to you..." she paused – shuddering at a sudden thought – "and the fear of losing you!" Selena concluded.

With his strength renewed, Steve replied "Selena, that is something that I have lived with throughout my entire life! For the first time in my life, I can say it at long last."

Unexpectedly, Steve and Selena spoke from their hearts with a sudden unified declaration "Death cannot stop *One True And Unconditional Love!* If I die tomorrow, I die knowing the warmth and tenderness of the one and only love that I have always dreamed of will live on forever – until the end of time. ***To Almighty God Be The Glory For All Of Eternity.***"

Touched, Steve smiled. In his heart, he knew that he could never and would never question the ethereal reality of Selena's love at any point in his entire life ever again. With a kiss, he continued "However, only a few words stand in comparison to these in relation to our love for one another."

"What words are those?" Selena wondered.

"The words of *One True And Unconditional Love* and promises that we will make tomorrow!" Steve declared. Suddenly, another complex concern within his mind surfaced. Terrified, Steve looked into Selena's eyes. "Selena! What if my medical condition is genetic? What if our children grow up with the same uncertainty and fears that I have?"

"Steve! Calm yourself! Do you not see that this is where we come in?" Selena asked.

"I do not understand," Steve admitted.

"I have lived my entire life with a powerful love for children. In fact, this love has been strengthened by the dream of becoming the mother of your children. I always knew that there is nothing that I would not do for my own!" Selena asserted. "However, that is a chance that everyone must take and a fear that everyone has. But, as far as you are concerned, you have lived through it – first of all. Second, in my heart, I know that there could never be a more sensitive and loving father to guide his children through any and all trials in life than you – many of which are beyond the control of everyone. With our hearts together as one, we will see our children through everything. **By The Power Of Almighty God,** with our stable family bond, guidance, and *One True And Unconditional Love,* they will grow up to be strong, healthy, dedicated, and loving - just as we are. Now, do you understand?" Selena asked.

Upon these words, Steve was already smiling. Looking into *The Eyes Of His One True And Unconditional Love,* he sealed Selena into a warm embrace and declared "Yes! Yes, I do! Thank you, *My Beloved Angel!* I love you so much!"

"I love you too, My Ever Romantic One!" Selena replied. "I love you too!" Secure in the greatest confidence that this fearful uncertainty was destroyed once and for all time, Steve and Selena rested in *The Arms Of One True And Unconditional Love* – sealing the moment with a passionate kiss.

All at once, it was clear that for the first time within Steve's lonely existence, all of his darkest fears and trials had ceased. He had realized his lifelong dreams of literary success and *One True And Unconditional Love,* and his insecurity about the unknown haunted him no longer. Strengthened by the reality of an infinite love through **The Blessings Of Almighty God,** Steve believed that the worst of times were behind him at long last.

By the force of habit, Selena looked at her watch. "Steve, do you realize what time it is?" she asked.

With his eyes closed, Steve continued to rest in the warm tenderness of her arms.

"No, what time is it, *My Poetic Angel?*" he whispered.

"It's 3:00A.M.! Time to get some sleep! We have to meet Pastor Kiplinger in a few short hours!" Selena answered.

"Right you are!" Steve declared. "Kiss me one last time!"

"I love it when you are so…" Selena paused with an amused grin. "you!" she concluded. "Then again, I love everything about you. I always have and I always will!" At the last possible second, she proceeded with a passionate kiss. "For all of Eternity!" she whispered.

"I love you too!" Steve answered. He was about to bring one of his two remaining silent mysteries to life. "First, I am going to do something that I have waited to do one more time since the moment that I had first done it!"

"What would that be?" Selena giggled – amidst the excitement of anticipation.

Steve did not answer. All that he did, was take her hand. Gently, he removed her engagement ring. As he descended onto one knee, Steve's eyes blinded with tears of love, sentiment, and happiness. In a final instant, he took notice of the charming intimacy of Selena's ethereal beauty once more. The wave of love swept over them.

Placing her other hand upon his heart, Steve spoke. "I am asking you, Selena Ferriday - as the ethereal vision of beauty, charm, and elegance, warm and sensitive kindness, and *One True And Unconditional Love* that I have always dreamed of, will you marry me?"

Smiling amidst this cherished love, Selena blushed and answered "As I stand witness to the most intimate sense of deja vu that I have ever known, I say to you now…" She paused for a sweet kiss. "Yes!" she accepted. By now, both of them were crying. As they sealed one another into a warm embrace, Steve and Selena spoke blessings of tender love and sentiment upon this moment.

"Heavenly Father, Just As You Turn Darkness Into Light Upon Each New Day That We Serve You With Gratitude And Love As Your Children, We Thank You For The Warm Glow Of Enlightenment Upon This Moment Of Uncertainty And Ask You, In The Blessed Name Of Your Son, Our Lord And Savior Jesus Christ That It Remain As A Source Of Strength And Comfort To All Challenges Ahead – Trial Or Triumph - Past, Present, And Future From This Day Onward. We Speak Faith In

You And Cast Out Fear By The Power Of Your Word And Declare Our Love In Mind, Body, Heart, And Soul For All Of Eternity. Amen."

As two birds flew across the moon, Steve and Selena joined hands and arose in unified surprise – a familiar green flicker sparkled in gentle glow in the center of the moon. In recollection of their previous moment of cherished love together on the previous night and the ethereal truth within it, they closed their eyes in deep reflection. As their composure restored, Steve and Selena found the words to speak in a kiss. They spoke of dreams not to be had for themselves – but for their children. Without reservation, Steve spoke first. *"If It Is God's Will*, I believe that our children to be blessed with your beauty!"

As she glanced at the ring upon her finger, Selena declared *"If It Is God's Will*, I believe that our children to be brought into the world to live the love that can be found in but one place – your heart." As they sealed their special dreams for the future with a kiss, the wind cast the intimate scent of a familiar perfume upon Steve's senses. He glanced. In an instant, his face flooded with sweat as the vision of his *One True And Unconditional Love* cast her ethereal presence upon him as she kissed him softly and caressed his face - stepping toward the boat. The gentle moonlight cast upon the sparkling medallion about her neck.

Selena blew a kiss and ran her fingers through her sparkling pink hair. She traveled in stride with the beauty of an *Angel*. The vision of her elegance became so powerful, that Steve was rubbing his eyes. Selena laughed and raised her eyebrows.

As they joined hands in their gentle stride, Steve and Selena ventured onto the boat amidst a passage of soft kisses. Once on their way, Steve turned the boat around for one last look at the scenic beauty of the island. As they closed their eyes in deep reflection, Steve and Selena spoke.

205

"Almighty Father God, We Ask You For Continued Peace And Safety In Our Travels At This Time In The Name Of Passage Onto The Declaration Of One True And Unconditional Love For One Another That You Alone Have Blessed Us With And Look To You With Gratitude And Love In The Cherished Name Of Our Beloved Lord And Savior, Jesus Christ Your Son Always And Forever. Amen." As Steve blinked his eyes and Selena blew a kiss, *The Eternal Capsule Of Time* was sealed once more.

The evening shade cast across the horizon. As Steve and Selena cruised through the cool darkness, they traveled a scenic path of return to their beachside hotel. As they gazed onto the ethereal essence above them, they witnessed a truly awesome visionary spectacle. Amongst the sparkling haven, the stars reflected in the formation of a familiar monogram. For Steve and Selena, this ethereal declaration would come to serve as an endless representation of *The Blessing Of Almighty God* that united them. As Steve and Selena joined hands, the distant spirits spoke their final prophesy – *S XO S.*

The tenderness of the evening hours would crystallize the intimacy within the hearts of Steve and Selena upon the solid foundation of their love for one another and the promise of a future to be shared by them in the idealistic sentiment of a few simple words. As they stepped into the elevator, a mesmerized gaze into *The Eyes Of One True And Unconditional Love* blinded their visual senses into a sweet kiss. As Steve's sensory perception searched for their floor number, Selena began to sigh and speak his name. Fortunate in his entrance of his suite security code upon their entrance, Steve's entire body was flooded with sweat. Selena was caressing the back of his neck.

As he stepped deeper into the cool darkness, Steve proceeded with a futile attempt to snap his fingers. With a silent giggle, Selena clasped his hand and held it close to her heart. Steve reclined her delicate body onto his waterbed. As he removed his sunglasses, Selena removed her own. "Take me, I am yours!" she sighed. The room sparkled in the glow of her beautiful eyes. "You do not know how good it feels to hear you say that! After all, I have been waiting for you all of my life. Now, you are all mine!" he whispered.

"Promise?" Selena inquired.

Placing her hand upon his heart in sentimental reflection upon a tender moment between them, Steve replied "Absolutely!"

He began to mix two familiar drinks into frosted glasses of sparkling green heart formations. Presenting one to Selena, Steve said, ""Sweet Paradise," for The Future Mrs. Fitzsimmons!"

"You know me too well, Mr. Fitzsimmons!" Selena replied in acceptance.

In a toast to their future children, Steve said "Here's to Sandra Rebecca!"

Smiling in approval, Selena added "And Michael Roy!" As Steve's eyes glowed in acceptance, he placed his glass to Selena's lips. As she placed her glass to his, they drank and proceeded to sweeten the moment with an even sweeter kiss.

As Selena caressed his face, Steve ran the tips of his fingers down her neck. Softly, he began soothing her tummy. Closing her eyes, Selena reclined her body – relaxing in the intimate tenderness of the moment.

As Steve encircled her navel in a heart formation, Selena proceeded with a silent giggle. Upon kissing her soft lips once more, Steve watched as Selena encircled the tender beauty of her tummy in a heart formation as well. With a smile, she spoke four simple words from a short time ago that would remain inscribed upon their loving hearts from this moment onward and into Eternity. These words would be the first words to be spoken from their hearts upon the birth of their twins – "Sandra Rebecca" and "Michael Roy!"

As their eyes blinded with tears, Steve and Selena reached for the dreams spoken in a tender moment from a short time ago, but cherished once again in the tender touch of this *One True And Unconditional Love*. With a unified expression of love, Steve caressed the smooth elegance of Selena's face in a gesture of assurance that such pure beauty will touch the lives of their beloved children **By The Power Of Almighty God** as it has touched his with the ethereal reflection of their mother and his *One True And Unconditional Love*, Selena.

As they reclined into *The Arms Of One True And Unconditional Love*, they relieved themselves of deep sobs in powerful communication of their feelings and dreams. With a kiss, Selena placed her soft hand upon Steve's loving heart – secure in **The Guiding Light Of Almighty God** to shine upon their sweet children with the heart that beats with the love of their father and her *One True And Unconditional Love*, Steve.

Within a few moments, Selena was near sleep. As Steve kissed her and touched her face in a gesture of relaxation, Selena expressed her love for him once more. As she slept, Steve checked his watch. The first light of **The New Day That The Lord Made In The Name Of One True And Unconditional Love** would shine its warmth across the horizon – soon.

A short time later, Steve woke Selena with a kiss. As she rubbed the sleep from her eyes, Selena could not see anything – Steve was shielding her vision. Amusingly, Steve declared "You are blinded by my love! Come with me, and I will shed a new light upon yet another **Blessing From Almighty God!**"

"Take me, I am yours!" Selena laughed as he helped her to her feet and led her outside and onto the veranda. As he kissed her once more, Steve removed his hand. Selena could not believe her eyes.

The morning star reflected its orange brilliance across *The State Of Orange* in ethereal ascension of the clear blue. The fresh air swept its soft purity across the beach in peaceful calm. Selena rested her head upon Steve's shoulder.

The beauty could not be spoken with words. Instead, a kiss delivered its visionary sentiment. As Selena stepped toward the door, Steve pulled her close to him once more. As he gazed into her beautiful eyes, they were surprised by the idealistic meeting of their minds through this final declaration. "Within a few short hours, through *The Blessing Almighty God,* I will unite with you in the name of *One True And Unconditional Love* for all of Eternity. *"Heavenly Father, We Thank You For Leading Us In Accordance With Your Will Onto The Discovery Of The Warmth And Tenderness Of A Cherished Union That We Declare Here And Now In The Name Of Our Beloved Lord And Savior Jesus Christ, Your Son Will Bring Glory And Honor To Your Holy Name For All Of Eternity. Amen."*

"I love you, Selena Ferriday!" Steve sighed.

"I love you too, Steve Fitzsimmons!" Selena replied with a tender kiss. Upon these words, they gazed into *The Eyes Of One True And Unconditional Love* once more. Slowly, Selena stepped toward the door once more and blew a kiss. "See you soon!" she whispered and departed.

Chapter Nine

As Steve began to ease his restless frame of mind in deep focus upon the matter of paramount importance that was at hand, he began to reflect upon everything that he had gone through in the name of this *One True And Unconditional Love.* Within a few short hours, he would experience one of the greatest moments in his entire life. As his visual senses elapsed into a restful sleep for a short while longer, he soon heard a knock at the door.

Upon opening it, Steve found a note – secured to the door with a sticker in the unique formation of a pink carnation. It was written in green letters of Old English - upon a cloth of yellow velvet. It was sealed with another pink carnation. With a smile, he opened it and read.

To Steve, My Ever Romantic One,

"By The Blessing Of Almighty God," *You Are My One True And Unconditional Love. I Love You Always And Forever. Use This Final Kiss To Guide You To My Heart. I Will See You In The Sunlight!*

Forever Yours, Selena

Your Poetic Angel

Steve's eyes blinded with tears. The entire cloth was flooded with the intimate scent of a familiar perfume. He ran his fingers across the bottom. Next to Selena's beautiful signature, he noticed a precious print of her tender lips with the cherished monogram *S XO S* beneath it. Closing his eyes for a moment of reflection, Steve held the letter close to his heart. Stepping toward Selena's door, he knocked three times and shouted "I love you, *Angel!*"

The day was July 10, 1984. As Steve looked out across the horizon, he could see **The Creations Of Almighty God** in the beautiful setting all around him in preparation to guide him onto one of the greatest moments in his entire life. On this day, the unified dream that he and Selena had sought throughout their many years of powerful dedication to its ethereal vision would stand in triumph against the inevitable trials of life and love – by *The Blessing Of Almighty God.*

On this day, Steve would gaze into *The Beautiful Eyes Of His One True And Unconditional Love* and fall in love with her once more – in eternal dedication to a love to last for all time. On this day, Steve Fitzsimmons and Selena Ferriday would unite as one for all of Eternity. On this day, July 10, 1984, Steve and Selena would profess their love for one another before *The Blessing Of Almighty God* that had united them – within the sacred institution of marriage.

Steve wore a tuxedo of a sparkling white shade with a bow tie and cummerbund of a unique yellow, red, orange, and green design. As he looked at the nightstand, he noticed a bright reflection of Selena's expedience. Inside of a yellow vase, a pink carnation sat in soft beauty. Next to the familiar commemoration of their special victory the day before, Steve noticed a photographic image of their tender love. All at once, he knew that this was a special request from his *One True And Unconditional Love.*

Smiling, Steve placed the finishing touch upon his wardrobe. As he placed the sparkling medallion around his neck as well, Steve laughed at the idealistic meeting of their minds. In his thoughts, he knew that the intimate powers of *"The Romantic Avenger And Romantic Visionary"* would unite again - very soon.

As he reached into the pocket of his jacket from *"The Legion Of Love,"* Steve retrieved a familiar box of yellow, orange, and green velvet. Opening it, he held the box close to his heart. Smiling, he gazed at a charming image of Selena that sparkled in ethereal beauty upon the wall amongst his other photographic sentiments. With a snap of his fingers, the suite stood in cool darkness. Steve proceeded toward his dream.

As he breathed the fresh air, Steve gazed at the scenic beauty across the horizon. With a smile, he held the medallion close to his heart. Pacific waves drifted across his feet. Steve closed his eyes. The wave of love had swept the intimate scent of a familiar perfume across his senses. With a deep breath, Steve blinked his eyes. "I am on my way, *My Beautiful Angel And Dream Come True!*" he declared. Steve's heart drifted upon *The Wings Of Love.*

His destination would be the island where two minds reflected upon the sentiment of *One True And Unconditional Love*, two hearts believed in the strength of that love and would now unite as one for all of Eternity. **The Power Of Almighty God** had united them, and **The Power Of His Infinite Love** had brought them to this – *"The Next Vision Of Love."*

In his travels, Steve was guided **By The Power Of Almighty God** – which he reflected upon in these few words of praise. ***"Father God, You Have Always Been There For Me. I Declare Here And Now That Everything I Have Been Through In The Name Of This One Moment In Time Has Been A Dedication To The Vision Of One True And Unconditional Love That I Always Knew In Mind, Body, Heart, And Soul Would Be Realized In Your Time. I Thank You, In The Precious Name Of My Lord And Savior Jesus Christ, Your Son And Declare Love And Praise To Your Holy Name Now And Forever. Amen."***

Steve docked near the sandbar. Behind a green pulpit of marble structure, a crucifix of pink and white carnations stood in sacred reflection upon a beautiful palm tree. Bowing his head in gratitude and deep reflection upon the blessing of love granted to him by **The Power Of Almighty God** once more, Steve smiled as he heard the soft melody of familiar singing voices from behind the trees.

In an instant, Roy appeared with a smile of warm happiness and best wishes. He was dressed in a tuxedo similar to Steve's. "Well, you made it, Buddy!" he chuckled. Shaking his hand, Steve replied "Yes, My Beloved Selena has made all of my dreams come true! I am the second luckiest man to have ever lived. In my heart, I know that Selena and I will be just as happy as you and your two *Angels* are! I love you, Roy Dawson!"

213

Upon these words, they embraced. "I love you too, Steve Fitzsimmons! She is very sweet and beautiful! You two are a truly ideal match! I just wanted to take this one last moment to wish you the best of luck and to let you know that Rebecca and I have a very special surprise for you," Roy replied.

As the sea breeze drifted across their senses, Steve and Roy watched as the pontoon plane landed. As Pastor Samuel Kiplinger stepped from the aircraft, Steve smiled. *"God Bless You, Pastor!"* he declared. Upon these words, Steve presented the minister with his latest financial offering in recognition of *The Spiritual Blessing* of his literary success and declared "Blessings upon you and everyone at *Faith, Hope, And Love Christian Haven* as I share blessings of my literary success bestowed upon me by *Almighty God!"*

"God Bless You, As Well, Brother In Christ, Steve Fitzsimmons!" the minister replied. Upon these words, they shook hands. Beneath the floral crucifix, Pastor Kiplinger lit a spiritual candle. In a final dispensation of the sentimental pursuit of *One True And Unconditional Love,* Steve placed a familiar ceramic heart beneath it and smiled as he noticed a familiar coral shell sparkling in remarkable glow beside it.

In an instant, Rebecca and Angel Starr appeared in beautiful green evening gowns. As they sang a final sentiment of love, Rebecca smiled at Steve and said "Good Luck, Steve! I love you!"

"I love you too, Uncle Steve!" Angel Starr declared.

As he laughed, Steve embraced each of them and replied "I love you too!" Roy and Rebecca kissed and stood next to one another – softly singing together in sentimental recollection of their own wedding day. As *The Creations Of Almighty God* in this beautiful setting united with him in the vision of this *One True And Unconditional Love* once more, Steve saw his *Beautiful Angel And Dream Come True* – defined and personified right before his eyes.

Selena shined with the gorgeous elegance of *His Dream Come True* that had been lost in a distant silver star – so close and yet so far - for so long. Her blue eyes illuminated with the light of intimate reflection. Her delicate skin sparkled in ethereal beauty – defined and personified right before his mesmerized eyes. She sparkled amidst an intimate rainbow of glamorous beauty in a gorgeous evening gown that reflected the most enchanting design of yellow, red, orange, and green in full and complete personification of pure beauty, charm, and tenderness, far beyond anything that Steve would have ever envisioned – vented in glamorous enhancement of her beautiful breasts and tender accentuation of her navel. Beneath a halo of white carnations, her beautiful long hair flowed with a long, soft, and gentle mirage of sparkling pink carnation. Her smile exuded warmth and happiness. Around her neck, she wore the beautiful pink carnation that Steve had given her and sparkling medallion in sentimental declaration of a love to last for all time. In her arms, she cradled a bouquet of beautiful pink carnations.

As they joined hands, Steve Fitzsimmons and Selena Ferriday whispered, "I love you!" in unison.

Pastor Kiplinger smiled. ***"God Bless You, Sister In Christ,*** Selena Ferriday!"

"May God Bless You, Pastor!" Selena replied.

Upon blessing them, Pastor Mulholland spoke:

As they joined hands, Steve and Selena whispered "I love you!" in unison. Pastor Kiplinger blessed them. Their eyes blinded with the tears of *One True And Unconditional Love.* Only love remained.

Pastor Kiplinger spoke. "In the beginning, ***To Almighty God Be The Glory,*** for *The Essence Of Creation* was an *Eternal Flame.* On ***"The First Day,"*** the breath of life touched the heart of this flame. With a brilliant flash from deep within this sparkling green light, *The Eternal Capsule Of Time* emerged. On ***"The Second Day,"*** a man and a woman began their search for *One True And Unconditional Love.* Despite

215

many trials, their sole source of strength and guidance was the passion that burned within *The Eternal Flame*. On *"The Third Day,"* the man and woman saw the light of ethereal reflection within *The Eyes Of One True And Unconditional Love*. As they reached for each other, *The First Kiss Of One True And Unconditional Love* united them together as one for all of Eternity. Together, they loved, laughed, and cried by the light of *The Eternal Flame*. In *The Arms Of One True And Unconditional Love*, they created children by the light of *The Eternal Flame*. Upon the dawn of each new day, they lived in dedication to **The Love And Spiritual Blessing Of Almighty God** by the light of *The Eternal Flame*. Together as one, they shined in cherished union with the light of *The Eternal Flame* until the end of time. Before the light faded on the mortality of these loving beings, they spoke a prophesy that was to remain sealed within *The Eternal Capsule Of Time* until the brilliant *Eternal Flame Of One True And Unconditional Love* sparkles once again within two loving hearts who travel the path that they did in search of their dream, believe in the power from within by **The Guiding Light Of Almighty God** to find it, and give of themselves to each other in representation of *"The Next Vision Of Love."* Only then, would their final prophesy be revealed **By The Power Of Almighty God** that had united them."

Suddenly, a dark shadow cast across the horizon. Amidst the splendor of glorious wonder, Roy and Rebecca placed their hands upon Steve's shoulders as the five of them gazed at the moon in its ascension before them. As Roy and Rebecca gazed at Selena with a smile of happiness and encouragement, Selena smiled at Steve. In her thoughts, she knew exactly what was happening. The moment of truth was upon her.

In an instant, Steve was blinded and fell to his knees. Upon Selena's tender touch, his visual senses restored. Gazing into her beautiful eyes, Steve would witness a visionary spectacle and solve the complex *Mystery Of Romance* by the sparkling light of *One True And Unconditional Love*.

216

Within the central glow of the moon, a familiar green flicker could be seen. In an instant, it exploded. A mass of beautiful stars drifted across the sky. As the wind blew, the stars seemed to take on the shape of a familiar monogram. Steve could not believe his eyes. Amidst **The Ethereal Essence Of Heaven**, the final prophesy of *"The First Vision Of Love"* blazed in ethereal splendor. Within a heart of green fire, the stars proclaimed *S XO S.*

As a gentle glow cast across Selena's entire body, Steve was mesmerized by the melodious echo of her ethereal declaration *"Steve, I Am Here For You – And Will Always Be. On The Day That You Reached For The Light, You Found Me."*

As his eyes blinded with tears, Steve arose in his soft pledge *"Distant Spirit, Now That I Know That You Stand Before Me, Dedicated To Your Ethereal Vision Of This One True And Unconditional Love – Forever I Will Be!"* Upon these words, Steve and Selena sealed one another into a loving embrace. Both of them were crying. "It was you all along!" Steve sighed.

"I tried to tell you but…" Selena began. "Oh, Steve…"

"We knew too, Steve!" Rebecca admitted.

"We could not tell you because we knew in our hearts that one day, **By The Power Of Almighty God** - you would find one another!" Roy continued.

As Roy and Rebecca kissed and gazed at the ethereal prophesy, they concluded in unison "We were right all along!"

"Explain no further! All that matters…" he paused for a final gaze into Selena's gorgeous eyes. "is our love!" Steve concluded.

"Do you really believe in *Love At First Sight?*" Selena asked.

"Yes! You and I are living proof of that! How about you?" Steve replied.

"Now more than ever!" Selena answered.

United in this *One True And Unconditional Love,* Steve and Selena whispered ***"Enlightened By The Power Of Your***

Love That Will Always Be My True Source Of Strength, With All Of My Mind, Body, Heart, And Soul, Thank You, Almighty Father God!" in blessed unison. Amidst this powerful sense of love and passion, Steve knew that he was dreaming no longer.

Upon these words, the five of them laughed in united happiness. As Steve and Selena sealed the moment with a unified expression of their love, Pastor Kiplinger proceeded. *" "True Love Is Only Found In The Heart."* This universal truism burned within *The Eternal Flame Of One True And Unconditional Love* and provided the brilliant visionary focus for *"The First Vision Of Love."* At this moment, it was spoken once more by the two beings that lived that vision *By The Power Of Almighty God* from their spirits that have traveled onto *The Ethereal Essence Of Heaven* that united them. In profession of their love for one another, Steve Fitzsimmons and Selena Ferriday seek to live their lives by the light of *The Eternal Flame Of One True And Unconditional Love* – the same which shed its brilliance upon *"The First Vision Of Love"* - and has brought them to this one moment in time to unite together as one for all of Eternity – *By The Power Of Almighty God."*

In a final instant, Steve glanced at the ethereal prophesy once more. His eyes blinded with the tears of *One True And Unconditional Love*. Relieving himself of a deep sob, Steve took notice of the beauty of Selena's loving eyes one last time. As the wave of love swept over them, the sparkling warmth of daylight was restored. Softly, Steve spoke.

"I, Steve Fitzsimmons, take you, Selena Ferriday, to be my wife. As my *One True And Unconditional Love*, I pledge to love, honor, cherish, and nurture you for better or for worse, for richer or for poorer, in good times and in bad, and in sickness and in health for as long as we both shall live. From this day onward and into Eternity, I pledge to live my life with you by *The Spiritual Blessing Of Almighty God* and the light of *The Eternal Flame Of One True And Unconditional Love* and that has united us."

With a smile, Steve reached into his pocket – all of the while, his eyes never left hers. As he retrieved a familiar box of yellow, orange, and green velvet, Steve opened it. Inside, was a glamorous diamond wedding band that reflected the intimate glow of emerald and diamond stars across a central band of gold. As he took Selena's hand, Steve placed it upon his heart for a brief moment in a final reflection upon a special moment between them – now cherished once more in realization of his dream once and for all time. Placing the ring upon her finger, Steve spoke a final declaration of his love – "From this day forward, I declare that we are united in the bond of *One True And Unconditional Love* for all of Eternity."

In intimate reply, Selena spoke. "I, Selena Ferriday, take you, Steve Fitzsimmons, to be my husband. As my *One True And Unconditional Love,* I pledge to love, honor, cherish, and nurture you for better or for worse, for richer or for poorer, in good times and in bad, and in sickness and in health for as long as we both shall live. From this day onward and into Eternity, I pledge to live my life with you by **The Spiritual Blessing Of Almighty God** and the light of *The Eternal Flame Of One True And Unconditional Love* that has united us."

Reaching into the center of the bouquet, Selena retrieved something that rested upon an ivory baby's breath bud. As she looked into Steve's eyes, Selena raised her eyebrows. In her hand, was a solid gold wedding band that sparkled in the cherished reflection of emerald stars across a central band of diamonds. Taking Steve's hand, Selena placed it upon her heart for a brief moment – amidst the same sentiment of cherished reflection as Steve. As she placed the ring upon his finger, Selena spoke a final declaration of her love – "From this day forward, I declare that we are united in the bond of *One True And Unconditional Love* for all of Eternity."

Pastor Kiplinger smiled. As he blessed them once more, he said "In exchange of these vows and rings, you have given of yourselves in representation of the love that the hearts of *"The First Vision Of Love"* had cherished before you – a vision that lives on within you. Thus, by the authority vested in me by *The State Of Orange, The Faith, Hope, And Love Christian Haven*, and **The Power Of Almighty God** that has united you, I now declare that you have become one within the institution of marriage. ***May The Good Lord And His Son Jesus Christ Bless You In Mind, Body, Heart, And Soul For All Of Eternity."*** Looking at the new couple before him with a warm smile, Pastor Kiplinger concluded with ***"All God's People*** said…"

Upon these words, Roy, Rebecca, and Angel Starr Dawson united with Steve and Selena Fitzsimmons and declared ***"Amen!!!"***

"Thank you! ***May God Bless You, Pastor!"*** Steve and Selena asserted.

"You as well, ***My Brother And Sister In Christ!"*** Upon shaking their hands, Pastor Samuel Kiplinger departed.

The wave of love swept across the horizon. Steve and Selena reached for each other. Moving their lips toward one another in tender intimacy, they kissed. Upon gazing into the eyes of his own *Everlasting Love,* Roy whispered "Are you thinking what I am thinking?"

"Absolutely!" Rebecca replied.

As Steve and Selena continued to kiss, they turned their hearts over to ***"The Ethereal Essence Of Heaven"*** and *"The First Vision Of Love"* in cherished gratitude as Roy and Rebecca sang a few tender words in sentimental reflection upon the *One True And Unconditional Love* of the new husband and wife.

Inspired by those two hearts, we found this One True Love...
With their blessing shining up above...
Their two hearts lived a love that cannot ever end...
Now we live it, My Love And My Best Friend...
Almighty God *brought us together... forever...*
And now, the rest is in our hands...
So many years, we searched...
God *sent this One True Love...*
Our two hearts represent "The Next Vision Of Love..."
We send our love and thanks to those people...
Our True Love cannot be denied...
I declare my love from me to you...
Through our hearts joined together...
"First Vision Of Love," we send our love to you...
We pledge Eternal Love to each other...

Upon completion of the song, Steve and Selena gazed into *The Eyes Of One True And Unconditional Love.* "I love you, *"My Romantic Visionary And Poetic Angel!"* Steve declared.

As Selena giggled in recognition of the song as the one that Steve had placed into her musical box the day before, she sighed "I love you too, *"My Ever Romantic Avenger!"*"

As Roy, Rebecca, and Angel Starr began to cheer and blow bubbles, Roy suggested "We should leave you two alone!"

"Right you are, My Marvelous Minstrel!" Rebecca responded to Roy – in sentimental declaration of her nickname for him. "Besides, we have to ride like the wind for our next concert!"

"In five days, I turn five years old!" Angel Starr shouted – extending five fingers to Steve and Selena.

"You can count on us, Sweetheart!" Steve assured her.

As Roy and Steve shook hands, Roy said "I hope that our words from the heart showed in some small way just how glad we are that you two have finally found each other. Although you have been through a great deal to reach this moment, you deserve all of the happiness in the world!"

"I could not have done it without you, Roy! Thank you for everything! You are the greatest!" Steve replied. Upon these words, they exchanged a high-five and embraced.

As they looked at Rebecca, Selena, and Angel Starr, Roy and Steve looked at one another once more. With a sudden look of concern upon his face, Roy said "You know that if there is ever anything that you need, just call us! Are you going to be OK?"

"Fear not, My Friend! The reality that twelve years have passed since anything has happened to me made last night all of the more special!" Steve assured him.

"What happened?" Roy asked.

Upon these words, Steve's eyes blinded with tears. With a warm smile upon his face, he replied "All that I know is that **By The Power Of Almighty God,** I am the second man to come face to face with *My Angel*. In my heart, I know that as long as we are together, I will never have to be afraid again!"

"Truer words were never spoken!" Roy asserted.

"You should know!" Steve replied.

As Roy looked at his beloved wife and daughter once more, he smiled and sighed "Yes, I do!"

As Rebecca and Angel Starr embraced Selena, Rebecca sighed "*Some Dreams Really Do Come True!*"

"If you only knew!" Selena replied.

"Take care of him!" Rebecca concluded.

"You know I will!" Selena assured her.

As Steve kissed Rebecca and Angel Starr, Selena kissed Roy. The tears of gratitude, love, and happiness reflected the loving bond between all of them. As they stood together in firm declaration, *"The Legion Of Love"* stared out across the horizon and shouted "Fear not, *State Of Orange!* Soon, *"The Legion Of Love"* will reunite!"

Standing together in spiritual sentiment, the five of them joined hands in gratitude for their reunion – united in their **Faith In Almighty God** – knowing that they would be together again very soon.

222

"Heavenly Father, We Thank You For The Cherished Time That We Have Shared Together. We Look To You With Gratitude And Love In The Cherished Name Of Our Lord And Savior, Your Son Jesus Christ For The Everlasting Bond Of Friendship That Has Continued To Bring Strength, Comfort, and Happiness To All Of Us In Mind, Body, Heart, And Soul And We Declare Praise To Your Name As We Part – Standing On Faith In You Upon The Peace And Safety That You Will Sustain In Our Travels Onto A Path Of Return Together Again By Your Will Alone. Amen."

As Steve and Selena embraced, they turned to Roy, Rebecca, and Angel Starr and said "Thanks for everything!"

As they turned to leave, Roy turned back once more. Grinning, he shouted "Anything for you! But remember – do not do anything that goes against our *"Laws of Love!"*"

As Angel Starr blew kisses at them and waved, Rebecca snickered "But if you do, be careful!" Upon these words, *"The Triangle Of True Love"* departed.

In their first united prayer as husband and wife, Steve and Selena Fitzsimmons gazed into *The Eyes Of One True And Unconditional Love* and spoke. *"Heavenly Father, We Thank You For Your Faithfulness In This Moment Yet Again – As You Have Declared That It Is Not Good For People To Be Alone. The One True And Unconditional Love That You Alone Have Blessed Us With Will Live On Within Our Minds, Bodies, Hearts, And Souls Together As One For All Of Eternity. We Love And Praise You In The Name Of Jesus Christ Your Son, Our Beloved Lord And Savior Now And Forever. Amen."* As Steve and Selena reached for each other, they sealed the moment with a tender kiss.

Suddenly, Steve and Selena witnessed a visionary spectacle that would shed the light of ethereal strength upon their inevitable trials of life and love, warm their hearts with the gentle glow of intimacy, and provide a brilliant reflection of

223

their endless love for one another. Unexpectedly, the brilliance of daylight faded into cool darkness once more. The sparkling prophesy of *"The First Vision Of Love"* appeared in ethereal splendor once more. Mesmerized, Steve and Selena watched as the heart of fire united with the stars of ethereal declaration – all that remained was the flicker of a green star. As Steve and Selena held each other close, they marveled the vision. In an instant, they were blinded and fell to their knees.

When their visual senses restored, Steve and Selena could not believe their eyes. The ceramic heart was sealed in a frosted crystal. Steve and Selena rubbed their eyes. The heart blazed in the brilliant glow of a green flame. A solid gold inscription sparkled upon the crystal.

As the sun arose across the horizon once more, Steve and Selena stared into *The Eyes Of One True And Unconditional Love.* They had united together as one in the light of *One True And Unconditional Love.* Tears flooded their eyes. As they relieved themselves of deep sobs, Steve sighed "I love you, Mrs. Selena Fitzsimmons!"

"I love you too, Mr. Steve Fitzsimmons!" Selena replied.

Steve ran his fingers through her hair of beautiful pink carnation. Slowly, they began to kiss. Amidst this cherished union, Steve and Selena reclined into *The Arms Of One True And Unconditional Love* – united as one for all of Eternity. There were no words left to speak.

As they gazed into *The Eyes Of One True And Unconditional Love,* their tender caresses communicated their deepest thoughts and feelings. With a tender kiss, the tears of *One True And Unconditional Love* returned. Their dream had come true at long last. Only love remained.

Upon returning to their hotel, neither of them would have ever suspected that they were about to take center stage – all due to the fact that they had neglected to exercise their method of ensuring a heightened sense of security by wearing sunglasses. In an instant, Steve and Selena were surrounded by a crowd of adoring fans – cheering and blowing bubbles. In the distance, they noticed Roy, Rebecca, and Angel Starr – grinning.

Suddenly, a banner descended from the ceiling. They laughed. The banner read *"Congratulations Steve And Selena Fitzsimmons 'The Next Vision Of Love.'"* With a microphone in his hand, Roy stepped forward and declared "Friends, please join us in extending our warmest congratulations and best wishes to our newlywed friends - best selling Romance author, Steve Fitzsimmons and successful poet, Selena Ferriday Fitzsimmons."

As the crowd cheered, Rebecca noticed their surprised grin and said "Come forward, legends of the written word - your public awaits you! Everyone here requested that you take a few moments to sign a few more copies of your best-selling work for them."

As Steve and Selena looked at one another with a sweet kiss, they stepped forward. "I accept on one condition," Steve declared. Turning to Selena, he explained. "There was a time in my life when I thought that *One True And Unconditional Love* was a vision that I could only dream about and communicate through my writing. Three days ago, I found it in the beautiful woman that now stands beside me as *My Dream Come True And Beautiful Wife*. All that I ask is your acceptance of her signature next to my own in sentimental reflection of the *One True And Unconditional Love* that has united us as one for all of Eternity. I love you, Selena."

As silent tears fell from her eyes, Selena replied, "I love you too, Steve! But I too will only do this if you inscribe your name next to mine on my poem. After all, I have realized the love within it at long last – all because of you."

"I would do anything for you, *My Beautiful And Poetic Angel And Dream Come True*!" Steve accepted. Upon these words, Steve and Selena sealed one another into a warm embrace.

Grinning, Rebecca glanced at Roy and Angel Starr and said "One more thing!"

"We would like to propose a toast!" Roy declared. As Steve and Selena were presented with two familiar drinks, Roy concluded with "Steve and Selena Fitzsimmons, here's to things worth waiting for! *May Almighty God Bless You Always And Forever!*" With a drink, Steve and Selena sealed the moment with a tender kiss. Steve knew that he was dreaming no longer. Upon completion of the unique bonding experience, they shared a large wedding cake of luscious yellow mixture with white butter cream and red, yellow, orange, and green frosting that Roy had prepared – decorated with a beautiful novel and poetry scroll centerpiece upon it.

Finally, Roy and Rebecca had a final gift for them. As they carried a large rectangle that was covered in drapery of green satin to the center of the room, Roy and Rebecca declared in unison "Here's to *The Next Vision Of Love!*" – and removed the cloth. Steve and Selena could not believe their eyes.

Their images appeared upon a canvas in cherished sentimentality. The reflection of their love sparkled in union with a bright illumination around them that shed light upon an ethereal inscription. Steve and Selena would come to regard this declaration as the final blessing from the hearts of Roy, Rebecca, and Angel Starr – as well as *The Blessing Of Almighty God* that had touched their lives with the presence of *Their Dream Come True*, provided them with the courage to believe in it, and strengthened them with the *One True And Unconditional Love* that would live on throughout all of the days of their lives together until the end of time.

They kissed. As their eyes blinded with tears, Steve and Selena joined hands. *"Every picture tells a story!"* Steve declared.

Smiling, Selena whispered "Clearly, this one maintains that we truly are an ideal match!" With a gentle sigh, they spoke the painted prophesy – *"Some Dreams Really Do Come True."* Only love remained.

Chapter Ten

Unfortunately, the warmth and tenderness of their love would soon be clouded by an unexpected shadow of painful fear and sadness. Despite all that Steve and Selena had gone through in the name of this *One True And Unconditional Love*, nothing could have ever prepared them for the terrifying moment of uncertainty that was about to occur.

In the middle of the night, Steve woke Selena – shaking in a bitter sweat. In a weak voice, he said "Selena, wake up! I am not feeling well!" Before Selena realized what was happening, Steve's face was flooded with painful tears.

"Come here, My Love! Are you hurt?" Selena asked.

"I have a terrible headache! I need to feel your arms around me! I am so scared!" Steve replied. Gently, Selena took Steve into her arms and placed his hand upon her heart.

"I am right here! Let me get some aspirin for you!" Selena replied – reaching into the nightstand.

"I feel so weak!" Steve breathed as Selena wiped the sweat from his forehead.

"OK! You do not have a fever. Just relax for a minute because you should not take these pills on an empty stomach. I will be right back!" Selena replied. With a gentle kiss upon his forehead, she arose for a brief moment.

Soon, she returned with a glass of ice water in one hand, and a plate with crackers and white bread in the other. Gently, she slipped the pills into his mouth. As Steve gulped the water – slowly – he was still shaking. "Thank you! I love you so much!" he whispered.

Taking him into her arms, Selena rested his head upon her chest so that he could feel the beating of her heart. Slowly, she began to feed the bread and crackers to him. Trying to remain calm amidst her deepest fears, Selena continued to caress Steve's face and assured him "I love you too! I always have and I always will. Please, try to calm yourself and rest. When you wake up, I will be right here!"

"I Love You, My Beautiful Wife!" Steve whispered – caressing her heart.

"Fear not, My Love! *I Am Here For You – And Will Always Be!*" Selena assured him. Upon these words, Steve drifted into a restless sleep – slowly. As he slept, Selena cried silent tears in desperate hope that her loving touch would somehow heal him and that neither of them would have to fear the worst. Softly, she began to pray *"Father God, I Implore You, In The Precious Name Of Our Lord And Savior, Your Son Jesus Christ To Deliver My Husband From This Uncertainty And Pain. We Love And Praise You Now And Forever. Amen."*

In a few hours, Steve was still drifting in and out of a very uncomfortable sleep. Suddenly, he arose and said "My head is spinning and I have to vomit!"

"Stay right where you are!" Selena replied – reaching for the wastebasket by the nightstand. In an instant, Steve was vomiting. With her arms around him, Selena noticed that he was keeping his eyes closed. "Can you open your eyes?" she asked.

As he tried, Steve breathed "No! It hurts too much!" – and proceeded to vomit again. With her hands trembling, Selena reached for the telephone. Amidst her sudden thought, her eyes blinded with tears – she remembered that Roy, Rebecca, and Angel Starr were gone. Desperate, she tried to reach them anyway. Unfortunately, their cellular phones were temporarily out of service.

In his weak condition, Steve began to pray softly. *"Almighty Father God And My Lord And Savior, Jesus Christ, I Implore You To Comfort, Strengthen, And Keep Me..."* Suddenly, Steve collapsed against her – unable to move. "Help me, Selena! Help me, *Angel!* Help me!" he breathed.

Frantically, Selena called for the emergency response service. "Steve, hang on! I love you! I love you!" was all that she could say.

Chapter Eleven

As they rode in the ambulance, Selena was thankful that they were close enough to Steve's health care facility. As he was rushed into the emergency room, Selena continued to hold his hand. Nothing could have ever prepared her for what was about to occur. After recounting Steve's medical history, Selena continued her desperate pleas for expedited help. As they sat in a room for hours because a room for a CT scan was not accessible, Selena had only been told that Steve's neurosurgeon was on call and that a CT scan would be performed as soon as possible.

In Steve's painful state, he drifted in and out of consciousness. As he was transported for a CT scan at long last, Selena was frightened because she did not want to leave him. Suddenly, she received the best encouragement that she could in this intense moment of uncertainty. Slightly, Steve opened his eyes and rested her hand upon his heart. As tears flooded her face, Selena smiled as Steve rested his face against her gentle caress and whispered "I love you, *Angel.* **"*God Is Good To Us!*"**

Unable to take her eyes off of him, Selena kept his hand in hers and caressed his forehead. "I love you too! **Yes! Yes He is!*"** she sighed. Upon these words, Steve was taken in for the CT scan.

As time passed, Selena held Steve's hand – in desperate hope that everything would be alright. Softly, they continued to pray. ***"Father God, I Speak Healing Onto My Husband,"*** Selena declared.

"Be With Me, Lord. I Pray In The Name Of Jesus," Steve asserted – in spite of his pain and weakness.

Completely unaware of the passage of time Selena was horrified to learn that Steve had experienced a shunt malfunction and would need a revision. Suddenly, she was consumed by anger and shouted "I will not agree to anything until I speak to his neurosurgeon!"

As her declaration of anger echoed throughout the entire room, a tall man stepped through the revolving door. He had black hair and brown eyes with a look of confidence that could set anyone at ease - even amidst the most difficult medical circumstances. He was dressed in a long blue doctor's coat, a white shirt, and a black tie and pants. He was carrying a large manila envelope with Steve's scans. Stepping toward her with a warm smile, he said "Hello! My name is…"

Before he could finish, the tears in Selena's eyes glowed with sudden relief as she read his identification. "Dr. Winston!" she breathed as she shook his hand with powerful gratitude. "I am glad to see you! I am Selena, Steve's wife."

With a smile, Dr. Winston replied, "It is a genuine pleasure to meet you! He always dreamed of finding love and happiness. I am certainly glad that he has at long last!"

Through rapid breaths, Selena declared "Words could never express the gratitude that I feel toward you through your selfless actions in saving Steve's life sixteen years ago and then again twelve years ago. If it had not been for you and *"The Blessing Of Almighty God,"* I would have never found *My One True And Unconditional Love.* Thank you so much!"

As he stepped toward Steve, Dr. Winston took his hand. Looking at Selena once more, he spoke. "It has been my pleasure. He is one of the most successful patients that I have ever had the pleasure to care for. He is very talented as well!"

Selena relieved herself of a deep sob. "It just hit him so fast!" she cried. He has not been sick for twelve years! Is he going to be alright?"

"Of course he will be. If there is one thing that I know about Steve, it is that his *Faith In Almighty God* has always carried him through." Dr. Winston assured her – opening the folder. As he held the film up to the light, he did not even have to place it onto the viewing screen.

"It's true!" Selena shuddered through her tears.

"Yes! He will need a shunt revision. Please, do not be afraid. Although Hydrocephalus is very complex and frightening, I promise you that he will recover before you both know it. Am I correct in assuming that he has explained the procedure to you?" Dr. Winston asked.

"Yes, of course! I just did not expect that if this ever had to happen to him again that it would happen so soon. We just got married yesterday. We met at his last book signing. I love him so much!" Selena declared.

As he looked down at Steve, Dr. Winston looked at Selena with a warm smile and replied "In my heart, I know that he loves you as well!" Looking at Steve once more, he tried to get Steve's attention. "Hello, Steve! This is Dr. Winston. You are going to be just fine." Unable to get a response in Steve's weak condition, Dr. Winston looked at Selena and admitted "The only problem is that we need his permission before operating. Perhaps, you can help!"

"Explain no further!" Selena replied – wiping her eyes and clearing her throat. Taking a deep breath, Selena smiled and took one of Steve's hands into hers and gently placed the other one upon her tummy. "Steve, My Ever Romantic One, listen to me very carefully. Do you like how this feels?" she asked.

As a sudden smile appeared upon Steve's sweating face, he breathed "Yes!"

"Do you want to feel better so that you can cover me with kisses?" she asked – in slight embarrassment as she noticed Dr. Winston's grin.

"Yes!" Steve breathed once more.

"OK! Then go to sleep and dream about me and I will be here when you wake up. OK?" she explained.

"I love you, *Angel*!" Steve whispered.

Kissing his forehead with one final caress, Selena replied "I love you too!"

"That is all that we need and the best that we can expect at this moment in time! Although that was the most

231

unique approval that I have ever heard, in my professional opinion, he just proved how much he loves you!" Dr. Winston asserted. "Thank you Selena! By the way, has he eaten anything recently?" he asked.

"Besides our wedding cake many hours ago, I just gave him some crackers and bread to ease his stomach with the aspirin!" Selena replied. "But, he did vomit before I called the ambulance."

"That is to be expected. He should be ready for surgery in an hour," Dr. Winston explained.

"Can I stay with him until then?" Selena asked.

"Yes, of course! Besides, he needs you right now and it appears that nothing and no one can stand in the way of the special love that you share!" Dr. Winston said.

"Thank you! Thank you very much!" Selena breathed.

"It is my pleasure!" Dr. Winston assured her once more. Although the tears of anticipation returned, she was secure in the confidence that Steve's life would be in the best and most capable of hands – guided by **The Strength Of Almighty God.**

. As he turned to leave, Dr. Winston turned around and asked "By any chance, are you the author of a very recent and famous poem?"

Shocked, Selena replied "Yes, *'Forever We Will Be...'*"

"Could I have your autograph?" Dr. Winston requested.

"Yes, of course!" Selena replied – signing an index card for him with the same sentiment of gratitude that she spoke from her heart only moments ago.

"Thank you very much. That was a truly beautiful poem!" Dr. Winston asserted in gratitude.

"You are very welcome! Thank you!" Selena replied with a smile.

Upon these words, Selena sat next to Steve. As he cringed in pain as blood was drawn from his arm, Selena tenderly held his hand. Unable to take her eyes off of him,

Selena resolved to try one last time to contact Roy and Rebecca. Reaching for her cellular phone, she kept one of Steve's hands in hers.

Unexpectedly, Roy answered at last. Intent on speaking as clearly as the distorted connection and her nervous frame of mind would allow her, Selena spoke. "Hello, Roy! Listen, I do not know how to tell you this, so I am just going to tell you – Steve had a shunt malfunction. We are at the hospital right now and Dr. Winston is going to perform surgery in an hour."

Shocked, Roy spoke by his first instinct. "Do you want us to turn around and come back?"

Selena could hear Rebecca's inquiry in the background. Suddenly concerned that the news would frighten the young and innocent heart of Angel Starr, Selena inquired "Roy, is Angel Starr asleep?"

"Yes, she is!" Roy replied – proceeding to communicate his fearful response as to the situation at the present time to Rebecca.

"Well, let me think…" Selena began – suddenly surprised by Steve's whisper.

"Tell him no! I will be OK! Rock on! *The Good Lord Will Carry Me Through!*" he declared.

Smiling, Selena kissed him in approval. "Mr. Fitzsimmons just told me to tell you that he will be fine and Rock on!"

"That is Steve, true to his form! Always thinking of others before himself! OK! Please let us know as soon as he gets into recovery, OK?" Roy asked.

"Of course! Thank you again, Roy!" Selena replied.

"For what?" Roy asked.

"All that I know is that because of the three of you, I am the second woman to come face to face with *My Angel*! I love you all so much!" Selena replied.

"We love you too! Tell Steve that we love him!" Roy concluded.

"You can tell him that yourself!" Selena replied. Placing the phone to Steve's ear, she whispered "Steve My Love, Roy and Rebecca have something to say to you!" As she heard Roy and Rebecca declare their love, Selena saw Steve smile and whisper, "I love you too! *Almighty God Is Good! Jesus Christ Is The Truth, The Light, And The Way!*"

Amidst silent tears, Selena returned the phone to her own ear and sighed "Did you hear him?"

"Absolutely! Take care of yourself and each other! *God Bless!*" Roy said.

"You do the same and remember, that if Steve said that he will be fine, *By The Blessing Of Almighty God,* he will! *God Bless!*" Selena replied. Upon these words, the conversation ended. Gently, Selena wrapped herself into Steve's arms and rested her head upon his heart – softly kissing his cheek and wiping sweat from his forehead every few moments with a cool washcloth. Only love remained.

"Comfort, Strengthen, And Keep Us, Almighty God Now And Forever!" they declared in soft unison.

Before long, Selena had received a briefing on the anesthetic procedure and was relaxing with a glass of ice water as Steve was about to be taken into surgery. In her thoughts, she was thankful that sterilization tape had been placed over Steve's wedding band so that it did not have to be removed. As Steve gripped her hand, he opened his eyes slightly once more and whispered. "I love you, *Angel*." In a final moment of united prayer, Steve and Selena spoke. *"Heavenly Father, We Are Your Loving Children And Are Now Faced With Something That Is More Difficult Than Anything We Have Been Through Together. Through Our Faith In You And Our Precious Lord And Savior, Your Son Jesus Christ, We Shall Have No Fear. Thank You, Almighty Father God! Amen!"*

As the silent tears of anticipation returned, Selena kissed Steve once more and sighed "I love always and forever! *May Almighty God Be With You,* My Beloved Husband!"

234

Upon these words, Selena watched as Steve was brought down the long hallway and into the double doors to the operating room. Gazing at the intimate reflection of Steve's love for her that sparkled upon her finger, Selena held the sentimental medallion and beautiful carnation to her heart and whispered once more "I love you!"

Once in the operating room, Steve smiled at Dr. Winston. As he took his hand, Steve said "Thank you again for everything, Doctor!"

"It has been my pleasure, Steve!" Dr. Winston replied.

"Before we begin, I want to say one final prayer," Steve declared.

"Please do!" Dr. Winston asserted.

In spite of his pain and weakness, Steve found the strength to speak a few final words of *Faith, Hope, And Love*. *"Almighty Father God, You Have Always Been There For Me. I Ask You In The Blessed Name Of Your Son, My Lord And Savior Jesus Christ To Speak Healing To My Body, Continued Guidance And Wisdom To Dr. Winston, And Strength And Comfort To My Beloved Wife Selena. I Accept All Challenges With A Powerful And Dedicated Mind, Body, Heart, And Soul – Always Ready To Do Your Will. I Have Always Believed That Everything Happens For A Reason. As I Accept This Challenge, I Implore You To Continue To Comfort, Strengthen, And Keep Me. Father God, Realize My Appreciation And Gratitude For The Life That You Have Given Me, And Know That I Will Continue To Become A Better Person For It. With Praise And Glory To Your Holy Name, I Love You In Mind, Body, Heart, And Soul Always And Forever. Amen!"*

Upon these words, Dr. Winston said "Relax now, and think about these two things – you have an impeccable writing talent and a beautiful wife who loves you very much! What is her name again?" Dr. Winston asked to focus Steve's mind into a state of ease as he began drifting into an anesthetic state – slowly.

"I Love You, Almighty Father God And My Blessed Lord And Savior Jesus Christ!" Steve declared. As he paused for a brief moment, Steve concluded with "Selena! "I love you, *Angel*" Upon these words, his last thoughts of his *One True And Unconditional Love* elapsed into a restful sleep.

Chapter Twelve

Steve began walking through a long and dark tunnel with a brilliant light in front of him. Clouds of steam rose upward and touched his hands every step of the way. At a comfortable stride, he remained uncertain as to the direction ahead of him. As his mind began to wander, he began to think about Selena and his *One True And Unconditional Love* for her. Smiling, he shouted "Selena! Where are you? Everything is fine, *My Beautiful And Poetic Angel!* Come to me and let me hold you in my arms – forever until the end of time." Suddenly, the light projected in a rapid flash - blinding him. Shocked and nervous, Steve fell to his knees. A sharp pain shot through his head and throughout his entire body. In an instant, his heart was beating faster than he had ever felt before. His face flooded with sweat. A frightening chill rushed through his entire body. Paralyzed with pain, uncertainty, and fear, he declared ***"Heavenly Father, In The Cherished Name Of My Lord And Savior, Your Son Jesus Christ, I Implore You Be With Me Lord. I Pray..."*** As he concluded with "I love you, Selena!!!" Steve's eyes blinded with tears and his vision faded to black. He elapsed into unconsciousness.

The next thing he knew, Steve found himself surrounded by total darkness – with the exception of a brilliant green flicker in the distance. Wiping tears from his eyes, the pain remained in his head and he could not move. Suddenly, he heard a faint voice in the distance calling to him – that became easier to understand with the passage of these words - *"Steve! I Am Here For You – And Will Always Be! Reach For The Light And Let Us Be Together – Forever You And Me."* With a sudden warm smile of *One True And Unconditional Love,* Steve knew at last that it was Selena's voice. As his strength slowly returned, Steve crawled toward his visionary assumption.

"Thank You, Lord!" he declared. As he reached, the distant green glow materialized into the formation of a star.

Upon touching it, the star began to flicker in his hand and spread across the darkness – shedding light upon it. In an instant, his surroundings stood in a warm and brilliant light. Overcome by exhaustion – but at peace at last, Steve rested upon his back. Above him, a distant shadow was emerging upon him. As Steve reached once more, a sparkling green light began to flicker in the distance. As he rubbed his eyes, the shadow began to materialize. Steve smiled and whispered, *"Thank You, Almighty Father God!"* Amidst the gentle glow of sparkling green light around her entire body, Selena drifted toward him.

Chapter Thirteen

Within the endless duration of two hours, Dr. Winston appeared in the waiting room with the same smile and look of confidence that he had presented only hours ago. As Selena took his hand, Dr. Winston placed his other hand upon her shoulder and said "The surgery was successful! However, I must admit that it was far more complex than I had anticipated..." As he paused, Dr. Winston asked with sudden concern "Forgive me, but do you want to hear all of this?"

"Yes, of course!" Selena breathed - with a smile of relief.

"Well, the truth of the matter is that scar tissue was growing at such a rapid rate around the shunt that his body was literally attacking it and trying to push it out of him – gradually obstructing the pathway and closing the drainage holes. Unfortunately, the reality as to its sudden appearance is a mystery. However, you should not concern yourself with that!" Dr. Winston asserted – in acknowledgement of the relief that he knew that Selena was experiencing.

Softly, Selena relieved herself of a deep sob. Amidst gratitude, she sighed "All that matters is that he is out of danger. Is he in any pain?"

"The incision on his head did require deeper attention," Dr. Winston admitted. "However, there was a very minimal loss of blood and he had no problems with the anesthesia. Even so, he is very weak – so he must be kept with oxygen and it is essential to monitor his heart rate. So, I am requiring the usual 24-hour period in intensive care and a minimum of one day in a regular hospital room."

Taking his hand once more in powerful gratitude, Selena sighed "Anything to ensure his health, safety, and a rapid recovery! Thank you so much. When do you suppose I can see him?"

"If it is not too soon, immediately!" Dr. Winston replied.

Placing his hand upon her shoulder once more, Dr. Winston escorted Selena toward the intensive care unit and said "If there is anything that I or anyone else here can do for you, please do not hesitate to ask!"

"Thank you very much again, Dr. Winston!" Selena replied. Amidst powerful gratitude, Selena whispered *"Thank You, Almighty Father God And My Blessed Lord And Savior Jesus Christ!"* and stepped into the room.

Chapter Fourteen

Steve saw his *Beautiful Angel And Dream Come True* – defined and personified right before his eyes. Selena was dressed in a white transparent shirt – vented in glamorous enhancement of her beautiful breasts and tied in tender accentuation of her navel – and white denim shorts. Amidst the same sentiment of elegance and charm as the day that they met, sparkling red gloss reflected upon her fingers and toes. As she ran her fingers through her beautiful long hair of gorgeous pink carnation, Selena stretched in revelation of an intimate mystery – releasing her navel from the constraint of her shorts. As Steve reached for her, they joined hands. Slowly, she drifted on top of him and into a tender embrace - resting gently in his arms.

As his eyes blinded with tears, the light continued to sparkle around her as she caressed his face. With the tears of this *One True And Unconditional Love* in her eyes, Selena smiled and whispered "I love you, Steve – My Beloved Husband!" – caressing his forehead.

"I love you…" Before he could finish, Selena kissed Steve's unsuspecting lips and gazed into his loving eyes once more. "I love you too, Selena – My Beloved Wife!" he breathed in conclusion. In an instant, Steve's strength returned and the pain in his head was gone.

"Thank You Almighty Father God And Our Cherished Lord And Savior Jesus Christ!" Steve and Selena declared in blessed unison. With a final gaze into *The Eyes Of One True And Unconditional Love,* they sealed the moment with a tender kiss.

As his visualization elapsed, all that he could hear was her soft and tender voice whispering his name – "Steve… Steve… Steve…"

Chapter Fifteen

Steve was resting comfortably – attached to a heart monitor that was reading from the pulse in his finger. The right side of his head had been shaved for the incision that had been covered by a thick bandage. Although she had every confidence that she was prepared to face this moment, Selena felt faint and collapsed into a chair. As she began to breathe heavily, Selena heard a soft whisper – "Selena!" In instant focus, Selena relieved herself of a deep sob and gained enough composure to glance at Steve – he was resuming consciousness.

Gently, she took his hand. Although the silent tears of relief, gratitude, and love remained, Selena smiled and spoke. "Yes, Steve. I am here – waiting for you to come back to me. Wake up, My Love. I love you so much! Steve... Steve... Steve... " As his visualization elapsed, Steve awoke.

Chapter Sixteen

Although the room was dark, it sparkled in the brilliant glow of Selena's beautiful eyes. As she held one of Steve's hands to her heart, Selena caressed his face - softly. In gratitude and praise, Selena turned to ***The Ethereal Essence Of Heaven*** and whispered ***"Thank You, Lord!"*** Glancing at Steve amidst the tender vision of *One True And Unconditional Love,* she spoke. "Hey there! Are you OK?" Before Steve could respond, Selena kissed him.

"I am now!" he whispered. Mesmerized by the *One True And Unconditional Love* between them, nothing could have ever prepared them for the moment of truth that was about to occur.

Blinded with tears, Steve placed Selena's hand upon his heart and relieved himself of a deep sob. As his hands began shaking, he spoke. "Selena, I love you so much. Please do not ever forget that. Although I knew that this had to be done, I had a fear that I was not going to survive. Fortunately, my weakness and the anesthesia prevented it, until…" Upon these words, Steve told her about his frightening journey. As she listened, Selena was mesmerized by his spiritual declaration "I realize now more than ever that ***The Good Lord Truly Did Bring Us Together. The Power Of Almighty God And His Son Jesus Christ, In Blessed Union With Your One True And Unconditional Love Saved Me!"***

Upon these words, Selena arose. Amidst passionate kisses, she slipped into the bed next to him - slowly. All of the while, Steve and Selena maintained their tender touch upon the heart of this *One True And Unconditional Love.* Amidst deep sentiment, she replied "Yes!" Smiling at her silent thoughts of idealistic reflection upon the ethereal and spiritual connection between them once more, she concluded with "After all, remember what I told you before: *I Am Here For You And Will Always Be!* ***By The Blessing Of Almighty God,*** together as

245

one, there is nothing that we cannot accomplish! I love you always and forever!"

"I love you too!" Steve whispered – caressing her sparkling pink hair and resting her hand upon his heart once more. "I love you always and forever!"

Upon gazing into *The Eyes Of One True And Unconditional Love* once more, Selena held Steve in a tender embrace and replied "I love you too, Steve! I love you too!" Softly, she began to whisper the tender sentiment of a familiar poem. These were the very words that she wrote from her heart in a now famous moment of cherished reflection – *"Forever We Will Be..."*

All through my lonely, sad years...
I never knew of the love that I would find...
No one to share in my triumphs and fears...
I could not see that you would be mine...
The moment I saw you, my heart became full of love so true...
You gave me hope and ease to my mind...
Now we stand here, Love – and cannot be denied...
My True Love, And My Best Friend...
Here with you, I will pledge One True And Unconditional Love...
And I pledge to you, My Tender Dream Come True...
Forever, We Will Be...

Upon these cherished words, Steve spoke a prayer of love and gratitude for the peace and safety of his recovery. ***"Almighty Father God And My Blessed Lord And Savior Jesus Christ, I Thank You For The Miracle That You Have Fulfilled Through The Restoration Of My Health Yet Again. I Thank You For The Cherished Love Of My Beautiful Wife Selena Whom I Now Hold Close To Me And Declare In Mind, Body, Heart, And Soul That As I Always Have, I Will Stand On My Faith In You And Never Fear. With Love, Gratitude, And Praise To You Now And Forever. Amen."***

In cherished sentiment, Steve whispered "I love you, *Angel*."

As she caressed and kissed his forehead, Selena replied "I love you too! Rest now, My Love!" With a final kiss, these tender thoughts and the soft beating of their united hearts drifted Steve and Selena Fitzsimmons into a restful sleep.

Chapter Seventeen

In their dream, the wave of love swept them into the future. The day was August 1, 1987. One year prior to this visionary day, Steve and Selena experienced something that would come to represent another dimension to their cherished relationship. They were more than a husband and wife united in the ethereal absolute of *One True And Unconditional Love*. Now, they were business partners.

In the summer of 1985, Steve and Selena published a collection of her poetry from the heart. Its title was a sentimental reflection of the first words that she spoke from her heart in declaration of her own vision of cherished love – *"Forever We Will Be…"* After a successful book promotion tour, Roy and Rebecca invited Steve and Selena to the same recording studio in which they united their voices of love for the first time through their debut album as *Lucky Seven*. This recording studio was located in the basement of *The Solid Gold Hotel And Casino* where Roy and Rebecca lived in *The City Of Lights*. This recording studio had been given to Rebecca in recognition of her beautiful singing talent as an inspiration to return and realize her melodious *Gift Of Song* from **Almighty God** after the tragic death of her sister, Reese when the city's radio station – *LUCK.7 Radio* – needed to relocate.

Within a few short hours, every poem that Selena had spoken from her heart transformed into the most magical demonstration of poetic duets to ever be recorded in song – including their unified version of the very first poem that Selena had ever written – *"Forever We Will Be…"* Within a week, their first promotional deal was signed with *LUCK.7* and their affiliate in *The State Of Orange – Sun Wave Radio*.

For Selena, this achievement instilled her with personal fulfillment on two levels. First, she and Steve were united by their **Gift From Almighty God** – Writing. However, neither of them would have ever believed that they could communicate the same powerful and intimate message through a hidden singing talent. Second, these poems began as cherished representations of the love within her heart prior to and after meeting and falling in love with Steve. Now, she felt the warmth of pledging her *One True And Unconditional Love* for him to the entire world – forever by his side. Their debut album was entitled *"True Love Is Only Found In The Heart"* – in reflection of the special words that brought them together through Steve's literary vision.

For Steve, Selena was more than his *One True And Unconditional Love*. She was more than his partner – united in their melodious voices in declaration of that love. Now, she was the source of his literary inspiration. Within one year after his recovery from the surgery, Steve had written his second literary masterpiece. This work focused upon his life with Selena and their love for one another. Its title was a reflection of the loving intimacy that would become their stage name - *Love At First Sight*.

In all of the days of their intimate union, one day that stood out for its solid foundation and focus upon the future occurred one month prior to this visionary day – Steve and Selena became the loving parents of a healthy and happy twin son and daughter. Their names would be none other than those cherished words spoken on the morning of their marriage – shining in the warm glow of the beautiful Orange sunrise – after returning from the place that they would come to recognize as *The Island Of Love*, Sandra Rebecca and Michael Roy.

After an appearance with Roy and Rebecca at *The Orange Grove Theatre* the day before, this day shined in the warm and tender intimacy of a passionate desire to take some time off and experience the tender warmth of their cherished family bond – and their *One True And Unconditional Love* for each other that continued to grow with the passage of each new day. Amidst their cherished reflection upon the song within their hearts and the tender touch of this *One True And Unconditional Love*, Steve held Sandra Rebecca in his arms. Selena held

Michael Roy. As the children rested upon the shoulders of their loving parents, Steve and Selena looked at one another. The children shined with adorable charm – smiling at one another. Their blue eyes sparkled in the cherished reflection of the dreams of two people that had been granted in their sweet images of beautiful innocence. They were dressed in pajamas that reflected the tender beauty of the charming floral sentiment that Steve had given to Selena in their first special day together that remained about her neck and the colorful brilliance of Steve and Selena's bedroom – Sandra Rebecca in pink carnation and Michael Roy in green.

As they walked toward one another, Steve and Selena's eyes blinded with the tears of *One True And Unconditional Love*. Softly, they relieved themselves of deep sobs of love and happiness and kissed. Steve declared "They have your eyes!"

"They have your heart!" Selena replied.

"The ideal combination!" they sighed amidst the unison of this *One True And Unconditional Love*. With soft sighs, the children drifted into the peaceful comfort of Dreamland. Steve and Selena soothed them into slumber with the tender words of a loving family bond that they wrote and recorded during Selena's pregnancy.

> *Loving our children...*
> *The best days begin...*
> *Though they are growing fast...*
> *We will give them love to last...*
> *Throughout life, they will never fear...*
> *Our love will always be near...*
> *They will be safe from danger...*
> *With the love of Mother and Father...*

Kissing their adorable children once more, Steve and Selena reclined Sandra Rebecca and Michael Roy to rest. Whispering a unified expression of their love for them, Steve and Selena activated the sound monitor and proceeded into the recreation room.

Quickly, Selena raised her eyebrows and pointed at the amusing pastimes that they had cherished from their childhood and used in the hospital once Steve's strength returned and as exercise during Selena's pregnancy – air hockey and ski-ball. "Let's see how hot you are, Hot Stuff!" she giggled.

Chuckling in amused acceptance, Steve declared "Game on!" With a draw declared in air hockey, they launched into the amusing competitive spirit of fun in ski-ball. As the game progressed, Selena declared "My competitive edge is my love for you!"

"What a coincidence! Mine is the exact same thing!" Steve replied.

Unexpectedly, the stakes would raise higher than Steve could have ever imagined through Selena's words "The winner claims that distinction!"

Snickering with a rapid throw, Steve replied in acceptance "For the moment!"

"If you only knew!" Selena giggled in excitement.

"Knew what?" Steve asked. When Selena did not respond, Steve continued to play – by mesmerized instinct.

Lost in the moment, they neglected to keep track of their scores. Suddenly, the end of the game resounded in red and green lights. Steve and Selena had identical scores of 777.

"Look at that! Roy and Rebecca would be proud!" Steve chuckled.

As they gazed into *The Eyes Of One True And Unconditional Love*, Selena sighed "Tied! Just like the two of us were meant to be – to each other."

Raising his eyebrows, Steve declared "Come to me, *My Beautiful Angel And Dream Come True!* Let us settle this cute competition right here and right now!" Upon soft activation of the stereo, the nostalgic intimacy of their cherished love poetry began its sweet melody. Steve took Selena's hand. With a kiss, they danced to the rhythm of reflection of their *One True And Unconditional Love*. As one poem faded into another – softly – Steve took Selena into his arms and reclined her onto the couch.

Unable to take his eyes off of her, Steve mixed two vanilla milkshakes into two familiar green glasses of heart formation. His sentiment was an amusing reflection of a new mother's need for calcium. In accentuation of their smooth sweetness, Steve poured a splash of "Smooth And Sweet Whipped Cream" into each one. As the tenderness of the moment elapsed into a sweet kiss, Steve and Selena toasted in unison "Here's to Sandra Rebecca and Michael Roy – the ideal combination!" Upon these words, Steve placed his glass to Selena's lips and she placed her glass to his. With a drink, they sealed the moment with a passionate kiss.

In tender melody, Steve sang his declaration of Selena's ethereal beauty and charming intimacy. "Time will pass. My love will never end. You will always be beautiful to me. *My Sweet Angel And Dream Come True*, I will cherish you always and forever." As they moved their lips toward each other, Steve and Selena began to kiss.

With his eyes never leaving hers, Steve took another drink and lowered himself onto his knees. All of the while, Selena watched in mysterious anticipation. He placed his hands upon her face - descending onto her neck. Caressing her tummy, he slowly raised her thick sweater of beautiful green – it was stained with talcum powder. "I can see that some things will never change!" Selena giggled.

"Yes, you are as beautiful as the first moment that I was touched by your ethereal image of *One True And Unconditional Love!*" Steve replied.

"Take me, I am yours!" Selena giggled once more.

Selena's tummy accentuated its tender beauty with pure intimacy. As she stretched, Steve's face flooded with sweat – Selena had released her navel from the constraint of her sweatpants of sparkling yellow. Gently, he caressed her beautiful pink hair – sealing the vision of her elegance into a kiss.

Looking into her beautiful eyes once more, Steve encircled her navel with a heart formation. Selena giggled. He was soothing her stretch marks of motherhood with peaceful comfort. Steve began to cover her tummy with soft kisses. Mesmerized by her ethereal beauty, charm, and tenderness, Steve watched as Selena gazed into his eyes and whispered a few familiar words in a final reflection upon the creation of Steve's most recent literary masterpiece and their melodious poetic bond. "Do you really believe in *Love At First Sight?*"

Caressing her hair, Steve answered "Yes, I do! As you know full well by now, **The Blessing Of Almighty God And Our Lord And Savior Jesus Christ,** as well as the sentiment of your inspiration, ethereal beauty, and *One True And Unconditional Love* between us made it even more special to write and sing about! How about you?"

"So do I! Fortunately, I live it all over again throughout every day of my life. I love you, Steve!" was Selena's tender response.

Steve whispered "I love you too, Selena!" - sealing the moment with a passionate kiss.

With a final gaze into *The Eyes Of One True And Unconditional Love,* the loving hearts of Steve and Selena Fitzsimmons united by the warm glow of a brilliant green light. Steve and Selena rested in the peaceful silence. All that they could hear was the beating of their hearts.

As they cried silent tears of a love to last for all time, Selena caressed Steve's forehead and kissed it. In sentimental gratitude, Steve began to reflect upon the ethereal reality of *Unconditional Love* and acceptance that had made *His Dream Come True* at long last. Mesmerized by the warm and tender love that had brought him through pain, uncertainty, and fear, shined the light of *One True And Unconditional Love* upon him for all of Eternity, and existed in pure intimacy in his loving arms, Steve knew that he was dreaming no longer. "I love you, Selena – *My Beautiful And Poetic Angel!*" he whispered.

"I love you too, Steve – My Ever Romantic One!" she replied.

In cherished gratitude, Steve and Selena united in prayer for the blessing of *One True And Unconditional Love.* **"Almighty Father God, We Thank You For The Love That We Share Throughout All Days Of The Past, Present, And Future And The Spiritual Blessing That You Alone Have Provided Through Our Two Beautiful Children Sandra Rebecca And Michael Roy. Through Now And Forever As We Continue To Do Your Will Throughout The Ages, We Declare Our Love In Mind, Body, Heart, And Soul In The Blessed Name Of Our Lord And Savior, Your Son Jesus Christ For All Of Eternity. Amen!"**

In a final moment of reflection upon everything that they had gone through to reach this one moment in time, Steve asked "**By The Power Of Almighty God**, united in this *One True And Unconditional Love* together as one, we will never have to be afraid again, will we?"

As Selena smiled, they gazed at the brilliant green sparkle of *The Eternal Flame Of One True And Unconditional Love* sealed in the frosted crystal before their eyes. Softly, Selena replied **"By The Power Of Almighty God And Our Lord And Savior Jesus Christ,** *Our One True And Unconditional Love* is strong enough to overcome absolutely anything because…" Upon these words, Steve and Selena Fitzsimmons gazed into *The Eyes Of One True And Unconditional Love* and united as one for all of Eternity through these final words that would remain inscribed upon *The Eternal Capsule Of Time* for all of Eternity – shining in the beautiful glow of a sparkling green flame – **"True Love Is Realized But Once In A Lifetime."**

CPSIA information can be obtained at www.ICGtesting.com
Printed in the USA
LVOW10s0353210816

501188LV00033B/663/P